KILLING ZONE

Hiram Rockingham looked up at the plane. Big black-painted sucker. Had guns stickin' out all along the left side, out of the nose, out of the tail and out of the bottom. Sucker looked bad.

He watched as the gunship circled the Randall place and then started trembling, unleashing its firepower: four 20mm Vulcan cannons, six-barreled Gatlin guns, four pairs of 7.62 machine guns, two 40mm Bofors.

Billy Randall's house and barns and sheds disentangled in front of Hiram's eyes.

Goldie Lorraine came running out of the fields, hollering to her father. "Hit's the wrath of God, Daddy!"

"No it ain't," Hiram said disgustedly. "It's the wrath of Ben Raines!"

ASHES
by William W. Johnstone

OUT OF THE ASHES (1137, $3.50)

Ben Raines hadn't looked forward to the War, but he knew it was coming. After the balloons went up, Ben was one of the survivors, fighting his way across the country, searching for his family, and leading a band of new pioneers attempting to bring American OUT OF THE ASHES.

FIRE IN THE ASHES (1310, $3.50)

It's 1999 and the world as we know it no longer exists. Ben Raines, leader of the Resistance, must regroup his rebels and prep them for bloody guerrilla war. But are they ready to face an even fiercer foe—the human mutants threatening to overpower the world!

ANARCHY IN THE ASHES (1387, $3.50)

Out of the smoldering nuclear wreckage of World War III, Ben Raines has emerged as the strong leader the Resistance needs. When Sam Hartline, the mercenary, joins forces with an invading army of Russians, Ben and his people raise a bloody banner of defiance to defend earth's last bastion of freedom.

SMOKE FROM THE ASHES (2191, $3.50)

Swarming across America's Southern tier march the avenging soldiers of Libyan blood terrorist Khamsin. Lurking in the blackened ruins of once-great cities are the mutant Night People, crazed killers of all who dare enter their domain. Only Ben Raines, his son Buddy, and a handful of Ben's Rebel Army remain to strike a blow for the survival of America and the future of the free world!

ALONE IN THE ASHES (1721, $3.50)

In this hellish new world there are human animals and Ben Raines—famed soldier and survival expert—soon becomes their hunted prey. He desperately tries to stay one step ahead of death, but no one can survive ALONE IN THE ASHES.

Available wherever paperbacks are sold, or order direct from the Publisher. Send cover price plus 50¢ per copy for mailing and handling to Zebra Books, Dept. 2311, 475 Park Avenue South, New York, N.Y. 10016. Residents of New York, New Jersey and Pennsylvania must include sales tax. DO NOT SEND CASH.

DANGER IN THE ASHES

WILLIAM W. JOHNSTONE

ZEBRA BOOKS
KENSINGTON PUBLISHING CORP.

ZEBRA BOOKS

are published by

Kensington Publishing Corp.
475 Park Avenue South
New York, NY 10016

First printing: March, 1988

Printed in the United States of America

We are not weak if we make a proper use of those means which the God of Nature has placed in our power. . . . The battle, sir, is not to the strong alone; it is to the vigilant, the active, the brave.

Patrick Henry

Madame Montholon, having inquired what troops he considered the best. "Those which are victorious, Madame," replied Napoleon.

Napoleon Bonaparte

Dedicated to Mike and Debbie Foster

Prologue

It began one summer's morning; one gorgeous day when the world went mad. It began when the Soviet plan to take over America with germ warfare back-fired . . . but millions and millions of people around the world died horribly because of man's inability to get along with his fellow man.

It was a time of great confusion, of panic and little brush wars that sprang up all over the once most powerful nation in all the world.

One man finally saw his duty, and seized the moment. That man was Ben Raines.

In years to come, Ben would be called many things: anarchist, dictator, murderer . . . and those were the kind things said about him.

Actually, Ben Raines was a walking contradiction; one of those rare types that fit no title. He could lean so far to the right that "anarchist" might fit him — inaccurately — for a moment. Then he would confuse and irritate his critics by embracing the most liberal of thoughts.

But regardless of his lack of titles, Ben Raines and a number of people who thought as he did formed Tri-

States and based its running on a common-sense type of government—common sense being something that the Congress of the United States had lacked for decades, back when there was a United States and a Congress.

The thousands of men and women who joined with Ben Raines had many things in common . . . and that was the reason for their working so well together. Ben Raines's critics complained that he had taken the best of the survivors into the Tri-States. Ben always got a kick out of that because after taking a breath, those same people would loudly proclaim that the people living in Tri-States were nothing more than savages and murderers and the like.

Actually, what they were was a group of people, of all colors, all races, all religions, who felt they could put together a society and make it work to the satisfaction of all concerned—and they didn't much give a damn what those living outside of Tri-States thought about it, or anything else, for that matter.

It was an approach toward living that had never before been tried. And it had worked.

Would it have worked in a nation the size of the United States? No one knew.

And now there was no United States of America—or a Tri-States.

But there was still Ben Raines.

There had been few jails in the Tri-States, because there had been virtually no crime. It had not been tolerated. And it was just that simple.

Everybody had a job. Everybody who was able to work, worked. People who were not able to work were taken care of. No one went hungry; no one had to lock their doors at any time. The life expectancy of a criminal in the Tri-States had been a matter of seconds, if that criminal even remotely considered the thought of resisting.

Justice was harsh, but it was not cruel. A murderer had a choice: hanging or shooting. A rapist fared no better. It was assumed in the Tri-States that if a person used a weapon during the commission of a crime, that person meant to use that weapon. That person also had a choice: hanging or shooting.

After only a year of existence, those inclined toward criminal activities learned to avoid Tri-States, at any cost. It wouldn't have done them much good not to avoid it . . . for the Tri-States' borders were closed.

Outside of Tri-States, the world was still reeling about, in shock after a germ and limited nuclear war. Inside Tri-States, people were humming right along; putting factories back into operation, raising crops and kids, building a nice little society.

One thing that might have contributed to the success of Tri-States was that there were so few lawyers allowed in to screw up matters.

For as Ben was fond of saying, "If you want to know what Jesus thought about lawyers, just read Luke 11:46 and 11:52."

So, naturally, lawyers hated the Tri-States.

But President Hilton Logan hated Ben Raines. Hated the fact that the maverick Tri-States refused to come under the banner of the United States. Hated Ben because of Ben's success in rebuilding a sane and sensible community.

And after a few years, by sheer numbers alone, the armies of the United States crushed the Tri-States.

But the victory was short-lived for Hilton Logan. Ben sent his Zero Squads after the President and any who voted along with him to destroy the Tri-States.

And a few years after the world had been nearly destroyed by global warfare, Ben Raines and his army of Rebels launched a guerrilla war within the borders of America.

But the gods of fate must have been shrieking with wild laughter, for a flea-borne disease struck hard, nearly wiping out civilization . . . or so Ben and his Rebels initially thought. When it was all over, there was not a working government anywhere in the world.

But there was still Ben Raines.

Book One

One

On the morning of his second day back in Louisiana, Ben drove out to see his old house. He knew it would be a bitter disappointment to him . . . and it was. The house was in disrepair; looked like a band of trash had been living in it.

"Maybe they have," Ben muttered.

Ben's Thompson SMG was lying on the seat next to him in the Jeep. One could not safely venture out unarmed. There was danger everywhere. All sorts of cults had sprung up, so-called religious orders, preaching all sorts of semireligious bullshit. Most of it hate-filled, and most of it directed toward Ben Raines and his Rebels.

The far northeast was out of bounds for any exploration . . . so far as Ben knew. And he didn't know that for a fact. Someday he meant to go and see for himself; maybe soon. He'd like to get away; off by himself.

And there were mutants that roamed the land, products of the germ and chemical and nuclear bombs. Part human, part animal, and God alone knew what else. Great beasts, the adults larger than the biggest polar bears, and twice as dangerous because they had some capacity for thought and reason.

There were the Night People, too. They lived mostly in the cities, and the cities were called Cities of the Dead.

Physically scarred and mentally traumatized by the bombings and aftermath of the Great War—as it was called—and the awful sickness that followed, the Night People banded together, electing to hate and despise those who were not like them. To make matters even worse, the Night People were practicing cannibals.

Yes, there was danger everywhere one turned.

Movement caught Ben's eyes; movement behind the rags that once were curtains.

"Good God," Ben muttered. "Somebody is actually living amid all that squalor."

"Whut you want, boy?" The question was called out from behind the rags.

"I'm not here to harm you," Ben shouted. "Just looking around."

"You bes' carry your ass on, soldier-boy! 'Fore I take a notion to shoot it off."

"I'm not on . . . your property." Ben's hackles began to rise. "I'm in the road. And you don't own that. Furthermore, I doubt seriously that you actually own anything. Very few people do, nowadays."

"Haw?"

"Are you a native of this area?" Ben changed the subject, hoping to get some kind of sense from the man, but beginning to realize that might be a hopeless task.

14

"I'm from the parish, yeah. What be your name?"

"Ben Raines."

"You the feller who writ all them books back yonder?"

"Yes. I used to live in the house you're presently occupying."

"You don't no more."

Ben realized then that he was not exactly in conversation with a mental giant. Or even a mental midget, for that matter. Ben asked the man if he was from a certain part of the parish.

"Yep!"

"That figures," Ben muttered. Back when the parish had built a new library, several residents of that area had said it was the most useless building in the parish.

Ben knew then when he was going to build the first westward-stretching outpost. Right here.

"I've got several thousand troops camped just outside of Morriston. Going to be lots of activity around here."

The voice behind the ragged curtains was silent for a time. "I reckon with you comin' back, we're gonna have all sorts of laws and rules and sich as that again, rat?"

"That is correct."

" 'Posin' I don't wanna foller 'em?"

"Then I imagine somebody will shoot you," Ben called cheerfully.

As his words were fading away, Ben saw the muzzle of a rifle poked through the rags. He rolled out of the Jeep, grabbing his Thompson as he went over the side. A rifle cracked, the slug popping through the windshield. Ben caught movement by the side of the house. A man stepped into view, carrying an M-16. Ben stitched him across the belly and then lifted the SMG, emptying a clip through the ragged curtains. A scream came from within the house.

Ben waited; no more shots came his way. He ran, zigzagging across the tree-filled and weed-grown yard, coming up to the edge of the house. Moaning could be heard through the broken windows. Ben thought: I put a lot of money into this house, only to have these trashy bastards screw it all up.

He kicked in the door, which wasn't all that difficult a task . . . it was hanging by one hinge. Ben looked down at the badly wounded man. The .45 caliber slugs had taken him in the chest. He lay amid filth on the floor. "You're not exactly a paragon of neatness, are you?"

"Fuck you, Raines! I didn't lak your arrogant ass when you lived here 'fore."

"Hell, man. I don't know you."

"I knowed you," the man managed to gasp. "Always lookin' down your damn snooty nose at the res' of us."

"The word is reserved, not arrogant." Ben felt a little silly, standing there discussing word meaning with a dying man.

"Whure's my brudder?"

"Was he carrying an M-16?"

"Yeah."

"He's dead."

The man cursed Ben.

"If you're quite finished. . . ." Ben looked down

at him. "Anything else I can do for you?"

"Whut you gonna do with me?"

"Nothing." Ben turned and walked back outside, across the lawn—loosely called—and got into his Jeep.

"You jist gonna leave me here?" the redneck hollered.

"That is correct," Ben muttered. He cranked the Jeep and drove off.

It was a hard time, and Ben Raines was a hard man when he had to be. Even when world conditions had been at their best, before the Great War, Ben could not tolerate ignorance, and he was doubly contemptuous of those people who were ignorant and proud of that ignorance. There had been too many schools, both traditional and Vo-Tech, for anyone to remain ignorant; therefore, he had no patience with anyone who chose to muck around in blind mental blankness.

He met a patrol driving fast up the old blacktop road.

"We heard shots. What happened, general?"

"A couple of people just learned a hard lesson about the value of knowledge and civility," Ben told the lieutenant.

The Rebel smiled. "Yes, sir. Will they be needing medical assistance, sir?"

"If you want to mess with them, go ahead." Ben drove on.

Used to be a lot of people living in this area, Ben mused, driving slowly along the rutted road. By and large, good people. We're going to be starting from scratch. He thought of the monumental task ahead of them all.

First we build the outposts, one every hundred miles, stretching from the Mississippi River to the coast of California. Little oases of civilization, where men and women could live in some higher degree of safety and build schools and homes and once more begin the job of pulling themselves out of the ashes of destruction.

After the recent battles, the Libyan terrorist Khamsin — the "Hot Wind," as he called himself — would be weeks, maybe months, rebuilding his army. Khansim was of no immediate worry to Ben.

Getting the first real outpost set up and working was Ben's main concern at the moment. That, and staying alive long enough to do it.

Hiram Rockingham stepped out onto his front porch and surveyed his own personal little kingdom. It began some twenty miles from Morriston — south. That area had been called, back before the Great War, the last bastion of ignorance, intermarriage, and intolerance in that part of the country. And that was only a mild exaggeration. Every state, and probably a large percentage of the counties therein, had something to compare to this region. Albeit not something the Chamber of Commerce would want to include in any tourist packet.

Hiram knew that Ben Raines was back, and Hiram knew also that with Ben's return, things were going to change.

The two men had hated each other for twenty years. Ben, because Hiram was the personification of an ignorant redneck. And Hiram, even though he would never admit it, indeed, probably didn't even realize it, had always felt threatened by Ben Raines.

Both men were strong-willed individualists. Both felt that their way was the best. The similarity ended there.

Hiram was ignorant. Ben was a man of books and knowledge. Ben preferred to talk matters over and reach some sort of gentlemen's understanding. Hiram, if he felt slighted, would burn the other party's house down or shoot his dogs. And then go home and feel very smug about it.

To Ben's way of thinking, people like Hiram took much more from society than they gave.

To Hiram, Ben had always been uppity and snooty. Read books and watched that silly stuff on the Public Broadcasting TV. Ben Raines felt that animals had rights. To Hiram's way of thinking, that was nonsense; animals didn't have no rights a-tall.

Back when the world still was spinning in some degree of order, Hiram and his ilk hated the men who worked for the Wildlife and Fisheries Department; 'specially them bastards in the enforcement arm of it. To Hiram's way of thinking, a man had a right to shoot a deer anytime he damn pleased. To try to convince Hiram that if everybody felt that way, there would soon be no game left was tantamount to beating your head against a brick wall.

Ben felt that the wilderness areas and the forests and streams were for the enjoyment of every citizen. And it had not improved relations between the men when it got back to Hiram that Ben had suggested an open season on rednecks. Then you could shoot one, strap it on the hood of your car or truck, and ride around town, showing off your kill.

" 'at damn feller's plumb crazy!" was Hiram's response to Ben's remark.

"That suggestion of yours is a little extreme, Ben," a friend told him. " 'Necks are human beings, you know?"

"They walk upright," was Ben's reply.

Hiram believed that there never was and never would be no damn colored man as good as or as smart as a white man. Period. Wasn't no Jew worth a damn; the Holocaust never happened. Mexicans was lazy and no good. You couldn't trust them slant-eyed folks. All Wops belonged to the mafia. Anyone who didn't like black-eyed peas and cornbread was ignorant. And so on, and on . . . imparting his dubious wisdom to his kids and anyone else who cared to listen.

Ben, on the other hand, believed, along with a growing number of people, before and after the Great War, that the time was coming when the nation as a whole would be forced to see that people of Hiram's ilk, regardless of color, could no longer be tolerated, socially, morally, economically, and probably most important, intellectually.

"Whut the hale's far does all that mean?" Hiram blustered, upon hearing Ben's comments.

"Hit means he'd lak to shoot you," a slightly more intelligent neighbor informed him. "Ifn you won't change."

" 'at bassard's crazy!" Hiram hollered.

As Ben drove the old country roads, Hiram sat on his front porch and looked out over the fields he and his kind worked.

They were good farmers; not even Ben would take that from them.

The weather had been good and the crops looked fine. Hiram wondered if Ben Raines was going to let him live long enough to get his crops in.

One thing Ben Raines wouldn't have to worry about was gettin' colored folks to join up with him. There wasn't no colored folks left around these parts. Hiram and his buddies had seen to that. There was some lived over to Morriston, but they stayed to themselves and didn't mess with white folks.

That was the way it ought to be.

Hiram remembered when that damn Kasim and his bunch come in; gonna make this whole place something called New Africa.

But President Logan had sent mercenaries in and wiped most of them out.

Then Ben Raines had killed Logan. Funny, Hiram pondered . . . the word he'd got was that Ben didn't even like Kasim.

Hiram sighed. All that was four-five years back, at least. He couldn't 'member 'xactly. Didn't make no difference noways.

Ben Raines showed his ass down in this area, and Ben wasn't gonna show it no more.

Hiram looked up as a pickup rattled over his cattle guard. Frank Monroe from up the road got out and come walking up to the porch.

"Mornin', Hiram."

"Frank. What's on your mind?"

"Ben Raines is back."

21

"I know it."

"Got an army with him."

"I hear he had him some soldier-boys. Don't worry me none." That was a damn lie, but Hiram wouldn't admit it for the world. If he hadn't been worried about it, he never would have thought about Ben killing him.

Frank spat tobacco juice on the ground. "Five or six thousand strong."

Hiram gripped the arms of his rocking chair so hard his knuckles whitened. "You a liar!"

Frank backed up and looked at Hiram. "We elected you leader here, Hiram. But that don't give you no right to call me no liar."

Hiram took several deep breaths. "You rat, Frank. You rat. I 'pologize. You seen this army with yore own eyes?"

"I seen 'um. Just got back from up there. Looked like a bunch of beavers workin' live. Stringin' wire for phones. Cleanin' out houses and sich. They's wimmin soldiers, too. Some of them givin' orders. They tough, Hiram. They lean and they mean and they tough. You know the very first thang they done yesterday morning?"

Hiram waited.

"Started school for they kids. Whole passel of kids come in yesterday, right after the Rebels hit the parish."

There were no schools in Hiram's little kingdom. Hiram never saw much use for them. But he knew, with a sinking feeling in his guts, he *knew*, that once Ben came into this area, and Ben would, there would be schools built. Right then and there.

The goddamned pushy son of a bitch!

"Git the people together, Frank. We'll have us a preachin' and a singin' and a prayin' and a eatin' on the grounds this night. Then we'll have us a meetin' of the men."

"Hiram," Frank said softly, carefully choosing his words, for he knew how much Hiram hated Ben Raines, "you thinkin' about fightin' Ben Raines and his Rebels?"

Hiram stood up. "This is our land, Frank. Our community. My great-grandfather come in here and cleared this land with mules and muscles and sweat. After the Great War, Frank, you and me, and all the others, we formed up and fought the outlaws and the trash. We ain't botherin' nobody down here, Frank. . . ."

That was not exactly true. Travelers had been shot dead for simply walking along the roads. If for no other reason than the parents of those who pulled the trigger had imparted to their offspring that they were "better than others."

". . . we got our own law here, and by God no fancy-soldier-suited blue-nose is gonna tell me and mine what we can or cain't do. I ain't a-gonna have it!"

"I'll pass the word, Hiram."

"You do that. And git hold of Reed. Tell him to build us a cross. We'll burn it after the meetin'."

Ben connected with the old US highway and drove back into town. The scene that greeted him was one he had expected.

A large crowd of civilians had gathered around the Rebel's main CP; a mixture of black and white.

General Ike McGowan walked over to Ben's Jeep. Ike cradled his CAR-15.

"This it?" Ben asked.

"Most of the adults that live in town. 'Bout a hundred more live around the outskirts. They tell me the real trouble is south of here."

"Yeah, I know."

Ike smiled slowly. "I can hear the wheels turnin' in your head, boy."

Ike was Mississippi born and reared, and at times loved to talk as if he didn't have a thought in his head. But he was highly educated and a former Navy SEAL. One of the original members of Raines's Rebels.

"Oh?" Ben smiled at his old friend. "And what do you make out of all the turning and grinding, Ike?"

"That you are going to step out of character, and when you do, you're going to do it up right."

"You've been talking to some of the townspeople?"

"Oh, yeah!"

"Which one?"

"Several. Black guy name of John Simmons. White feller name of Rich. Several of the townspeople who knew you from 'way back when. They told me some interestin' stories about you and a 'neck name of Hiram Rockingham."

"John Simmons. Got to be in his sixties now. He was a young man out in L.A. when Watts exploded. He and several other blacks guarded their businesses with rifles until the trouble was over."

24

"Yeah? He kill anybody?"

Ben grinned. "John told me that an L.A. cop got all upset when he saw them guarding their places of business with guns. Asked them what was going on. John told him that if any nigger tried to burn his place, he was gonna get shot. Cop told him, 'Yeah. Well, just don't wound anyone.' "

Ike laughed. "Cecil's been talkin' with John ever since you pulled out this mornin'. I imagine he's told Cec the story."

General Cecil Jefferys was yet another Rebel who had been with Ben for years. A former Green Beret. The black man was one of the most honorable men that Ben had ever known.

Ben walked over to the knot of people and shook hands with those that he remembered. John Simmons smiled at him.

"Been a while, Ben."

"Fifteen years, John. Might have known you'd still be kicking. You're too damn ornery to die."

"Been close a couple of times, though. I made the mistake of driving down into the Stanford Community one day." He met Ben's eyes and let Ben figure out the rest.

"They put lead in you, John?"

"Sure did."

"Why, John?"

The man shrugged still muscular shoulders. "Because I'm not the right color, Ben. They asked me what the hell was I doing down there? I told them it wasn't any of their fucking business."

Ben laughed aloud at that. "John, had you been drinking?"

25

"No. I was just driving around. Hell, I wasn't bothering a soul, Ben. But rednecks and white trash and niggers irritate the hell out of me."

Ben clasped him on the arm. "You won't do, John. You just won't do. Let's talk about something more pleasant than Hiram Rockingham. Who's the leader of Morriston now?"

"No one. And that's the shame of it all. The town is still divided . . . just like it was twenty years ago. Hell, a hundred years ago!"

"That's going to change, John." Ben's words had steel behind them.

"I knew that when we got word your columns were heading this way. But I warn you, Ben. It's going to be one bloody son of a bitch."

"I expect so, John." He looked at Richmond Harris, who had been standing quietly, listening. "Rich. You and John are now the administrators of this area. Appointed by me. Start drawing up plans for this community."

"How much area, general?"

"What used to be the entire parish."

Rich arched an eyebrow. "I can tell you a bunch of people who won't like that at all."

Ben smiled. But it was not a nice smile. "I'm counting on that, Rich."

Ike looked at his friend. He knew that Ben Raines was not a man you wanted to get crossed-up with . . . for Ben had said that if this nation was ever to be rebuilt, ignorance and prejudice were two things that would have to be eradicated. Either educated out, or killed out.

Two

Ben had called a meeting of his top personnel. He thumped a part of a parish map. "Stanford Community. We'll have a little resistance from a few people in and around Morriston; but not very much. They're starved for progress. They were starved for progress twenty years ago," he added drily. Again he thumped the map. "But here is where we'll have the fighting. And don't, don't, sell these ol' boys short. They may be trash and 'necks and people you might not want your sister or brother to marry, but they're woodsmen . . . every one of them. Keep that in mind at all times."

He looked at his daughter, Tina, who commanded a unit of her own. "Excuse me. Woodspeople."

"Thank you, general." She smiled at him.

"These people living in that area, general," Colonel Dan Gray said. "How would you best describe them? Cretinous, backward, savage, superstitious? . . ."

"All of that you just named."

"My word!" The Englishman frowned. "What a dreadful grouping."

"Now, then," Ben said, "to lighten up some. Further on westward, along the old interstate, we have our old friend, Emil Hite. He's back in business."

Everyone laughed at that.

"Emil is running his scams again. He is of no danger to us. Leave him alone. As long as he stays out of our immediate area. OK. Ike, order a fly-by of this area. If the pilots are fired on, return the fire and return it hard!" He looked at Cecil. "Are all the planes in?"

"Yes, Ben. They're out at the regional airport."

"I want a Puff along with them. First light tomorrow."

"Right."

A Puff was a truly awesome piece of flying machine. A twin-engine prop job that was filled with weapons of war: .60 caliber machine guns, .50 caliber machine guns, electrically fired, along with numerous rocket launchers. One Puff could effectively neutralize an area roughly the size of three football fields. Neutralize: meaning its firepower would kill any living thing within a given area.

When all the armament on a Puff was being fired simultaneously, the plane would rattle and shake and look like it might fall out of the sky. But nothing lived under its flight path. Nothing at all.

"I want the guards at the Mississippi River bridge to stay alert," Ben ordered. "Vicksburg proper, so I'm told, has been taken over by the Night People." He shook his head. "What puzzles me is where these people are coming from; why we haven't seen more of them over the months."

"We haven't been in the cities much in years,

Dad," Tina said.

"That's true," Ben acknowledged. "But why are they suddenly popping out of the woodwork?"

"I have a theory, Father," Buddy spoke up. All heads turned to look at the handsome, heavily muscled young man. Ben's son; his flesh and blood.

Buddy had joined the Rebels a few months back, meeting his father for the very first time and immediately fitting in. The young man was very much aware that Ben would someday be forced to kill his mother, a nut who called herself Sister Voleta. The young man was not looking forward to that day.

Like his father, Buddy carried a Thompson SMG, .45 caliber. But unlike the other Rebels, Buddy did not wear a beret on his head. He wore a bandana tied around his forehead.

"Handsome, rakish-looking rogue, isn't he?" Colonel Gray had once remarked.

"And your theory, son?"

"Father, everything from the place once known as Washington, D.C. north is supposed to be destroyed, right?"

"That is my understanding, yes."

"Have you personally witnessed this?" the son asked.

"Well . . . no," Ben admitted. "But I have spoken with pilots who said it was."

"How reliable was their testimony?"

Ben thought on that. He had heard radio broadcasts just after the bombings, a decade back. The broadcasts said the eastern corridor of the United States had taken hot hits. Any number of people Ben had spoken with had confirmed that. And that

Air Force General he'd killed down at Shaw AFB
. . . hadn't he said that?

No, Ben thought, turning away from the group
and walking a bit, pacing the room. No, he had
intimated that. That's all.

Ben turned to face his son. "Neutron bombs," he
said. "They kill the people, but leave the buildings
intact."

"That is my theory, sir." Buddy confirmed Ben's
statement.

"Go on, son. No! Wait! I personally got very
close to the eastern corridor. I had instruments with
me; they showed hot. Deadly, dangerous levels."

"Yes, but how long after the bombings did you
approach these areas?" Colonel Gray inquired.

Ben thought back over the years. "Just a few
months."

"Well, they probably would have still been hot
then. But not now," Ike mused aloud.

The room was silent.

"Every message we've ever received over the years
said that New York City was destroyed. Gone.
Nothing left. If that isn't the truth, then who? . . ."

He stopped, then smiled knowingly. "Sure," Ben
said, his voice no more than a whisper. "Who else
but the Night People. They've kept that area for
their own for years, simply by sending out false
messages."

"That is my theory, Father," Buddy said.

"Think of the treasures," Ben whispered. "The
museums, the libraries, the recordings, the art gal-
leries." He looked at Ike. "Two-hundred-man team,
Ike. Rations for an extended journey. I want you and

30

your people outfitted for hot areas. When can you pull out?"

"Two days, Ben."

"Go!"

Ike left the room as Ben's eyes touched the gaze of his daughter. Tina said, "There will have to be scouts, general."

"You think you can handle it, Tina?"

"If I didn't think so, I wouldn't have brought it up."

"Get your team together and get cracking. Pull out as quickly as possible."

Grinning, she tossed him a salute and ran from the room, yelling for her Scouts to group up.

Ben looked at Buddy. "You understand why I want you here with me, son?"

"Yes, sir. Besides, I think the people you're sending are better qualified to handle it than I."

Ben smiled. "Always the diplomat, aren't you, boy?"

"Full of shit, is the word," Cecil said drily. "Of course, he is your son, Ben."

"Oh, Lord!" Hiram Rockingham proclaimed, raising his hands heavenward. "Why have you sent us this human plague called Ben Raines? We have all been Your good and faithful servants, Lord. And we do not understand this."

Hiram, sixth-grade educated, and with about as much working knowledge of the Bible as a platypus duckbill, had, many years back, announced that he was taking over as God's Main Man in the Stanford

31

Community. There had been a preacher in the area, but he'd been defrocked after he was caught screwing the church piano player.

The piano player, one Mrs. Rosie May Helen Jean Seager, and the preacher had left the area shortly after that. Hiram Rockingham took over the duties behind the pulpit, and with that, religion reverted back to the dark ages.

Hiram's church, originally Baptist, had become the First Church of the Holiness, Praise Be. And Hiram differed somewhat from the teaching in the Bible. Since many of the residents of the Stanford Community could read but little, and none born during the past two decades could read at all, the folks accepted whatever Hiram said as straight out of the Gospel, not realizing it was Gospel according to Hiram.

And the Praise Be church of Hiram, after Hiram said it was OK, had taken to polygamy like a fish to water. Hiram had four wives, and fourteen children, the oldest in his thirties. Even Hiram had a hard time keeping up with what kid belonged to which wife.

But they were, to Hiram's way of thinking, all good kids. Bubba Willie was a tad on the crazy side, but that was to be expected, since his mother was Hiram's first cousin—or was it double-first cousin? Hiram couldn't remember—but that didn't make no difference. Not really. Hiram loved them all. Wives and kids. 'Course, ever now and then he had to take up a piece of stovewood and beat the hell out of the kids . . . and occasionally the wives. But that was something they all expected and accepted as normal.

Then, too, Bubba Willie's retardation just might have been caused when he was a little boy and Hiram popped him up side the head with a poker when Bubba Willie wouldn't mind. But even if a team of world-renowned doctors had said that was the cause, Hiram wouldn't have believed them. To say that Hiram was set in his ways would be like saying a mule is stubborn.

But a mule did have a few attributes that Hiram didn't have. You could teach a mule a few things.

"Oh, Lord!" Hiram squalled, just before the huge cross, wrapped in rags and soaked in kerosene, was ignited. "Give us a sign."

The Lord just might have been listening that night. For as soon as the cross was flaming, it began to rain, coming down in torrents.

"Piss on it," Hiram muttered.

"That was an unusual storm last night," Cecil said. He and Ben were having breakfast in one of the many mess tents around the area. "Blew in and blew out like none I'd ever seen before."

It was just breaking dawn. The sounds of planes low overhead rumbled through the early morning. "I hope those assholes in the Stanford area have enough sense to know not to fire on those planes," Ike said, sitting down at the table.

"They don't," Ben told him, taking a sip of coffee.

Colonel Gray joined the group. "If they fire on Puff, there will be some funerals soon."

Ben sipped his chicory-laced coffee. He was actually getting used to the stuff. "They'll fire on the

33

planes. Bet on it."

"Then they're awfully stupid people, general." Dan sipped his tea. The Englishman would only rarely drink coffee.

"That they are."

"Ben," Ike chewed on a biscuit, "I hate to dump cold water on your plans, but have you considered this: OK, we'll be successful in setting up the twenty-five or so outposts between here and the coast. That's only a little sweat. But there must be hundreds, maybe thousands of communities like this Stanford."

"I have considered that, yes."

"So we're going to have little communities of learning dotting the land. What's goin' to pull the thousands of ignorant assholes in?"

"Nothing." Ben lifted his eyes, meeting Ike's gaze. "Nothing at all."

Cecil waited in silence. He knew Ben's plans. And while in a civilized world they would be considered outrageous . . . the world was no longer civilized.

"Then? . . ." Ike lifted one eyebrow.

"I plan on giving the people a choice. Do I have to spell out to you what that choice is?"

"Ben, you can't! . . ." Ike choked it back in anger.

"Oh, hell, Ike! Give me credit for more compassion than that! I'm not going to send Rebels in to engage in wholesale slaughter. Good God, Ike."

"But you're sending a gunship down there right now! Damn, I can still hear them."

"Ike," Ben spoke softly. "Have you forgotten so soon the only thing a redneck understands?"

Ike shook a finger in Ben's face. "Boy, don't you

34

tell me about rednecks! I was born in rural Mississippi! You forgetting Megan?"

"I'm not forgetting anything, Ike. But apparently, you have."

"They ought to be there in about a minute." Ike rose from the table and walked outside.

"What's wrong with Ike?" Cecil asked.

"Nina's pregnant." Doctor Lamar Chase spoke from the other end of the long table. "You all know how Ike is when it comes to kids. He's just thinking about the little children that might be hurt or killed down there today."

"And you think I haven't?" Ben asked.

The old doctor met Ben's eyes. "I know you have, Ben. And I know you're just as sick of it all as I am. But I also know that you have to make the decisions. And so does Ike. And," he sighed, "I also know that while your way might not always be the most humane, considering the time and place, it is certainly the most expedient."

"Big ol' flyin' machine a'comin', Daddy!" Axel Leroy yelled to Hiram. "Can I shoot at it?"

Hiram looked up at the plane and decided he didn't like the looks of it at all. Big black-painted sucker. Had guns stickin' out all along the left side, out of the nose and out of the tail and out of the bottom. Sucker looked bad.

"Axel Leroy!" Hiram hollered. "You lay that rifle on the ground and wave friendly-like to that plane. Don't you be makin' no hos-tile moves, boy."

"Awww, Daddy!"

"Shet your sassy mouth, boy. 'Fore I find me a chunk and bus' your head with it."

Axel Leroy put his .30-30 on the ground.

"You wave, boy," the father told him. "You grin and wave. Jist lak your daddy's doin'."

Father and son waved. The planes moved on. Hiram took a deep breath. "Somebody's fixin' to get killed this day," he prophesied correctly.

"Goddamn sorry-ass Ben Raines," he cursed, resisting an urge to shake his fist at the departing planes. He held back, knowing in his guts that them planes carried enough guns to blow Hiram and his kin clear into the next world. And Hiram was smart enough to know for an iron-clad fact that Ben Rains would just love to do that.

Hiram heard a single shot. He watched as the big black-painted plane started trembling, unleashing its firepower: four 20 mm Vulcan cannons, six-barreled Gatlin guns, capable of firing more than twenty-five hundred rounds per minute; four pairs of 7.62 machine gun modules, also six barreled, all capable of four thousand rounds a minute. Fore and aft were two 40 mm Bofors that could pump out a hundred two-pound rounds a minute.

Hiram watched as Billy Randell's house and barn and sheds disintegrated as the gunship made a slow circle around the grounds. Nothing was gonna live through all that, Hiram thought. Not nothing at all.

"Holy shit!" Axel Leroy said. The young man then pissed his pants and went running for the outhouse. He had a sudden urge to take a dump.

"That stupid Randell kid," Hiram said, as wife number two came rushing out of the house, her face

36

pale with fright. "He just had to take a shot at that plane."

Wife number two fell to her knees and began speaking in tongues.

Goldie Lorraine came running out of the fields, hollering to her father. "Hit's the wrath of God, Daddy!"

"No, it ain't," Hiram said disgustedly. "It's the wrath of Ben Raines."

Three

Hiram's spirits kept getting lower and lower the closer he got to Morriston. He had never seen so many soldier-people in all his born days. Men and women. And they all looked like they could take a tank on, with their bare hands.

And he just couldn't understand a lot of things about them. Oh, there was folks of all colors there; he would expect something like that from Ben Raines. But some of the men had beards; some had short hair, some had long hair. Just didn't look like no army Hiram had ever seen.

And Lord God Almighty . . . the guns! There was big guns and little guns; tanks and half-tracks and APCs and rocket launchers and, why, Hiram had never seen the like.

He began to taste the bitter copper sensation of defeat in his mouth.

He had tasted sickness in his mouth earlier that morning, when he and his boys couldn't find enough of the Randell boy to even bury proper. The whole area around the place was tore up so bad it looked like Ol' Scratch hisself had seared it.

Hiram spotted a black soldier and hollered at him. "You boy! Git over here."

Hiram suddenly found his chin being propped up by the muzzle of a .45, cocked and ready to bang.

"Did you wish to speak with me, sir," the man behind the gun asked.

"Yes, sir," Hiram said. First time in his life he'd ever said that to a colored. "I surely did."

"What is it you wish to know?"

"I would like to find Ben Raines, please."

"*General* Raines!"

"Yes, sir. That's him."

A crowd of Rebels had begun to gather around, and behind the Rebels, John Simmons and Richard Harris were standing, both of them smiling.

Hiram's oldest, Billy Bob, had accompanied his dad to town. It used to be a treat. Not this time.

"Poppa," Billy Bob said. "Don't do nothin' foolish. Les' us both swaller our pride and walk soft."

Billy Bob did have some sense. He did have a fourth-grade education.

The muzzle of the .45 was removed from under Hiram's chin. The Rebel said, "There is an old bank building just west of town. That is General Raines's CP. You'll find him there."

"Thankee kindly."

"You're welcome."

The crowd parted, and Hiram moved out, the old pickup smoking badly.

Ben saw them come in and told his aide to show them into his office. He waved Hiram and Billy Bob to seats, after Hiram had introduced his son.

"You just had to come back, didn't you, Ben?"

"I wasn't planning on it, Hiram. But then I got to thinking this place was as good as any place to start."

"Start whut?" Hiram asked, suspicion thick in his voice.

"Why, Hiram . . ." Ben could not suppress a smile, "the slow return to progress."

"Are you sayin' that we is backward?"

"Some of the worst I have ever witnessed, Hiram."

Hiram grunted. "You never did dance around no issue, did you, Raines?"

"Never did, Rockingham."

Hiram gave out a long sigh and rubbed his face. For a very brief instant, Ben almost felt sorry for the man. Almost. And it passed very quickly.

"Get it said, Ben."

Ben studied the man. There was no way he could put anything to Hiram in a subtle manner. Stupid people do not understand any form of nuance. As Ike knew only too well, rednecks understand force. Sort of like the mule and the two-by-four. You have to get their attention.

"I'm not just talking law and order, Hiram."

Hiram's eyes were filled with hate. It was something he made no effort to disguise. "Spell it out, Raines."

Oh, hell! Ben thought. Let's give it a try. He studied the man. Hiram and Ben were both middle-aged. And both were in fine physical condition. But back in the mid-seventies, when both had been young bucks, Hiram had made the mistake of trying Ben. Once. Just once. Ben, fresh out of one of the military's toughest outfits, had literally stomped the man into the ground. Hiram had never forgiven Ben. He had led the men who burned the cross on Ben's front yard; sent him threatening letters through the mail. Had shot one of Ben's dogs. And with that action, Ben knew then for fact what he had always suspected: People like Hiram were cowards. All night-riders are cowards. . . .

"Why you starin' at me, Ben?"

Ben told him the truth. "I'm trying to make up my mind whether to try reasoning with you, or just outright killing you and having done with it."

Billy Bob paled under his deep tan. Hiram shifted uncomfortably in his chair.

"You could have kilt me twenty years ago, Raines. Why didn't you do it then?"

Ben saw his opening and took it. "Because it was against the law, Hiram. Moral law and written law. Do you understand that?"

"You blamin' ever'thang that happened back yonder on me, Ben?"

"Who started it?"

"You come down where you wasn't wanted."

"Public roads, Hiram. I violated nobody's property rights."

"That ain't it." The man clung stubbornly to his lopsided philosophy.

Whatever the hell it is! Ben thought.

"Then what is it, Hiram?"

"Man's got a right."

"To do what, Hiram?"

The man struggled for words that he could not find.

"Hiram, perhaps if you'd had a bit more education, you might be able to tell me what's on your mind."

"I git along jist fine, Raines. I don't need no fancy education."

"Well, Hiram, I guess that is your right. You're a grown man."

Hiram couldn't believe that Ben Raines was sitting there agreeing with anything he had to say. Come as a surprise.

"We burred a boy this day, Raines. All that we could find of 'im."

"He fired on a low-flying plane, Hiram."

"His right."

Ben leaned back in his chair. Right there, he thought, sits the stumbling block to progress. And I don't have the time to go into each little bastion of ignorance and sit down and talk with the thousands of people like Hiram. So what the hell, then, do I do?

"Hiram, let me stop attempting to nicely step through that quagmire you call a mind and give it to you flat-out."

"I reckon you 'bout to start stompin' on my rights, ain't you, Raines?"

"Hiram," Ben said with a sigh, not really wanting to use verbal force with the man, although he knew that was inevitable. "When your self-proclaimed rights start conflicting with the rights of others, something has to give. You with me so far?"

"I got a right to 'tend the church I wanna 'tend, Raines."

Ben stared at him. "Hiram, I don't give a damn what church you attend."

Hiram blinked. "You don't?"

"No. That's your right under the Constitution of the United States. And I'm trying to keep as many rights as possible during this awful time."

"I got more'un one wife," Hiram said sullenly.

"I don't care, Hiram. I don't care if you have twenty wives."

"You *don't?*"

"No. That's none of my business."

"Wal, whut the hale do you want, Ben?"

"Civility, among other things."

"Haw?"

"Politeness. The respecting of other people as long as they respect you. The right to come and go as one pleases. The understanding of and the general observance of customs conducive to the welfare and the good of society as a whole. . . ."

"Haw?"

Ben lost his temper. Several of his aides had been listening outside the open door and all knew that the general had just about reached the blowing stage. "Goddamnit, Hiram, what in the name of God does it take to get through to you?"

"Wal, damnit, Ben, why don't you talk plain and maybe I could understand you?"

"Why don't you get some education so you can understand simple English, you ignorant bastard!" Ben roared.

"I never had no time for nothing lak 'at," Hiram mush-mouthed.

"That's a goddamn lie and you know it. That's the same bullshit that people of your ilk have been using for decades. I didn't buy it when we had a working society and I damn sure don't buy it now. The bottom line was and still is that you were too goddamned lazy to try to improve yourself. Under the myriad of laws we were wallowing in twenty years ago, there was damn little anybody could do with people like you . . . but I'm no longer bound by any of those laws."

"You cain't force me to learn no book-stuff."

"No, Hiram, I can't. But I can sure shoot you!"

It had been the most humiliating, degrading and disgusting, and horrible experience in all of Khansim's life. Damn Ben Raines!

Leading his men into Atlanta, knowing those disfigured and horrible creatures were there, waiting for them. Cannibalistic savages! Khansim was still trying to regrouped his shattered forces; number the dead.

They had fallen back to mid-Georgia, gradually working their way back to South Carolina. But since he had pulled nearly all his forces out of South Carolina, the Americans he had enslaved had now revolted, rising up, seizing arms, killing the troops Khansim had left behind. Everything was . . . it was just . . . well, all fucked up!

Lance Ashley Lantier had gathered his forces around him and beat it back to North Georgia. Piss on those disgusting Night People and piss on Khansim, too. Damn A-rab was nuts!

He thought he'd take his men and head on up

toward Kentucky. Set up there. Hell with Ben Raines
. . . at least for the time being.

Hiram looked at Ben. He felt something cold and
slimy, sort of an oily-feeling, turn over very slowly in
his stomach. Right then and there, Hiram realized
something that he should have known and seen in
Ben years back: Ben was dangerous. All them good
ol' boys he'd growed up with and knowed all his life
wasn't shit when held up to Ben Raines. Them ol'
boys liked to talk and brag a lot 'bout how bad they
was, but then they'd go run in packs, like killer dogs
. . . not none of them ever had the balls to go off
alone and try Ben.

He shoulda seen that.

Ben always had been a lone wolfer . . . and lone
wolves are dangerous.

"Lay it on the line for me, Ben," Hiram finally
said.

"It's really very simple, Hiram. Perhaps that is
why you've never been able to understand it."

"I reckon that's it, Ben." There was a subdued
note to Hiram's voice.

Tina stuck her head into Ben's office. "Runnin'
late, Dad. Pulling out now." She kissed him and
smiled at him.

"See you, kid. Stay out of trouble and keep in
daily contact with Ike. If the Big Apple is still there,
you and your team will be the first to see it. Take a
picture of it for me, will you?"

"Will do. 'Bye, Pop."

She was gone.

Hiram said, "Your daughter?"

"Yes. She commands a team of Scouts."

"Whut's 'at 'bout apples? They ain't ripe yet."

Ben softened his smile. "New York City is, was, often referred to as the Big Apple."

"Oh!"

"Hiram, have you ever really cared what went on outside of your own little world?"

"Not really. How's that gonna hep me put food on the table?"

Good question, Ben thought. "Other than broadening your level of knowledge, Hiram, it might not help you feed your family."

"Thought so."

Steady, now, Ben cautioned himself. Don't boggle his mind this early in the game. "Hiram, my Rebels are going to secure this parish. I mean make it secure so all residents current and future will be safe. You with me, Hiram?"

"I reckon. There's gonna be more people comin' in to live?"

"I hope so. Does that upset you?"

"More people means more trouble."

"Not if they're the right kind of people, it doesn't."

"Are we the right kind of people, Ben Raines? Me and Billy here?"

"You can be."

"Po-lite way of sayin' we ain't."

"You're right, Hiram."

"Why don't you jist go on, Ben? Go on to another spot and set up your fancy doin's?"

"Because this spot is ideal, Hiram. And if you

think I'm bad, Hiram . . . wait until you meet Khamsin. And you'll meet him."

"Khamsin . . . who?"

"Means the Hot Wind. He's a terrorist from Libya."

That got through to him. "Lak that fool that took our people hostage down in I-ran back a-ways?"

"Ten times worse."

"Why would he be comin' here, Ben Raines?"

"Because he doesn't like me, Hiram."

"I can understand that," Hiram said drily, and Ben had to laugh at the expression on the man's face.

"Hiram, we might never be friends, but that doesn't mean we have to be mortal enemies. I'll level with you: I don't like you. And I really don't see any change in that position. I don't know whether this shaky little truce of ours will last, or not. That is strictly up to you and your people."

Hiram was equally honest. "And I don't lak you worth no more than a pile of dog shit, Ben Raines. I personal thank all you gonna do is screw things up for me and mine."

"That's fair enough, Hiram. We've made our positions clear. School starts Monday morning at eight o'clock. Have any child between the ages of five and seventeen at the school complex on Matthew Road. School will run for six hours daily."

"And if I don't, Raines?"

"I will personally lead the troops into your community, take every child between six months and twelve years, and you will never see them again. I've done it before, Hiram. Don't ever doubt that. At least half of the children you'll see around here are adopted."

"You talk big about right and wrong and all your high and mighty ways, and you'd do that to mothers and fathers?"

Ben picked up a book from his desk and tossed it to Billy Bob. "Read it!"

Billy Bob could not. He could not make out half the words in the first sentence.

"He's at least thirty years old, Hiram. And he's illiterate."

"He ain't done it! Me and his ma was married in the church!"

"Goddamnit, Hiram! I said illiterate, not illegitimate. He can't read, man!"

"He can plow and plant and harvest. He can hunt and fish and trap! He don't need to know nothin' else."

"Hiram, are you aware that about half the game and fish you're eating have been, to one degree or the other, contaminated? Do you know how to check for it? Tell me, Hiram, of all the babies born during the last twelve years, how many were deformed; mentally retarded?"

Hiram would not meet Ben's eyes. "God's will," he finally muttered.

"God's will?" Ben shouted. "It isn't God's will! It's your own goddamned stupidity, man! Did you see all those cattle trucks arriving when you came in? We've been breeding a stronger, hardier breed for years . . . free of contamination. Did you ever think about things like that, Hiram?"

Hiram refused to answer.

"After the bombs came, Hiram . . . and the survivors began trickling in, did any of your people take them as wives or husbands?"

Hiram looked at Billy Bob.

"I see," Ben calmed down, leaning back in his chair. "Your kids, Billy . . . how are they?"

"Different," the man said.

"How different?"

"They ain't right. Some of them was borned blind; some of them born . . . all twisted and ugly. Only two of them lived."

"I'm sorry, Billy. Your wife?"

"First one died. I kept it in the family since then."

"No doubt," Ben muttered.

Keep that up, Ben thought, and you'll eventually get the same results.

"Start bringing your people in tomorrow morning, Hiram. First light. I want them all to have complete medical check-ups."

"I don't reckon I got no choice in the matter, does I, General Raines?"

"No, Hiram. I reckon you don't."

Four

"Makes me feel like some damned commandant of a concentration camp," Ben said to Dan, after Hiram and Billy Bob had left.

Dan nodded. "Sometimes, general, one has to do things that are distasteful, but for the good of the majority."

"Thank you, Dan. Take a battalion down tonight. You have parish maps?"

"Yes, sir. Found them at what used to be the Chamber of Commerce office."

Dr. Chase walked in, Cecil right behind him.

"You're late," Ben bitched.

"My, haven't we become the punctual one?" Chase sat down. "Blow it out your beret, general."

One thing Ben could always count on was Lamar Chase bringing him down to earth, and if he didn't do it, Ike would.

Ben outlined his plans.

Chase nodded his head in agreement. "I have teams cleaning up the hospital now. It really isn't in that bad a shape. Some progress was actually tried here in this community, Ben."

50

"Took a damn war to do it!"

"He's quite argumentative today," Dan said. "Comes with having something loosely called a conversation with cretins, I should imagine."

"Thank you, Dan," Ben said. "I couldn't have said it better."

Ike had been standing at the door. "Don't compliment that Limey too much, Ben. He gets the big head."

"Idiot!" the ex-SAS officer said to the ex-SEAL.

"Stuffed shirt!" Ike fired back.

"Hillbilly!"

"All right!" Ben ended it. "You getting your equipment lined out, Ike?"

"Right. It's goin' on so smoothly we'll be able to pull out in the morning. I'm taking Dr. Ling, Lamar."

"Good man. If there is something he doesn't know about radioactivity, it hasn't been written yet."

"Who have you chosen as XO, Ike?"

"Major Broadhurst. Tina's going to range out about two hundred miles ahead of us. Here's the route, Ben." He laid a map on the desk. "From here to Memphis, then we cut east to Nashville, Knoxville. We know D.C. took a hot one. That's fact. So we'll stay on Eighty-one all the way into Maryland. After that, we'll have to play it by ear."

"Sounds good, Ike."

"OK. I got things to do. I'll leave you boys to your roundin' up of rednecks. See you in the mornin', Ben." He grinned and left the office.

"You want me to take ten or twelve deuce and a halfs down into his wretched community, general?"

Dan asked. "To further hasten any recalcitrant recluses?"

"Yes. Good idea. Dan, I'll be blunt. These people have been borderline lawless for decades. Don't fuck around with them. First one to bow up, butt-stroke him and put him on the ground. Force is the one thing they understand."

"Yes, sir."

"Has Colonel West and his mercs pulled in yet, Cec?"

"Yes, Ben. They're bivouacked about ten miles east of town. Strange man, that Colonel West."

"Yes. Lamar, how are we fixed for medicines?"

"Pretty good. It's doubtful these people have been inoculated against anything. So that is the first order of business. This area has reverted back swiftly since the bombings. Malaria and typhoid fever worry me. But my big concern is typhus."

"Why typhus, Lamar?"

"Transmitted by fleas and lice."

"I agree." He called for an aide. He stuck his head into the room. "Have the school grounds and buildings sprayed top to bottom. And have a delousing tent set up."

"Yes, sir."

"Dan? After the people have been moved out tomorrow, have teams sent out to inspect each home. If they're living in squalor . . . burn it."

"Yes, sir."

"That's not going to win you any friends, Ben," Cecil reminded him.

"I am well aware of that, Cec. It's just a matter of time before Hiram and his bunch elect to do one of two things. They'll either pull out in the middle of the night, or they'll fight."

"You're that sure, Ben?" Lamar asked.

"Yes. Hiram despises me. Always has. The first time some kid tells him that we're teaching against his philosophy, that's when it's going to hit the fan."

"The children are the hope for the future, general," Dan spoke up. "We cannot allow a child to be brought up in ignorance."

"I don't intend to allow it, Dan. That is why most of the time, just a whole lot of those kids from the Stanford Community will be spending the night with various Rebel families here in town."

"That isn't going to make you any more popular with the 'necks, Ben," Cecil told him. "But I have to applaud your plan."

"I never cared about being popular with trash, Cec. They have no place in my plans."

"You know, Raines," Dr. Chase said, "it's just a damn wonder somebody didn't shoot you back when you were ranting and raving with the written word."

"They tried, Lamar. They tried. It was then that I knew I'd touched a raw nerve." He turned to look out the still-dirty window of the old bank building. "It was only then that I fully grasped the seriousness of the problem. Ninety-five percent of the people like Hiram will never change. But there is hope for the kids. And whether it's right or moral for me to do what I'm doing . . . God will have to judge me on that point. For now, I can do only what I think is best for future generations."

* * *

"What are we gonna do, Hiram?" The question was thrown at him from amid the white-robed and coned-hatted crowd who had gathered in the darkness. The cross had burned down to only a faint glow.

"We got to go along with Raines till we can come up with a plan." Hiram's oldest, Billy, had refused to attend the meeting this night, and that both confused and hurt Hiram. Since the meeting earlier in the day with Raines, Billy had been moody and untouchable. The boy acted like he had something heavy on his mind.

"They's too many of 'em for us to fight, Hiram. And that's what I think Ben Raines wants . . . a fight."

"In a way he do," Hiram agreed. "If it was jist us, he would. But Ben's got plans for the younguns. I don't know what they is, but that sneaky bastard's got somethang up his sleeve. Y'all can jist bet on that."

"Furst time one of them nigger Rebels gives me an order, I'm a-gonna bus' his head," a pus-gutted man loudly proclaimed.

Hiram remembered the muzzle of that gun stuck up under his chin. Humiliating! "No, you won't, neither, Carl. You'll jist do 'xactly whut he tells you to do. We're so bad outnumbered by them Rebels we ain't even in the ballpark, much less in the game. I don't know yet what we're gonna do. And until I can come up with somethang, we just play 'er easy-like."

Billy sat on his front porch and thought of the

54

man called Ben Raines. There was something about the man that both drew and frightened Billy Bob. And it was embarrassing about that book. Billy had never told his father, but he didn't like not being able to read right. Billy always thought that all them books he'd seen all piled up in stores and libraries and homes had to have been writ for some reason. And he figured that there was good to be had in a lot of them.

Problem was, he couldn't make out the words.

And them Rebel soldiers; they just seemed so, well, busy, he reckoned. Like they knowed they had a good purpose in life and was right eager to get crackin' on it. And ever'where he'd looked that day, he'd seen men and women and kids with books in they hands. There had to be something to it, or else all them folks wouldn't be foolin' with it.

And what was that word General Raines had used? Yeah . . . civility. Nice-sounded word, Billy thought. Felt good on the tongue. Problem was, he didn't know what it meant. Get right down to the truth of it, Billy didn't know half of what General Raines had said.

And it just, by golly, shouldn't oughta be that way. A man ought to be able to have sense enough to know what the other feller is talking about.

Billy watched as his brother, Grover Neal, rode his horse up to the porch of the house. "Billy," the young man said. "Daddy was some put-out 'bout you not goin' to the gatherin' this night."

"Had things to do, Grover."

"Whut?"

"Mind things."

"Whut kind of thangs?"

"Thinkin' to do."

"Oh."

Billy's older boy, by wife number two, came out onto the porch and sat down in front of the old TV set that rested on the porch. "Magic box," the boy said.

For some unexplainable reason, that statement got all over Billy. "It isn't a magic box, Richard Lee. It's just an old television set."

"Mister G.B. says it's a magic box," the boy said.

Billy almost said that Mister G.B. was a fool and had been for as long as Billy had known him. But then he remembered that G.B. was his pa's best friend.

"Yeah, it's a magic box, Richard Lee," Grover spoke up.

"Shut up!" Billy's tone was harsh toward his brother. "Don't be fillin' the boy's head with crap. No such thing as magic."

"Ummmm!" Grover backed up. "I bet you won't say that to Old Lady Pauly. She put a hex on you, boy."

"Go on back home, Grover. You're talkin' like a fool!"

"I'm a-gonna tale Daddy on you, boy!" Grover swung back into the saddle.

"You do that. Right now, you bes' just get on out of here."

"If this here ain't a magic box," the boy asked, after his uncle had ridden off into the night, "what then be it?"

Billy sighed. "Son, back when I was just about

56

your age, we had something called TV. Folks could send pitchers . . . *pictures,* through the air and they'd form up on that screen and we could watch shows that come all the way from, well, Mon-roe."

The child drew back from the set, suddenly fearful of the set. "No!"

"Oh, yeah, Richard. But it wasn't nothing to be afraid of."

"Can you make it do it agin?"

"No, boy. I'm . . ." Then he admitted the truth. "I'm not smart enough."

"I bet Grandpaw could do it!"

"No, boy. He can't do it, neither."

"But Grandpaw knows ever'thang."

He just thinks he do, Billy thought. If I was a big enough man to tell you the truth, Grandpaw is nearabouts as dumb as I am.

"But I seen a man today that probably could make that thing light up. Or if he couldn't, I betcha he's got some people with him that can."

"Who he be?"

"Man name of Ben Raines."

The boy looked at his father. "But Grandpaw says Ben Raines is evil."

Billy then took the first step toward breaking out of the bonds of ignorance and near-barbarism. "Your Grandpaw is wrong, boy. General Ben Raines ain't evil."

"Then what he be, Pa?"

"Smart. I think he's got the in-sight, boy."

The boy gasped. "I be fearful of that man, Pa."

Billy shook his head. "No need to be. What you need to do is learn from him and his kind."

57

Behind the screen door, wife number two was standing in silence, hands to her mouth, listening in shock. Her husband was talking agin the leader.

And it was the code that she had to report him.

An hour before dawn, and Ben and Ike were sitting alone in a mess tent, having breakfast and talking.

"If New York City is still intact, Ike, it's a good bet that's the headquarters of the Night People. What was it we were told in Atlanta. The Judges. Yes. The Judges are the council; they make the rules for the Night People."

"And the place is gonna be swarmin' with those heathens."

"Yes. I think that's why they eventually had to branch out. New York couldn't support them all. So they began fanning out. If what we're saying is true, the Night People could be the biggest threat we've ever faced."

Ike shuddered. "Can you just imagine a *million* of those creatures, Ben?"

"Mind-boggling, isn't it?"

"To say the least."

"I'm thinking that if New York City is intact, and inhabited, the city is probably cordoned off by various groups. Street punks and warlords probably control parts of it; Night People control other parts; decent citizens might have a stronghold there. We just don't know."

"I'll find out, Ben."

"Ike, I am giving you a direct order. Keep your big

ass out of the city. Do you understand me, Ike?"

"That's a big ten-four, Ben." The ex-SEAL grinned at Ben.

Ben stuck out his hand and Ike took it. "Luck to you, Ike. And look after my little girl."

"Will do, Ben. I spoke to Cecil and Chase and Dan last night."

"I'll keep an eye on Nina for you."

Ike smiled. "Tell you what, Ben. As testy as she's been the last few days, I'm glad to get gone!"

Laughing, the two men moved out into the quiet of early morning.

Ben stood in the darkness and watched as Ike linked up with his two-hundred-person unit. They had a long and dirty and dangerous route ahead of them. Ben knew Cecil was mildly pissed at him for not having been chosen to go; but Ben needed Cec here. Cecil had a calming influence about him. The man almost never lost his temper—however when he did, one had better stand aside, for the former Green Bennie was awesome in a fight, and for his age, still amazingly powerful. When it come to administration and logistical problems, Cecil was the best.

When the last vehicle in Ike's column was gone, Ben walked back into the mess tent and drew himself another mug of what currently passed for coffee. He sat alone with his thoughts.

Hiram had taken everything too calmly to suit Ben; he figured the man's brain was working overtime, trying to come up with a plan to outfox the man he hated more than anything on the face of the earth. Ben's thoughts went winging back, sailing through the years. . . .

. . . " 'at's him over yonder." Ben heard the voice come from behind him. He did not look around.

"The skinny feller with the beer?"

"Yeah."

"He don't look lak much to me."

Favorite redneck game; bait the stranger and see if he'll fight.

All real men fistfight. Ever'body knows that. If he won't fight, he's probably a queer.

Late afternoon, years before the Great War would alter the lives of every human being on the face of the earth for untold generations to come. Ben had stopped, against his better judgment, at a 'neck honky-tonk a few miles from Morriston.

"Bring us a beer, Carol," Hiram had called. "A long neck. Ast that lanky drank of water at the bar ifn he'd lak a sodee pop. He looks too sissy to be drankin' a man's drank."

Ben smiled at the waitress. "I'll pass."

Ben knew exactly what was coming next, and Hiram didn't disappoint him.

"You too good to drank with us, boy?"

"That's Hiram Rockingham, mister," the barmaid said in a hoarse whisper. "He's bad."

"He certainly smells that way," Ben said, raising his voice.

"Whut's 'at?" Hiram hollered. "Whut'd he say 'bout me?"

"I said you stink like shit, you ignorant mother-fucker," Ben said. He still had not turned around.

He was watching the 'neck in the mirror.

Hiram stood up and balled his hands into fists. "Ah thank ah'll jist whup your ass for that."

"I doubt it."

When Hiram was two steps away from him, Ben turned and hit the redneck in the face with the beer mug. Blood and beer went flying. Ben grabbed Hiram by the seat of his dirty jeans, the other hand on his equally dirty neck, and drove him headfirst into a wall.

Turning, Ben picked up a pool cue and hit the first 'neck he could find in the teeth. Tobacco-stained pearlies went flying. The other 'neck went racing for the door. Ben jammed the business end of the cue stick between the man's cowboy boots and brought him down . . . then kicked him in the head.

The others in the joint had not moved. But Ben heard one say, "Best pass the word to leave that son of a bitch alone."

Ben ordered another beer and sipped on it until Hiram began to groan and move. Ben then poured the rest of the beer on his head.

Ben stepped back and waited; stepped back far enough so that Hiram could not kick or grab him.

"We was only funnin' wift you," Hiram said, getting to his feet.

"It is a joke only when all parties find it amusing. But I don't suppose someone as ignorant as you could ever possibly comprehend that."

Hiram swung. Ben grabbed the forearm and put Hiram on the floor with a bit of applied judo.

Then he kicked Hiram right on the ass just as hard as he could.

Hiram squalled and cussed. He rolled to his feet and charged Ben, trying to get him in a bearhug. Ben tripped him and once more sent the 'neck to the floor.

Ben kicked him in the face. The sound of bones crunching was loud in the barroom. Hiram fell back, unconscious, blood and tissue and gum and bits of teeth leaking out of his swollen mouth.

"Call the sheriff's department," Ben told the barmaid.

The deputy was amused. Obviously, he had little use for the people of Stanford . . . probably even less than most, since Ben was sure he had answered many calls to that area.

"So Hiram said he was gonna whip your ass, huh, Mr. Raines?"

"That's what he said."

"You want to file any complaints, Carol?"

"Not a one. Hiram and his buddies got exactly what they deserved."

"But we was only a-funnin', deputy!" one 'neck hollered.

"Shut up," the deputy told him. He swung his eyes to Ben. "You want to file a complaint, Mr. Raines?"

Ben shook his head. "No, it's over as far as I'm concerned."

The deputy smiled. "Maybe the fight is, but you don't know this bunch, mister. You're from Illinois, so I'll bring you up to date. These guys are Kluckers."

"I beg your pardon?"

"KKK."

"Is that supposed to fill me with fear?"

The deputy laughed. "You may be a Yankee, Mr. Raines, but you're all right. Just watch your back from now on, 'cause they ain't never gonna forget or forgive you for this. They're white trash, Mr. Raines."

Ben looked at the deputy.

"You see, Mr. Raines, here's the way it is. You got black people, you got colored people, and you got niggers. You got white people, you got rednecks, and you got trash. Blacks and whites never have had any trouble." He turned around and left the dark barroom.

"Well, I'll be damned!" Ben said.

Five

Hiram rinsed off his dentures and stuck them in his mouth. He'd worn them ever since that goddamned Ben Raines had kicked his teeth out, years ago.

Son of a bitch didn't fight fair.

Hell, they'd only been jokin'. Man couldn't take a joke, either.

Hiram had heard the trucks and Jeeps go by his place during the night. And he knew what they was without even having to get up out of the bed.

Them damn soldier-people come to see that all the folks around here got into town like good little boys and girls.

He'd been too busy today to go and see Billy; something was sure wrong with him. Grover Neal come by after the cross-burnin' and said his brother got all uppity with him. Hiram wasn't going to have that. Not none of it.

He sat down and ate his breakfast, conscious of the Jeep parked in front of his house, with a machine gun stuck up in the rear of it.

Goddamned Ben Raines was pushin'. That's what he was doin'. Pushin'.

But already, Hiram could see by looking out his kitchen window, people were leaving for Morriston.

Just like good little boys and girls.

Hiram sat, his stomach sour, and cursed Ben Raines.

Tina had halted her Scouts just south of Memphis. The team, to a person, sat in their vehicles and stared at the huge sign by the side of the road.

MEMPHIS — OFF LIMITS. DEATH TO ALL WHO ENTER.

"You think they're trying to tell us something?" a young man asked Tina, a smile on his face.

The Rebels were human; of course, they knew fear. But none of them lived with it on a day-to-day basis. Many had been raised in Rebel camps, from California to Georgia. Most of them had been fighting since they were barely into their teens. They were solid, hard-nosed, professional soldiers, and they did not frighten easily. They had, to a person, faced hideous mutants; armies of warlords; street gangs; they had faced the troops of the Russian, Striganov, and his IPF . . . and they had defeated them all.

More important, they had all been trained by Ben Raines . . . he had written the training manual. The Rebels could be totally ruthless in their seemingly never-ending quest to bring some form of stability back to the shattered nation. And they rarely took prisoners.

One either agreed with the Rebel philosophy, or the choices were plain. Leave the area or attend your own funeral.

"Well, whoever put that sign up can go right straight to hell. We've got to cut a route through Memphis. Matt, you and Chuck range out a mile in front of us. We've got to clear this two-forty loop for Ike. Move out."

The point men saw their first pile of bodies just after entering the city limits. They waited until Tina and her group had joined them.

"Damn," Tina said, eyeballing the pile of stinking bodies. "That's a fairly fresh pile. And they're all been carved up."

"The choice cuts taken," another Scout said.

Tina stood for a moment, pondering their situation. If they advanced further and got themselves cut off, surrounded by . . . whatever enemy was in the city, they could accomplish nothing. Getting themselves killed would prove or solve nothing. But on the other hand, if they didn't clear the route, Ike's main columns would have to cut off the Interstate somewhere around Batesville and wind their way north on secondary roads until reaching I-40.

"It's probably Night People responsible for this," she finally said. "I won't order any of you to your deaths. Let's vote."

That, also, was the Rebel way.

All voted to continue on into Memphis.

"We're not exactly traveling light, Tina," the ranking sergeant said. "We've got .50s and .60s and rocket launchers and explosives. And we've got daylight on our side. Let's put the vehicles fifty yards apart, everybody on alert, and roll in."

"Heads up, people," Tina ordered, clicking her M-16 off safety. She turned to her driver, Sharon. "Let's take the point."

And head into the unknown, she thought.

"And top of the morning to you, sir!" Dan called out cheerfully to Hiram. The man had just stepped out onto his front porch.

"Soldier," Hiram returned the greeting, sort of. "Don't trust us, soldier-boy?"

Dan smiled at the man. "Implicitly, sir."

Hiram grunted. He figured he'd been insulted but wasn't sure.

"Me and mine will be along directly," Hiram told him.

"We'll wait," Dan said pleasantly.

Hiram figured there wasn't no point in puttin' it off no longer. He plopped his hat on his head and started hollerin' for his wives and kids.

It was quite a parade that came rattling and banging and smoking into town.

"The western people had a name for people like Hiram," Ben said to Cecil. "Rawhiders. They didn't build anything to last; just laced it together with rawhide, knowing it was going to fall down sooner or later."

Even the normally mild-mannered Cecil was disgusted with the sight. "There are literally thousands of abandoned vehicles around the land. There is no need for vehicles to be pieced together with wire!"

"Yes, but that would require some initiative, Cec. It's easier to just . . . 'war hit up' and let it flap."

"And these people were like this when the world was whole?" Cec asked.

"To one degree or the other. There were, at one time, many good, decent families living in the Stanford Community. But they were always outnumbered by the Hirams of this earth."

"I wonder what happened to them?"

"They probably left after all semblance of law and order was gone. Wouldn't you?"

"No," the black man said, some heat in his voice. "I would have picked up a gun and fought the Hirams of this earth."

"My, my!" Ben kidded him. "How militaristic we've become."

"Stuff it, Raines!" the ex-teacher-turned-Rebel said with a grin. "Let's go see how Chase is doing."

"Fuming, I should imagine."

They found him at the delousing tents, arguing with Hiram and several other men.

Buddy Raines had walked along with his father and General Jefferys.

"I ain't gonna stand for bein' treated lak no gawddam cow!" Hiram hollered. "I jist ain't a-gonna do hit."

"Don't get too close, Ben," Chase warned. "The man is crawling with fleas."

"I know," Ben said drily. "I had to have my office fumigated after he left. Hiram, go to that tent over there and take a shower. Then come to this tent here for delousing."

68

"Ah'd lak to see you make me do that!"

Ben smiled. "I kicked your ass years ago, Hiram. You want me to do it again?"

With a low curse, the man glared at Ben, raw hate in his eyes. "You 'barrassin' me in front of my people deliberate, Raines."

"Everybody is being treated the same, Hiram. You singled yourself out by your behavior."

"Why don't you take the treatment, Raines. Show us how hit's done."

"Because I don't live in squalor. I take baths daily, and I don't have fleas and lice. Move, Hiram."

"I'll kill you someday, Raines," the 'neck swore.

"You'll try."

"What do we do with their clothes, general?" Ben was asked.

"Burn them."

"They's smoke down yonder!" a 'neck hollered, pointing.

"Lot's of smoke!" another yelled. "Whut the hale's goin' on?"

"Some of the homes are being burned," Ben told the group. "Your possessions were moved out and put in empty homes . . . after being deloused and fumigated," he added, more than a modicum of disgust in his voice.

"My daddy built that there house!" a man yelled.

"Yes," Ben told him. "And I knew your father. He was fine man. A good, decent man. He would have had no part in following scum like this," Ben jerked his thumb at Hiram. "I can't help but wonder what happened to change you." He looked at Buddy. "Take over here, Buddy. Delouse them."

69

"Yes, sir."

"Come on, Cec. The odor is overwhelming."

"See you in Hell, Raines!" Hiram swore.

"I hope it smells better than this," Ben called over his shoulder.

"Blow it," Tina finally said, after inspecting the barricade on the I-240 loop. "But be sure it isn't booby-trapped. Let's back off and put a rocket into the mess. If it's wired, that should tell us."

The rocket knocked a hole in the barricade and the rest was quickly shoved to one side. Rebels stood on both sides of the overpass, weapons at the ready, eyes constantly searching the area below them.

Tina checked the sky. It would be getting dark in a couple of hours. She did not want to be caught inside the city limits after dark.

Sergeant Wilson caught her glance. "It's going to be close, Tina."

"There's a barricade of some sort every mile," Tina's walkie talkie popped.

"We're not going to make it," Tina said. Then softly cursed. "The airport is right over there. Or what is left of it. Let's hole up there for the night and establish radio contact with Eagle Base and with Ike."

The twenty-five person team of Scouts made their way to the airport . . . and immediately ran into trouble.

"I do not wish anytime soon to go through another day like this one," Chase bitched, pouring himself a stiff drink of bourbon.

About an hour before dark, and the men were sitting in Ben's office. "I still feel like I've got lice crawling on me." Chase downed the drink in one gulp and poured another.

"I have to say this, general," Dan said. "Is it worth all this? To settle in this particular spot, that is?"

"I'll admit that some of it is purely personal," Ben said. "But we're going to be hitting pockets like this no matter where we go. We might as well practice here and get it down pat. We've got to show the people that we mean exactly what we say. We can't run a bluff."

"I can't begin to tell you all how much I miss the tranquility of the old Tri-States," Cecil said. "Talk about your good old days."

"We could do it again," Ben said. "But what would we have accomplished by doing so? We would be safe inside our sealed borders, but people like Hiram would be gaining strength outside. Very soon, we'd be even more outnumbered than we are now."

All present silently agreed with that.

"Father." Buddy spoke. "Why didn't you just send planes to do a fly-by of what is left of New York City?"

"I will eventually, son. But first the ground teams have to check out and clear runways; check fuel depots. We have to make certain the planes have a place to set down."

"I see." The young man rose and walked to the window. Somebody had washed it during the day. "Something on your mind, son?"

The son turned to face the father. "You speak of classes of people, father. I had never understood it fully until this day. But it's still confusing to me. A rational person would surely understand that if one is to prevent disease, one must bathe. Even animals make some attempt to clean themselves. What makes these people behave as they do?"

"Lack of education is part of it, Buddy. And the way their parents brought them up has something to do with it. For years, so-called experts did their best to convince people that there is no such thing as a person's being born bad. I never believed a damn thing those so-called experts had to say. I've seen too much proof otherwise. My belief is that once a person hits adulthood, few will change. Part of them might want to change, but something within them has overpowered that urge."

"Then . . . so we can change the children of these people, hopefully. But what about the adults?"

"Fear is the great motivator, Buddy. To cut through all the grease and get to the stew, you've got to understand that all governments are based, to one degree or another, on fear. Fear of punishment for breaking the rules."

The handsome young man was silent for a moment. Dan wore an amused look on his face. Chase was studying his glass of whiskey. Cecil kept looking from father to son.

"All right," Buddy said. "I can see where that is true. Governments must assume the same position as a parent toward a child; am I correct in that assumption, Father?"

"Unfortunately, yes, Buddy. I'm afraid that is the

case."

"But the Rebel philosophy is not so much to that degree."

"That's right. That's why it's so difficult for so many people to understand us."

"This Hiram person? . . ."

"He will never understand it. Hiram is the worst kind of person, Buddy. He is ignorant and very proud of that ignorance. And because of that, Hiram is very dangerous. He preys on the fear and superstitions of others like him. You ever seen a snakepit, son?"

"Oh, yes, sir!"

"That's what we're dealing with . . . with most of the adults of the Stanford Community."

"Then someday, Father, you will have to kill this Hiram person."

"I'm afraid so, son."

"It's a very distasteful business, isn't it, Father?"

"Yes. Yes, it is."

An aide stuck his head into the office. "Ike just called in. He can't make contact with Tina's Scouts."

Six

Tina and her team had pulled up under the canopy of steel and concrete, left guards with each vehicle, and slowly entered the littered airport concourse. Tina was the first to notice what appeared to be a bundle of rags behind a car rental counter, next to the wall. She motioned the other team members back to the shattered electric doors and lifted her M-16.

The creature came off the floor, out from under the rags, its horrible twisted face ugly with hate, the unnaturally white eyes hot with fury.

Tina pulled the trigger, the slugs catching the creature in the chest, stopping the horrible howling. The lower concourse was suddenly filled with Night People. The Scouts sent a dozen of them into that long sleep and then rang out to their vehicles.

"That hangar over there!" Tina pointed. "It's small enough that we can clean it out quickly but large enough for us to store our vehicles."

There was still enough light in the sky to prevent the Night People from leaving the safe darkness of the airport's lower deck.

But a Scout sent a long burst of M-60 machine gun fire into the lower deck, just for insurance. The insurance paid off. A long while of agony erupted from the dimness of the concourse.

One horribly disfigured creature braved the light, running out just as the overhang was ending and the vehicles could break free of the dimness. Tina's Jeep struck the thing and sent it over the hood, to land in the small back seat, packed with supplies. Tina felt bloody fingers clawing at her neck.

They were accelerating fast out of a curve, and the driver had all she could do fighting the wheel. Tina twisted in the seat and came face to face with the foul-smelling and hideously deformed being. Clawing at her .45, cocked and locked, she fired through the seat, the big .45 slug striking the thing in the belly. With a howl of anguish, the Night Person toppled out of the Jeep, only to be run over by the truck behind Tina.

Her driver, Sharon, cut her eyes at her and grinned. "How'd you like to bed down with one of those beauties?"

"Pl-ease!" Tina took a deep breath. The fetid smell of the creature still lingered around her. She wrinkled her nose.

They made it to the hangar without seeing another Night Person, but with the darkness quickly gathering, all knew they were being watched.

"Chuck, take two and clear the hangar to the left," Tina shouted. "Matt, take two and do the same to the hangar on the right. Sharon, Bernie, Ham, come on!"

The rattle of gunfire was loud as the Rebels

cleaned out a nest of Night People in the left-side hangar. None were found in the other two buildings.

"Find buckets and barrels, people. Take your entrenching tools and fill them up with dirt. Ham, check out those pumps over there. See if the tanks still hold fuel. We'll saturate the dirt with jet fuel and set them around the outside of the hangar. Ignite them when the creatures come at us tonight. And you can bet they damn sure will. Let's go, people!"

"Eagle One to Shark," Ben spoke into the mic.

"Shark here."

"What's wrong with Tina, Ike?"

"Don't know, Ben. I'm about a hundred and twenty-five miles south of Memphis. Been trying to reach her for an hour. No response."

"Son of a bitch!" Ben cursed.

"You want me to pour on the juice and try to find her?"

Ben then made the decision that separated him from the others, placing him in that lonely position of commander. "No, Ike. Tina knew the risks when she volunteered. Your job is to get to New York City. I'll try to contact her with our equipment here. I'll get back to you. Eagle One out."

"Shark out."

Ike looked at his XO. Broadhurst shook his head. "That's one hard man, general."

"Most good soldiers are." Ike's reply was curt but not unfriendly. "It goes with the territory."

"Eagle One to Big Apple Scout. Do you read me,

Big Apple Scout?"

"Relax, Eagle One." Tina's voice came through the speaker. "I've been listening to you and Shark growl."

"Don't get smart-assed with me, girl!" Ben said with a grin, as relief flooded him. "What's the problem at your twenty?"

"Night People, and from what we've seen so far, Memphis is filled with them. We're holed up at the airport."

"Which one?"

"Big one just south of the Two-forty loop."

"How's your position?"

"Pretty good, I believe. It better be, 'cause we're sure socked in here for the night, and I got a hunch it's gonna get interesting."

"You still have about a half hour of light left. Have your people work in pairs and check for portable generators. Place should have plenty of them, especially in the hangars. Then find the plug for the outside floodlights. You ten four this?"

"Thanks, Eagle. I'd forgotten about that."

"Stay in contact. Eagle One out."

"Whut you gonna do 'bout Billy Bob's talkin' agin you, Pa?" Jimmy Luther asked his father.

"I don't know. Nothin' yet. Give him time. He'll screw up big the next time. Bet on it."

"And then, Pa?"

"You know what the code says, boy. Same as I do."

His son nodded his head. "I don't lak my new

house. Wife does, though. She's all thrilled with it."

"Wimmin would be. They ain't got no sense no how. If it wasn't for what they got 'tween their legs, we be huntin' them lak deer. We ain't gonna raise no fuss just yet. Play along with Raines, you hear?"

"Yes, Daddy. Uh, Daddy? . . ."

"Whut it is?"

"Precious was makin' eyes at one of them soldier-boys today. I seen her."

"I'll take a strop to her ass! My little baby Precious Thrill ain' gonna get in-volved with no nigger-lovin' soldier-boy. You see her doin' that agin, you come tell me, you hear, Jimmy Luther?"

"Yes, Daddy."

"An tell the others to watch Billy Bob. Ah thank he's all tooken with Ben Raines's big words and highfalutin' ways."

"Yes, Daddy."

"I hate that goddamned Ben Raines!"

At full dark, the Night People began to circle the hangar, moaning and filling the air with promises of dark and bloody torture. Inside, Tina had gone her dad one better. She'd had her team run three strands of wire completely around the building, ankle to chest high, securing it with insulators taken from light poles and other hangars.

The teams had found three portable generators, and Ham had connected them together and then grinned up at Tina.

"When they hit those naked wires, Tina, it's gonna be the last time for some of them."

"What do you mean, 'some of them'?"

"Enough of them grab it, it'll short out, probably. But not before it does a hell of a lot of damage."

"We save the wires for last," she ordered. "This building is metal; it isn't going to burn. We've got enough firepower among us to stand off one hell of a crowd. If it comes to it, we can bust out and take our chances outside. But that is really a last resort."

" 'Course there is something else you'd better know, too," Ham said.

"I don't like the sound of this." Tina tried a small smile.

"These are big-assed generators. They just might throw enough juice to melt those wires we strung up."

"Thanks, Ham. But I could have done without that knowledge."

"We can always try prayer," he suggested.

"Believe me," Sharon said, "I have!"

Then came the sound that chilled them all, cooling the blood and raising the hair on the back of their necks, making rational human flesh feel like it was crawling.

"Die . . . Die . . . Die . . . Die!"

The chanting was accompanied by the sounds of hundreds of marching feet.

"Snipers up on the scaffolding," Tina ordered. "Everybody else take your positions and stand hard."

The Rebels moved to preassigned posts. They waited.

The chanting became louder.

"Sweet Jesus Christ!" a sniper muttered.

"What do you see?" Tina called from the hangar floor.

"Hundreds of them. One great big human wave of robed and hooded . . . whatever the hell they are."

"Pick your targets and fire!" Tina ordered.

The hangar echoed and rocked with the sounds of .223, .308, .50, and .60 caliber ammo. The din was enormous inside the metal building.

Outside, the howling and crying of wounded was harsh in the night air. The first wave of Night People never even got close to the hangar. Those that had tried now lay in bloody heaps on the concrete, several hundred yards from the hangar. Those still alive had run back into the dark safety of the night.

"Cease firing!" Tina called. She walked the hangar floor, going to each position, chatting briefly with the Rebel stationed there. No one had been hurt by the Night People, although a couple of arrows had managed to penetrate the broken windows of the hangar.

"How far away is the nearest group?" Tina called to a Rebel on the scaffolding.

" 'Bout three hundred meters. Pretty good bunch of them."

"Ham, set up a mortar just outside the door and lob a couple of HEs into that knot of garbage. That might shake up their little world." She looked up at the Rebel on the scaffolding. "Give me coordinates."

The klicks were called out as Ham adjusted the leveling bubble. "Drop one in," he ordered.

The rocket slid down the tube. The high-explosive round rocked the night.

The spotter called down adjustments.

The second HE dropped right in the middle of the Night People, hurling bodies and pieces of bodies in all directions.

"Now start dropping in white phosphorous," Tina ordered. She stood just outside a small hangar door.

The WP rounds were cranked out as fast as could be dropped down the tube. The WP sparked the night, the burning shards igniting the clothing of the Night People, burning deep into flesh, sending the Night People screaming and squalling and running off in search of relief.

But there was no relief from WP; the shards would burn all the way through bone.

"Cease firing!" Tina said. "Back inside, Ham. That should give us some breathing room."

An hour passed in near silence. The Night People, up to this point, had been accustomed to dealing with civilians, without any effective organization, training, or leadership. This band of Night People had never before encountered anything like the Rebels.

Tina accepted a hand-rolled cigarette from Ham. The tobacco, years old and dry, was harsh against her throat. Like her father, she smoked but three or four cigarettes a day; she felt that she might add to that before this night was over.

The generators were rumbling, the racket reverberating around the hangar. Ham had not yet connected the insulated wire that was hooked into the naked wires around the hangar.

"Here they come," a Rebel called in a hoarse whisper. "They're crawling on their bellies."

She felt Ham's eyes on her. "This time, we give

81

them a taste of the wires."

He grinned in the gloom and nodded his head.

"Light rain outside," Pam called.

"That's even better," Ham said with a laugh. "They'll be wet when they hit the wire. Get ready for some fireworks."

"Get your welcoming cocktails ready," Tina called.

The Rebels had gathered up boxes of empty bottles and filled them with gasoline, stuffing rags down the necks of the bottles.

"I wish we had some flour," a Scout bitched.

"Yeah."

Flour added to the gasoline sticks when the cocktail blows, burning into flesh.

"They're close!" the spotter whispered. "They've got spears."

"Hit the juice, Ham."

Ham connected the wire and quickly ran around the inside of the hanger, briefly glancing out the broken windows, inspecting the wires. "They're holding."

"They're here!" a Rebel called softly.

A wild, hideous shrieking filled the night; more screaming was added as other Night People hit the naked voltage-charged wires around the hangar. Inhuman howlings filled the misty darkness as the juice was transmitted throughout damp bodies. The hangar was completely ringed by Night People.

"Give them everything you got!" Tina yelled, jerking her M-16 to her shoulder and squeezing off three-round bursts.

Moletov cocktails were hurled into the mass of stinking, hate-filled Night People. The burning rags hit stinking human rags and burst into flames. Once-human beings were turned into living torches, racing shrieking into the dark mist, briefly illuminating the night before falling to the concrete to lie kicking and howling as the flames ate the life from them.

Ham cut the juice to save the wires as the Night People began falling back. But this time, they were running away with a finality to their movements. They had had enough of the little band of Rebels. What had first looked so easy had turned into a death trap for them.

"Cease firing!" Tina called. She watched the misshapen and grotesque forms vanish into the gloom. "They've had it."

She walked to her Jeep and pulled out a food packet and a canteen of water. "Eat in shifts," she called. "Then we'll set up a guard schedule. We're pulling out at first light."

"Big Apple Scout to Shark," Tina radioed.

"Shark."

"What's your twenty, Shark? You sound awfully close."

"Hernando."

"Come on. We're just now clearing the last blockade. Try to ignore the buzzards around the airport."

"Ten-four. Be there in a few and then you can fill me in."

The Rebels in Ike's command looked at the circling and bloated buzzards as they passed the airport.

"Looks like they counted coup last night," Ike said to his driver.

"Sure does. Look over there." He pointed. "That buzzard's so full he can't even get off the ground."

They watched until they were past the point. The buzzard had given up trying to fly. He simply sat like an ugly blot, too bloated on human flesh to rise.

Tina's scouts were waiting for them on Interstate 40, just off the exit where the artery cut east. Ike halted his column and walked up to Tina.

"Fill me in, Tina."

She gave her report quietly and quickly.

"We're going to be doing this with every city we come to," Ike said. "And if I remember correctly, Nashville is a bitch to get through. But we've got to secure the Nashville airport for planes. Let's try to make it to just west of Nashville today, Tina. We'll bivouac outside the city and hit the airport at first light tomorrow."

"Yes, sir. Rolling now."

When Tina's team had pulled out, Ike radioed back to Base Camp One and brought Ben up to date.

"How's things with you and the rednecks, Ben?"

"Tense. Dan left some of his personnel down in that area and the folks resent the hell out their presence. It's only a matter of time before we're going to have to go in and kick ass."

"Any word from Khamsin?"

"From what we've been able to decode, Khamsin has his hands full. The citizens over there have risen up in revolt. I don't think we'll have to worry about the Libyan for a long time. Least I hope we don't."

"I'll check in with you just as soon as we make camp this evening, Ben. Shark out."

Ike walked the long column, inspecting the Jeeps and trucks. There hadn't been a vehicle of any type manufactured anywhere in the world in almost a decade and a half, and special care was given to Rebel vehicles. Wherever the Rebels went, parts trucks went along, with skilled mechanics accompanying. Something was always breaking down.

Ike spoke to every driver, every Rebel who met him during inspection. These men and women were Ike's special team. There were few among them who could be called young. Most were in their thirties and forties. They were all hardened combat veterans, survivors of half a hundred battles. Whatever weapon they handled, machine gun, mortar, rocket launcher, flame thrower, rifle . . . they were all experts. And they would stand to the last person. Most of the men had been in the U.S. military — years back — all in some hard-assed outfit. And the women were all highly trained guerrilla fighters, informal graduates of Raines's Rebel training courses.

"Hey, General Ike!" a man called. "When are we gonna see some action? Boring so far."

That was met by a laugh from all within hearing range.

"You'll get your chance, Lutty," Ike called. "Keep your pants on."

"He better," a woman laughed. "I didn't come along for romance."

"You think New York City is still there, Ike?" a man with a Bronx accent called. "I sure would like

85

to see my old neighborhood."

"If it is, Simon," Ike answered, "it's probably got rats as big as cats runnin' around."

"That'd be a definite improvement. Had rats as big as dogs when I lived there!"

More laughter.

"How you doin', Dana?" Ike asked a woman who sat behind the wheel of a pickup.

"Hangin' in, general."

Ike walked on. "Walt." He spoke to a black man. "You know we're gonna have to skirt Baltimore."

"I know, general. I just want to get close enough to see if anything is standing."

He had lost every member of his family when the bombs came.

"Lee," Ike spoke to an oriental man. "That's a hell of a big truck for someone as little as you are," he kidded him.

"I lowered the seat and put blocks on the pedals," Lee grinned at him.

Ike laughed and walked on, cradling his CAR-15. At the end of the long column, he waved for his driver to come pick him up.

His Jeep drove slowly back up to the front of the column, with Ike yelling out every few feet, "We're gonna push 'em hard, people. Heads up and stay alert."

At the head of the column, Ike balled his right hand into a fist and pumped his arm up and down. "Let's go!"

Seven

"You got anything to say to me?" Ben asked Dr. Lamar Chase.

Chase had marched into his office and plopped down without a word. Sat and glared at Ben.

"Ben, I am a tolerant man, you know that."

Ben laughed out loud.

"Just button your lip, Raines! Well . . . I'm usually a tolerant man."

"That's better."

"My doctors just finished with their report on that . . . freak show we conducted."

"You're speaking of the physicals on the people from the Stanford Community."

"Of course. It isn't time for your physical yet."

Ben smiled at the crusty old bastard.

"It came as a surprise to me, but the kids are not malnourished. Their diet could probably stand some variance. But by and large I found no problems there that can't be corrected. It's . . . the physical abuse that's bothering me."

"What the hell did you expect, Lamar? You saw

the caliber of parents."

"You do then agree that children of abusive parents usually grow up to abuse their own?"

"I'm going to surprise you, doctor . . . yes, I do believe that, for the most part."

"My God, Raines!" Chase feigned great shock. "There's hope for you yet. I can see it now: Ben Raines for President, on the Liberal ticket."

Ben waited until Chase finished hooing and hawing and slapping his knee. Get one over on the general . . . and Chase was good at it.

"What do you want me to do about it, Lamar?"

The doctor rose from his chair and poured a glass of water, then walked around the room, taking an occasional sip. He sat back down and looked at Ben. "Now I'm going to surprise you, Ben. What I am going to suggest is very Orwellian, and very out of character for me."

"You want me to physically take the kids and move them into Rebel families, right, Lamar?"

"Sometimes you spook me, Ben. I'm beginning to believe there might be some truth to those rumors about you."

"Horseshit!"

For years, beginning shortly after the Great War, rumors had persisted, then grown all out of proportion, about Ben Raines's being some sort of God. There were tribes of people in the deep timber and in the mountains and underground—those called the Underground People—who actively worshipped Ben Raines. Erected carved statues of him.

And even the old man who called himself the Prophet predicted dire things would happen if people persisted in worshipping Ben Raines.*

There were the Woods Children who lived in the timber, and they, too, worshipped, and on occasion, fought alongside the Rebels. They would never be convinced that Ben Raines was anything other than a God.

And so many more. . . .

"Will you do that, Ben?" Chase asked.

"No."

"I'm thinking of the children, Ben."

"So am I, Lamar. No. I'm going to take the kids, Lamar. I will not have them growing up to be like their parents. But the kids have to see that their parents are fools. They have to be shown, personally shown, that their parents are ignorant, and will never make any attempt to climb out of that dismal quagmire."

Chase sipped at his water and was silent in thought for a few heartbeats. He lifted his eyes. "Ben, that's tougher than just seizing the children."

"Yes, I know. But there is a reason for it, too, Lamar. I'm thinking that some, *some* of the parents will be so shamed by their ignorance, they'll learn just in order to keep their kids."

"And some of the parents will be so angry they'll try to kill you, Ben."

"They've tried before, Lamar."

"All right, Ben . . . we'll play it your way. Hell, my suggestion would just get us into a fight as quickly as your way." He sighed. "I've got years on

*Fire in the Ashes—Zebra

you, Ben. I'm an old man. I never understood a government who would allow children to grow up ignorant."

"Oh, I can answer that, Lamar."

"I just knew you could." Lamar's reply was as arid as Death Valley. "Well, don't just sit there, elucidate."

"Don't play the fool with me, Lamar. We've been together for too many years."

Lamar sighed deeply. "Problem is, Ben . . . I leaned that way myself for a good many years. My heart just broke over the plight of the poor, the homeless, the needy."

"And many of them did need help, Lamar. We're in agreement there."

"Finish it, Ben."

"There were some in our government who wanted a classless society. Unfortunately, while it looks good on paper, it's a lie. Anyone who doesn't believe there are classes of people is either very naive or a damned fool! But there was certainly no law that said a person couldn't climb out of their predicament. Thousands, millions, did. The problem was, and to many people, I suppose, still is, there were no guidelines to go by. It's like a good cop's hunch when he looks at a building and thinks, 'Something's wrong in there.' He knows it, or he feels it, but under the law, he's powerless to act. Same with what used to be called pornography. Remember the Justice who said that he couldn't define it, but he knew it when he saw it?"

Lamar chuckled and leaned over, pouring a cup of coffee. "You never had any political aspirations, did you, Ben?"

Ben shook his head. "Not a one, Lamar. Oh, I'd be lying if I said that I didn't, on occasion, think what I might do if I sat in that high office. But running for office . . . hell, no! No way."

"Since we're waxing philosophical, Ben . . . why not?"

"Run for office?"

"Yes."

"Hell, Lamar!" Ben laughed. "I was an ex-soldier for hire. A mercenary, if you will. I fought in brush wars all over Africa. Before that, I was a spook for the Company. Nothing more than a government hired gun. Politically, I was labeled an ultra-right-winger . . . which, to some extent, was true. The press would have destroyed me. You know as well as I do that a good segment of the press had set themselves up as the so-called Guardians of the American Way. Ah, hell, Lamar!" Ben waved his hand. "Don't get me started. We got a long day ahead of us."

Dan had been listening at the door, not eavesdropping, for both Chase and Ben had seen him. He stepped inside and took a seat. "Now we'll have a quorum," he said with a grin.

"Oh, Lord!" Ben rolled his eyes. "The English have arrived."

"Do continue, general," the Englishman urged him. "In retrospect, what could have been done to prevent the world from collapsing?"

"An astute awareness on the part of the American people would have helped. But that never happened. We were too busy merchandising ourselves into financial and moral bankruptcy."

All of his staff and half a dozen civilians from the Morriston area had stopped work and were listening outside the door.

Many of the Rebels were in their twenties; too young to be fully cognizant of what had happened before the Great War. One day there was a working government with everything looking good, the next day, millions around the world were dead.

Ben had started to write the history of what had happened. He'd had no thoughts of becoming a leader of anything. But since he was a well-known writer and sometimes commentator, whose views were hard-conservative, when the word got around that he was still alive, a movement grew to put Ben Raines in charge. For months Ben had ducked those people.

It had been Lamar Chase, among a few others, who had convinced him to grab the reins of leadership; shortly afterward, the Tri-States had been formed.

And the legend of Ben Raines had begun to grow, spreading all over the battered and shattered land once known as the United States of America.

And the people flocked to Ben Raines and his Rebels by the thousands; only about half of those would or could live under the Rebel philosophy. The rest would wander off and never be heard from again, falling victim to the ever-growing bands of outlaws and warlords and filth that lurked all over the ripped-apart nation.

And among those people who filled the hall outside Ben's office was Billy Bob Rockingham. He tried to blend in with the crowd, to listen, and to learn.

Ben refilled his coffee cup and leaned back in his chair. "I think many of the American people got exactly what they deserved."

"Why, general?" Dan asked. The ex-British SAS officer was a highly educated man, and like so many other Rebels, his quest for knowledge had never been extinguished. And perhaps that was one of the keys to fitting in with the Rebel movement. One's mind could not remain stagnant or in neutral.

"Because this nation was built on the beliefs in liberty and freedom; the pursuit of happiness; the right to be safe and secure in one's homes and possessions. But a certain group, or groups, always fought to take those rights from us. There were people who said it was wrong to defend oneself and one's possessions with a gun; they placed the rights of criminals above the rights of the law-abiding and taxpaying citizens."

"Why, general," a woman spoke from in the hall, "didn't the American people do something about it?"

"Because," Ben smiled, "never in the history of the world has a well-fed, well-clothed, and well-housed general populace ever risen up in armed revolt. And most of us were all of that.

"The nation either had to get mentally tough, or die. You all know what happened. Thinkers, those who weren't overcome by their own proported brilliance, saw the end coming . . . but nobody would listen to them. Toward the end, though, there were some people who opened their eyes to what was taking place around them. But they went about doing something about it in the wrong way. They became very vocal survivalists and founders of hate groups. And those types of groups always attract the wrong types of people. So, Big Brother stepped on them like bugs. Rightfully so. They blamed people not of their race or color or creed for all the nation's woes and ills. But the nation was rotting from within. We were given little direction by our elected officials. The machinations of government and of law became too ponderous. Many people just quit caring. I was one of those who dropped out in total frustration.

"Ours was a land filled with hypocrisy. We wanted the very best people to run for public office. But the best people never ran, for no one wanted their guts ripped out by the press, so consequently, the best people never sought the higher offices.

"And what did I do? Not much. Sat back and wrote my books and laughed while the world went to hell in a bucket of shit.

"And so here we are. Without a stable government anywhere in the world, that I know of. We—the Rebels—are the only group of people in this land who are trying to restore the nation to at least some of its greatness. I don't know if we can do it. But I will tell you all this: as long as there is breath left in my body, I am going to try. And we begin right here." Ben thumped the desk. "Here is where we start obliterating ignorance and prejudice. Right here is where we begin restoring the work ethic. There is no room for troublemakers. No room for ignorance. No room for those who want something for nothing.

94

The door is closed to them."

John Simmons stepped into the doorway. "There was a cross-burning last night, Ben. Do I have to tell you where?"

Ben stood up and picked up his Thompson. "Show me, John. You ride with me. Dan, get some people together."

"Yes, sir," the Englishman said. "Going to get interesting, general?"

"That's one way of putting it."

Eight

Billy Bob sat on the steps in front of the old two-story bank building, thinking about the General's speech. Made sense . . . as far as Billy Bob could understand it. He had missed a whole bunch of words. And, he realized, that wasn't nobody's fault 'cept his own.

Billy thought that no man had the right to be dumb. There was some, like his brother Bubba Willie, who couldn't help it. But if a person had a right-workin' brain, he owed it to everyone around him to get some learnin'.

And Billy also knew the shit was about to hit the fan down where he lived . . . and he knew he wasn't goin' to live there much longer. He'd get his families and move out. Get closer to town so's he could maybe go to a school for grown-ups. And he knew something else: he wasn't about to go back near home on this day. General Raines was fixin' to kick some ass.

Ben jerked Hiram off the front porch and tossed

him to the ground, knocking the breath out of the man. A whole gaggle of kids was peeking out of windows, out from under the house, from behind trees and even from behind and inside the outhouse.

Ben waited until Hiram had crawled to his feet. The man stood before Ben, so angry he was trembling with rage. "Whut for you do that to me, Raines?"

"Because you're a stupid fool! Among other things. All right, Hiram. I'm going to try one more time. Just . . . one . . . more . . . time. Hear me well. A new day is upon us, Hiram. We're all starting over. Fresh."

"Under your gawddamn rules, right, Raines?"

"You got it, Hiram."

"Maybe I don't want to play by your rules, Raines?"

"Then get out. But the kids stay. Just like I told you before."

About a hundred people had gathered, leaving their homes and following the Jeeps and trucks when they barreled past.

"No more cross-burnings, Hiram. Unless it's Halloween, if I catch anyone wearing a sheet, I'm going to shoot them on the spot."

"Gawddamn you, Raines! They's a whole passel of niggers in Morriston that's armed up and talkin' revolution. Talkin' about killin' whitey and makin' this place some sort of New Africa."

"Oh, I'll get to them, Hiram. Bet your boots on that. And I'll treat them the same way I'm treating you."

"What do you mean, sir?" a man asked, stepping

97

out of the crowd. "Do you mean you're comin' down just as hard on coloreds as you is on us?"

Ben turned to face him. "Nobody will be treated differently, mister. We're all going to obey the same set of rules."

The man looked at Hiram. "But Hiram, you said he was just pickin' on us."

"It is the truth!" Hiram hollered. "Y'all cain't see that Raines is playin' us for fools, that's all. Hell, he was onest married to a nigger gal. Don't believe me, ask him."

"Is that true, general?" the same man asked.

"That's what she told me. She called herself a zebra. Her father was white, her mother was black. So what?"

"What happened to her?"

"Government troops killed her during the battle for the Tri-States, back in 'ninety-eight. She was pregnant at the time," he added.

"The Klan's been strong down in this area for a hundred years, general," a man called out of the crowd.

"It just ceased to be," Ben said flatly. "And the same is going to apply for any black-militant, white-hating group. I told you, we're starting all over. Get it through your heads."

Hiram stuck out his chin. "You know what you is, Ben Raines. You a commonist. That's what you is. A damn commonist."

Ben smiled. "Are you attempting to say communist, Hiram?"

"That's whut I jist said. Commonist!"

"No, Hiram. A com*mun*ist is a member of the

Communist Party. There is no such word as commonist. A commoner is a person not of the nobility. Do you have all that straight now, Hiram?"

A child laughed. Hiram spun around and picked up a stick of wood, drawing back to throw it at the girl.

Ben jerked the wood out of the man's hand and spun him around. "She was laughing because you were made to look foolish, Hiram. And when people are made to look foolish it is usually because they are. If you would rather not look foolish, why don't you learn to speak English and get some education."

Without waiting for Hiram to stop sputtering long enough to reply, Ben walked to the young girl, about nine years old, and pretty. Kneeling down, Ben smiled at her. She shyly returned the smile.

"What's your name?"

"Betsy Ann."

"Well, Betsy Ann. Are you looking forward to going to school Monday morning?"

"No, sir."

"You're not! Why? Don't you want to learn about all sorts of things?"

"Yes, sir," she said with the honesty of a child. "But Grampaw Hiram says that book learnin' is all a bunch of nonsense."

Ben smiled. "Your Grandpaw Hiram looked and sounded a little silly a minute ago, didn't he, Betsy?"

She grinned. "Yes, sir."

"If he had him some book learning, he wouldn't have looked so silly."

"You learn that from books?"

"You can learn all sorts of things from books,

Betsy. You can learn everything from Azygous and Aye-Ayes to Zebus and Zwitterions."

She laughed out loud. "You're funnin' me!"

"No, I'm not, Betsy. Have you ever seen moving pictures?"

"Pitchers that move?"

"Pic-tures, Betsy. Say it."

"Pick-tures."

Ben laughed. "That's close. Ever seen one?"

"No, sir. Ain't that black magic?"

"There is no such thing as magic, Betsy." He started to explain about illusions, but didn't want to confuse the child. "Someone who believes in magic is not very smart."

"I'm gonna go fetch Old Lady Pauly!" Harry Larry Rockingham shouted. "Show you sumthang, Ben Raines. She put a hoo-doo on you."

Ben laughed at him. "OK. Go get her."

Harry Larry was gone in a rattle of fenders and a cloud of smoke.

Ben looked at Betsy. Then he glanced at a Rebel in Dan's command. Becky Carver. Her husband was an intelligence officer, and they were childless. He pointed at Becky and then pointed at Betsy. Becky grinned and nodded her head.

"Betsy, how'd you like to spend the weekend in town with that lady?" He pointed toward Becky. "I might be able to arrange for you to take a ride in an airplane. Would you like that?"

"Ooohhh, yes. Ifn it's all right with my dad."

"It's all right with him. Believe me, it is, child. I am absolutely totally positive he isn't going to open his mouth about it. You go over to Becky. You'll

100

like her. She speaks English and takes baths."

"Gawddamn you, Ben Raines!" Hiram hissed his hate. "You snake-sneaky bassard!"

Ben just grinned at him.

Ben turned to face the crowd of adults. "How many of you adults believe in black magic . . . voodoo and hoodoo?"

About two-thirds of those present raised their hands.

Ben turned to face the children. "Your parents are wrong. They've been teaching you nonsense. Would you believe me if I could prove it to you?"

The youngsters all solemnly nodded their heads in the affirmative.

Ben looked at Hiram. "Bring on your voodoo woman, Hiram."

Ashen-faced, shaking with rage, Hiram could but nod his head. "She'll be here. And when she come, she's a-gonna put a hex on you."

"Horseshit, Hiram!"

The crowd of kids giggled.

Ben turned his back to Hiram and walked off to stand beside Dan. "Here's what I'm going to do, Dan. And may the Lord God in Heaven forgive me."

The Englishman arched one eyebrow.

"This old woman deals with dried frogs and lizard legs and snakeskins, Dan. But you can bet your ass she's anything but ignorant. She's made a living off of these ignoramuses for years. And you can bet your boots she's heard all the rumors about me, too."

Dan smiled. "I love it, general."

"Let's see if it will work."

Harry Larry came roaring back, a woman dressed in black sitting beside him. The men helped her out of the truck. She looked at Ben and her face paled.

"She's heard," Dan whispered. "We should charge admission for this, general."

Ben stifled a laugh and walked toward the voodoo woman. She held up a hand. "I mean you no harm, Ben Raines. None at all."

The crowd hissed and drew back.

The kids were all knotted up together in fear.

Hiram was looking at the two of them, not understanding what in the hell was going on. Old Lady Pauly had never behaved like this before.

"I'm told you can put your magic to work on me, lady." Ben raised his voice so all could hear. "All right, shake your voodoo stick at me. Come on."

She shook her head. "I can put no hex on you, Ben Raines."

"Why?" Ben's word was harsh.

"I simply cannot." She knew better than to use the word magic.

Easy, Ben, he cautioned himself. Don't let this backfire on you. Avoid the words powers or magic. She's a smart old gal, and she'll twist those words around and use them against you. She is being careful not to use them herself.

Both were right to a degree.

"Don't you ever again fill these kid's heads full of garbage, old woman. You hear me?"

"I hear you and I will obey your commands. Shall I leave the country?"

"That won't be necessary. Just stay out of my way and keep your mumbo-jumbo to those ignorant enough to believe it." He looked straight at Hiram as he said it.

The man's mouth was open so wide it looked like his upper plate might fall out.

"Take her back, boy," Ben told Harry Larry.

Harry Larry got back in his rattletrap pickup so fast he lost one shoe.

"Betsy Ann," Ben looked at the little girl. "Do you live here in this . . . place?" He waved a hand at the shack.

"Yes, sir, Mr. Raines."

"Get your things. Just a few things. We're going to give you new clothes when we get to town."

"Yes, sir!" the girl ran into the shack.

Ben and Hiram walked around each other like a couple of stiff-legged dogs.

"That's cold, Ben Raines. Takin' folks kids from them."

"Come on, Hiram." Ben tossed his Thompson to a startled Rebel, who luckily managed to catch it. "Come on. Let's do it, Hiram. Fight for leadership. You and me. Best man wins, the other pulls out. How about it, redneck?"

Hiram wanted to do just that . . . sort of. But he still had very vivid memories of a barroom brawl with this man, during which not only did Ben kick his ass, but two other pretty salty ol' boys' as well.

"You'd lak 'at, wouldn't you, Ben?"

"Oh, yes, Hiram. Very much."

"If you thank you so much smarter than me, Ben Raines, how come it is you fight? I thought smart, uppity people didn't do sich thangs?"

"That's where you're wrong, Hiram. Boo!" Ben

suddenly jumped at Hiram and the man almost fell down trying to get away.

All the kids and a goodly number of adults got a laugh out of that.

"Smart people, Hiram, have had to fight, in one way or another, for thousands of years. Simply to keep ignorant assholes like you from taking over the world. The garnering of knowledge has always been an uphill struggle, Hiram. Because fools like you keep trying to push us back."

"Whup him, Daddy!" Efrom Silas yelled. "Whup his ass good!"

"I'm waiting, Hiram. Come on. Let's go a couple of rounds."

"Straight-up fistfightin', Raines? None of that tricky stuff?"

"Why, sure, Hiram." Ben then stepped forward and landed a right on Hiram's jaw, knocking the man down.

Hiram jumped up, shook his head, and came in flailing, both fists pumping.

Ben stepped aside and clubbed the man on the back of the neck, knocking him to the dirt again.

Hiram tried to knee-tackle Ben and got a boot in the belly for his efforts. He crawled around on the ground, gagging from the boot in the gut, until he caught his breath.

Ben took that time to take a drink of water from his canteen. He replaced the canteen in the canvas-covered cup and snapped it closed.

"Hiram, is this the best you can do? You want me to get one of my women Rebels to come finish the job?"

William Watson started jumpin' up and down. He threw his hat on the ground. "Ain't no damned woman gonna whup no man." He stepped out of the crowd and screamed. "Come on. Any of you bitches wanna fight me? Just step up here and have a go at it." He looked at his father. "I'll take over, Paw."

Hiram was sitting on the ground, both hands holding his aching stomach.

A Rebel stepped from the ranks, handing her Uzi to a friend. Ben smiled. Tama. One of Dan's close-combat instructors. An expert in judo.

Tama said, "Would it not grieve a woman to be overmastered with a piece of valiant dust? to make an account of her life to a clod of wayward marl?"

"Haw?" William Watson squalled.

"Shakespeare, you dumbass!" she told him, never stopping her walking toward him.

Tama kicked him on the kneecap with a boot, spun as gracefully as a ballet dancer and kicked him on the kidney. Willie went down squalling and did not make any attempt to get up.

She faced the crowd of stunned and silent people. "Any of you women who would like to learn to defend yourselves, come on into town and look me up. I'll be happy to teach you. It's something you should all know."

"Oh, shhiitt!" one man said.

Willie tried to grab hold of Tama's ankle. She stomped on his hand. The sounds of bones crunching was loud in the still air.

Willie rolled on the ground, screaming in agony, holding his broken hand.

"You!" Ben pointed at Charlie Jimmy.

"Sar?" Charlie Jimmy hollered. "I ain't done nothin'!"

"Did I say you had? Bring that fool there," he pointed to Willie, "into town, to our hospital. We'll fix up his hand." Ben walked to the porch and swept up Betsy Ann in his arms.

He looked at the knot of kids. "It will be all right with your parents if you come into town with us." He looked at the adults. "Won't it?"

They mumbled and nodded their heads.

"How many want to come in and spend some time with us?"

Nearly all of them.

"Well, then . . . pile in the trucks, and let's go!" Ben grinned. "You don't have to worry about getting anything. You'll get new clothes when we get to town."

After the sounds of the last vehicle had faded away, Hiram pounded his fists on the dirt and cursed Ben Raines. "I'll kill you, Ben Raines. Gawddamn you, I'll kill ya!"

But he was speaking to only a few people. Most had left. They wanted no more trouble with Ben Raines and his Rebels.

Nine

"It's eerie," Sharon said to Tina as they drove closer to Nashville. "The last human being we saw was a good forty-fifty miles back."

"Yeah. I know. And Nashville is just about fifty miles away. What are your thoughts on it?"

"I think people have moved away from the cities as far as they can."

"I'm with you." She checked her map. "Pull off at the Kingston Springs exit. Let's check it out."

The area was devoid of any living thing, human or animal.

But there was a good, easily defended place for a camp, and after testing the water, the Scouts found it safe to drink. At a service station by the Interstate they found a full underground tank of fuel; that would be used in topping off the tanker trucks that traveled with them and to fill up other vehicles.

By the time they had checked out the area and marked out the bivouac site, the first of Ike's convoy was pulling in, Ike in the lead Jeep.

"The last fifty miles was like traveling on the

moon," Ike said. "I didn't see any sign of life, Tina. How about you?"

"Same here. I think Nashville is going to be crawling with unfriendlies."

"Yeah." Ike looked around and nodded his approval of the bivouac site. "Double the guards tonight," he said, more to himself than anyone else. "Tina, when the camp is secured and everyone in, lay Claymores outside the perimeter."

"Yes, sir."

The electronically detonated Claymores would blow when any hostile came within a certain distance, breaking a beam.

Ike glanced up at the sky. "Be dark in less than two hours. Let's get cracking, gang."

The Rebels worked quickly but carefully in the setting up of camp; it was something all had done hundreds of times. There were no neat little rows of tents, which would allow any hostiles to smoke half the camp with one burst. Some slept under trucks; others pitched tents in staggered fashion; still others chose to utilize only a ground sheet and blanket.

The evening meal was cooked, then the fires extinguished. Guards would mount and stand a two-hour watch; two hours was long enough with all senses working overtime. Anything past that created a totally unnecessary strain. The camp became dark and silent.

At full dark, all were very much aware of quiet movement in the thick underbrush that had grown wild for years, some of it nearly impenetrable.

"Not going to be much sleep for us this night," Major Tom Broadhurst said.

"Christ!" a Rebel bitched. "Don't those . . . whatever they are out there ever bathe? The stench is sickening."

"They certainly seem to have an aversion to water," Tina said, sniffing. She remembered only too vividly the fetid body of the Night Person and the stinking hands clawing at her neck at the airport.

The night suddenly roared as the damning beam of light was broken and a Claymore unleashed its fury, sending hundreds of lead and steel pellets into the still air. The explosion was soon followed by the sounds of wailing and screaming as the mangled bodies coughed up blood and spat out life.

Automatic rifle fire split the darkness; few sparks could be seen, since the Rebels used flash suppressors. The biting barking of a .60 caliber machine gun yammered and the screaming of the wounded grew louder.

A spear jammed its steel head into the door of a pickup; arrows began slamming into the ground; a few hostile rifle and pistol shots came from outside the perimeter.

"Take positions and return the fire!" Ike yelled.

And the night roared and slammed with Rebel gunfire.

"Grenades!" Ike shouted. "Fire-frag."

The grenades, probably the most lethal ever manufactured, split the night with steel and fire. Burning, howling shapes could be seen racing through the woods and brush, some with their hair on fire, to fall shrieking to the earth, kicking out their life, illuminated by the glow from burning forms of other unfriendlies.

"Cease fire!" Ike shouted down the din of battle. "Report!"

The posts began calling in. Several wounded Rebels, none seriously, no dead.

"Put an end to any suffering that you can see," Ike ordered.

Well-placed single shots cut short the terrible shrieking of the wounded or burning Night People.

"Guard shifts change," Ike ordered. "Heads up and drop anything that moves outside our perimeter."

"You'll die like all the rest!" The shout came from the timber. "Only more slowly and horribly . . . I promise you all."

"Keep it quiet," Ike said. "Pass the word. Let's see if we can get a fix on his position. Tina, set up mortar teams. HE and WP."

"Yes, sir." She slipped away, into the gloom.

"Die, die, die, die!" The chanting began.

"Stubborn bastards, aren't they?" Broadhurst spoke softly.

"Let's keep them talking, Tom. I figure no more than a hundred yards out."

"Just about right. Hey, Stinky!" Ike yelled. "Why don't you crawl back into the hole where you came from before you piss us all off?"

Wild cursing ripped the night.

"Tell Tina to drop in a few. Let's see what happens."

In a few seconds, the area a hundred yards out was ripped and torn by mortar fire.

"Goddamn tubes are up all the way, general," a mortar crew chief called.

"Rake it with machine gun fire," Ike ordered.

The chugging of big .50s hammered, every third round a tracer, and the position of the Night People was spotted.

"Rifle grenades!" Ike yelled.

The area was blasted and pounded and torn until Ike yelled for a cease-fire.

No more chanting or cursing was heard.

"Get some sleep," Ike told his people. "We're gonna need some rest before we tackle that airport in the morning."

Ben shut down his office and stepped outside to sit on the steps of he old bank building. Dan had stopped by just before dusk to tell him that all the kids they'd brought back with them were housed and safe and content.

Ben hadn't seen Denise since the Rebels had pulled into the area. She had volunteered to work with some of Chase's medical people and was staying busy. And away from Ben.

The Rebels had set up one firm outpost, in Great Bend, Kansas, back early in the summer. And from all indications, the outpost was doing well. One tiny dot of civilization in the middle of ignorance and barbarism and the ashes of war. And soon, there would be another outpost.

One more tiny step toward restoring order out of ruin.

But we still have such a long, long way to go, Ben mused.

Buddy walked out of the gloom of night to sit

beside his father. Ben smiled at his son. Buddy was square-jawed and tanned, very heavily muscled. His hair was dark and curly. The young man was handsome, but not in the pretty-boy way. His was a solid, rugged handsomeness. And he was never without the bandana tied around his forehead. Like his father, Buddy carried a .45 caliber Thompson SMG.

"Have you had word on General Ike and Tina, Father?"

"Spoke with both of them about an hour ago. They're settled in just outside of Nashville. They'll clear the airport in the morning. Where the hell have you been all day?"

"Getting to know the lay of the land."

"And?"

"It's flat."

Ben laughed in the night. A friend of his had once said that flat, commercial land produces flat, commercial people. He wondered why he had thought of that now.

"How'd you get around, son?"

"Found a motorcycle. A Harley-Davidson. Took a little work, but I got it running. Monroe is filled with Night People." He added that last bit with no more emotion than if he were discussing a slice of apple pie.

"You went there?"

"Yes, sir."

"Don't do it again. Not by yourself. Do I have to make that an order?"

"No, sir. I will admit it was a bit rash on my part."

"No, son. It was just plain stupid."

"Yes, sir."

"I thought you found a girlfriend?"

He smiled in the night. "Several of them, Father."

"Going to play the field, huh?"

"What a quaint expression. But, yes, that sums it up rather well."

"Thank you. Since you seem to have a lot of time on your hands, and are not married with children to help look after, perhaps I'd best assign you something to do."

"I thought perhaps that would be coming."

Ben looked at him. The young man's expression was bland. But his eyes were twinkling.

"Tomorrow morning, first thing, you tell General Jefferys I've OK'd a full platoon for you. Draw rations for a full week. Double quota of ammo for each person."

"Yes, sir. And then what?"

"Clean out Monroe."

"Yes, sir. Consider it done. There are several houses that were filled with Night People. We won't have to worry about them, though."

"Why?"

"Because I took care of them today."

"Boy! You are foolhardy, you know that?"

"Like father, like son, some might say."

Ben grumbled under his breath.

"Any further orders, sir?"

"Why, you got a hot date?"

"Another quaint expression. No, I just thought I'd turn in early."

"Goodnight, son."

"Goodnight, Father."

Ben watched him walk away. He smiled, thinking: Oh, to be twenty-one again!

That primal sense that combat personnel soon develop took over as a warning light clicked on in Ben's head. He threw himself to one side just as the rifle barked, the slug whining off the concrete steps.

Ben burned a clip of .45 ammo just as Buddy's Thompson was barking out the same message. Both men saw a man stand up on his tiptoes and do an odd dance of death across the street. In less than thirty seconds, the area was ringed and sealed off by Rebels, and Ben and Buddy were standing over the bullet-riddled body of the man who had just tried to kill Ben from ambush.

"You know, him, general?" Ben was asked.

"Unfortunately. That's one of Hiram's sons. His name is, was, Harry Larry."

"Shame," Buddy said.

"You might say that," Ben replied, looking at his son. "Or you could say there is one less redneck in the world."

"Yes, one could."

Cecil pulled up in his Jeep and Ben climbed in. "Buddy will be in to see you in the morning. I've assigned him a full platoon."

"To do what?"

Ben explained. When Cecil remained silent, Ben asked, "Aren't you going to say what a fool thing it was for him to do?"

"No. Hell, you'd do the same damn thing. You're notorious for it."

For the second time that evening, Ben grumbled under his breath.

"No point in bitching about it. You know it's true."

"Are you aware there is a movement in town, among blacks, to start a New Africa?"

"I'd heard," Cecil said drily. "And no, I'm not going down to talk to them. I have absolutely no patience with those nitwits."

"Why, Cec! I thought you were all brothers?"

Cecil glared at him. "How would you like the troops to see two middle-aged men duking it out in the middle of the street, Raines?"

Ben threw back his head and laughed.

The smell of gunsmoke had not yet dissipated.

"All right, Cec. I just thought it'd be better if you did the talking."

"I'll talk to them, Ben."

Cecil put the Jeep in gear and drove off into the night.

The medics who were loading the body of Harry Larry into the back of a meat wagon looked at each other.

One said, "Have you ever noticed that all officers are weird?"

"Have the kids been told about Harry's shooting last night?" Ben asked Cecil over breakfast coffee. Still a good hour before dawn. They were the only ones in the mess tent.

"Not to my knowledge. And Hiram came for the body last night. He doesn't believe that his son took a shot at you. Their kind never does anything wrong. It's always the other person."

115

Cecil touched his arm. "You know, of course, Ben, that I am the exception when it comes to blacks?"

"I know it, Cec. So is John Simmons. So was Pal Elliot. Salina. Valerie and Lila. Megan. Major Johnson. The list is long; do you want me to repeat every name, Cec?"

"No. No, of course not. It's like being flayed with a tiny knife after you say each name. Ben, you know what? I sometimes think we should just quit trying to see that the races get along. Sometimes I just want to separate them; put the rednecks on one coast, the militant blacks on the other coast. Let the Latinos have the southwest and you and me and Ike and those who follow us carve something productive out of the center of the country . . . and keep the others away from each other."

Ben smiled down at the murky mess that was laughably called coffee. "And would that work, Cec?"

"Why, hell, no! We'd be fighting more then than we are now." Cecil sighed and pushed his empty plate from him. "I am really not looking forward to seeing Lamumba today."

"Seeing who?"

Cecil turned his head away so Ben would not see his smile. "Lamumba. The guy who heads up the local return-to-Africa group."

"Oh, shit! Another Kasim."

"Please. I just ate. I do my best not to remember that fool!"

"How many members does this Lamumba have?"

"You ready for this?"

116

"Do I have a choice?"

"No. About three hundred."

Ben stared at him. "Are you joking?"

"Unfortunately, no. And they're all well-armed, and they all hate whites."

"How come John didn't tell me about this?"

"He elected to tell me instead. I did not feel like kissing him at the news."

Ben watched Cecil's eyes as a young black woman entered the mess tent. She wore captain's bars on her collar. Her field pants fit her very well.

Cecil sighed and shook his head. "It's hell to be middle-aged, Ben."

Ben said, quite smugly and deliberately, "Hasn't bothered me a bit."

Cecil looked startled for a second, and then caught Ben's drift. "Look, honky . . . that's supposed to be *my* line!"

Chuckling, the two men emptied their trays and left the tent.

Captain Patrice Dubois watched the men leave. She had not been with the main force of Rebels long, having just come in from Old Camp One up in North Georgia. "Handsome man," she remarked to a sergeant, also a woman.

"Which one?"

"Both of them. But General Raines is untouchable, or so I've heard."

"Hang around," she was told. "Somebody's been feedin' you a line of bullshit."

"It doesn't matter. It's General Jefferys I was talking about."

"He's free. Lost his wife not too long ago. Cancer.

117

His first wife was killed during the government assault on Tri-States."

"Tough."

"You're new in camp."

"Yes. I've been up in North Carolina most of the time; attached to the North Georgia Rebels. I've been instructing in guerrilla warfare."

"What's your specialty?"

Captain Patrice Dubois smiled. "Silent killing."

"You ought to be assigned to Colonel Gray's bunch, then. Gray's Scouts. That bunch is randy, honey. Tina Raines is assigned to Gray's Scouts."

"The general's *daughter?*"

"That doesn't cut any ice around here, sister. You either pull your weight, or you're in deep shit."

The two women Rebels took their trays to a table and watched as a handsome young man entered the tent and joined the growing mess line.

"What a hunk!" Patrice said softly.

"The general's son. Buddy. He's taking a full platoon out today to clean the nests of Night People out of Monroe."

Patrice shook her head. "Where is General Raines's daughter?"

"Acting as CO of the Pathfinders on their way to see if New York City is still standing."

Patrice chewed thoughtfully for a moment. "Absolutely no favoritism in this army, is there?"

"None, honey. None at all. And no racism, either. General Jefferys hates a nigger as much as General Ben Raines hates a redneck."

"But isn't what you just said a form of racism?"

The sergeant smiled. "I really think you ought to

volunteer to go with the generals today, captain."

"Where are they going?"

"Down to talk to a bunch of goofballs who want to form a New Africa and kill all the whites around here."

The sergeant never stopped sprinkling a bit of salt and pepper on her eggs. She did not catch the odd look on Dubois's face.

"Maybe I'll just do that," the captain said.

Ten

"Blockade at Charlotte Pike exit, general," Tina radioed back. "And it's a good one."

"Hold what you've got, I'm right behind you."

The Rebels had inspected the bodies of the dead Night People at dawn, and found the same deformed, disfigured, and stinking men and women as Tina's Scouts had seen in Memphis. The Rebels had not been impressed.

"I hate to waste explosives blowing these damned things," Ike said. "Back off and put a rocket into it to see if it's wired, then we'll just ram it out of the way."

When the rocket hit the barricade, the whole mess went up with a roar that knocked several Rebels off their boots.

"Son of a bitch!" Ike said, shaking his head and thumping his ringing ears. "Well, piss on 'em. We don't need a Metro Airport to land the planes that will be resupplying us." He looked at his map. "We'll bypass this place and hit Seventy just outside of Dowelltown; take that all the way over to Crossville. We'll use that airport, if possible."

"And just maybe, along the way, we can pick up

some intell as to just what the hell is going on around the cities," Tina suggested.

"Yeah. All right, people, back it up and let's cut south. Blaze us a trail, Tina."

"Request permission to accompany the generals today," Patrice said, with a sharp salute.

"We're not much on saluting around here, captain," Ben told her. "When you get to know how we operate," he softened that with a smile, "you'll know when to salute, believe me. Permission granted."

"Thank you, sir. I'm Captain Patrice Dubois."

"Are you Creole?" Cecil asked.

"I'm not sure, sir. I don't remember much about my background. Only that I'm from New Orleans and I was ten when the Great War came."

Cec looked at Ben and smiled. "Ah, youth!"

"Yeah. A gathering of old men, that's us."

"Great movie."

"I liked the book."

"You would."

Patrice did not have the foggiest idea what either man was talking about.

"You have read Gaines, have you not, Captain Dubois?"

"I . . . ah, no sir."

"I have a copy. I'll lend it to you."

"And some Faulkner, too, Cec."

"Spare her that, Ben. You might like to study novels; I prefer to enjoy them."

"Faulkner is enjoyable."

"Right, Ben." He looked at Patrice. "Have you

had breakfast, captain?"

"You saw me in the tent, general."

Cec smiled. "Yes. So I did."

Ben started whistling "Some Enchanted Evening."

Cec gave him a dark look.

The look was wasted. Patrice Dubois had never heard of the smash hit *South Pacific*, or any of the music from it.

"How can it be an enchanted evening, Ben—it isn't even good dawn yet?"

"It's the mood that counts."

Ben walked off, humming "Matchmaker, Matchmaker."

"You two act more like brothers than friends," Patrice observed.

"We're both, Patrice."

"And yet you are going this day to run off a group of blacks who only wish to live as their ancestors lived."

She caught the shift behind Cecil's eyes, and knew she'd lost points.

"You have a lot to learn, captain."

"I'm a good student, general."

But the ice that had formed in Cecil's eyes was still there.

"Perhaps. Time will tell."

"General, I don't understand the Rebel philosophy."

"Then why did you join?"

"The truth?"

"I would prefer that."

"For survival, general. Oh, being a Rebel is a damn good way to get killed, sure; but it's also the best way I know of to stay alive . . . if you can make any sense out of that."

"I can. But you don't agree with what we're doing?"

"I didn't say that. I said I don't understand what you're doing."

"What about it confuses you?"

"I've been with the Rebels for over two years. This is the first time I've seen any one of the three generals of the Rebels. I still haven't seen General Ike. I've been sent to Michigan, to Florida, and to North Georgia, each time the units getting larger. And I'm fully trained. I have been the only black in an all-white outfit. And somehow I don't think that was an accident."

"It wasn't. Those are my orders. I also place a lone white in an all-black or all-Latin unit; just to see if they can cut it."

"I see. And have I 'cut it'?"

"Obviously. I've seen no bad reports on you."

"And you would see them, personally?"

"Oh, yes."

The camp was fully awake now. Those Rebels who were not in a family unit were lining up at the mess tents around the town, for breakfast.

"Are you going to order Lamumba and his followers out of the area, general?"

"No. Just tell them that we're all going to get along. Then if they can't see their way clear to do that, they can carry their asses."

"And you are absolutely convinced that this way, the Rebel way, is the best way?"

"Oh, yes, captain. If I was not certain, I wouldn't

be a part of the movement. And, Miss Dubois, I would suggest that you make up your mind . . . quickly."

Cecil turned and walked off.

"Had your breakfast, son?" Ben asked Buddy.

"Yes, sir. We'll be pulling out within the hour."

Ben inspected the gear Buddy was drawing from quartermaster. He added a few items and then nodded his approval. "The next outpost will be somewhere around the Shreveport area; just east of that city. When you're finished in Monroe, resupply and reconnoiter all the way to Shreveport. Clear the Interstate of any obstacles . . . stationary or living."

"Yes, sir."

Ben was startled to see the huge bulk of Command Sergeant Major James Riverson gearing up.

"What the hell are you doing, James?"

"Preparing to move out with Buddy, general."

Riverson was one of the original Rebels, having been with Ben since '88.

"On orders from whom?"

"My own," the big Top Kick said flatly.

"What if I need you here?"

"You don't."

Grunting, Ben walked away, toward the platoon of Rebels gearing up to confront the Night People. Somehow, it came as no surprise to find nearly all were hardened veterans of dozens of battles.

Ben spoke to one Rebel. "Looking after the general's son, Mike?"

"Why, no, sir!" the battle-hardened vet said, a

bland expression on his face. "Just followin' orders, sir."

"Whose orders?"

"General Jefferys, sir."

"Ummp," Ben grumbled. "But of course. Carry on."

"Yes, sir."

The Rebels smiled as Ben walked away. Damned if they were going to let anything happen to Buddy.

Ben caught up with Cecil. Captain Dubois was tagging along, some distance back. Ben commented on it.

"She doesn't as yet know where her loyalties lie, Ben."

"Ahhh. Got to the heart of the matter very quickly, did you?"

"It would appear so. How many personnel do we take with us on this . . . odyssey?"

"Hell, it wouldn't make any difference if I said none. Fifty would still be close by."

Cecil smiled. "True. I'll order a team."

"Good. We'll meet at your office at nine."

"See you then."

Ben walked to his already staffed and busy office, checked in, but found he could not concentrate on the paperwork: dozens of reports from roaming teams of Rebels all over the battered nation. He left them stacked on his desk and got into his Jeep, electing to drive through the town.

He wanted to tell Hiram that he had not gunned down his son without provocation. But he knew that Hiram's hate was so great he would never believe him. Ben made up his mind just to let it lie and wait for Hiram to make his move.

He drove the streets, conscious of the Rebels in Jeeps behind him . . . always with him. Ben had reached the point where he paid no attention to them . . . almost.

He drove past the town's factory buildings, now empty, their windows broken-glass-mute eyes. And again, the thought came to him: why, if a building is empty, do certain types of assholes and crapheads feel compelled to break the windows? Having grown up in a rural area, during a time when vandalism was not tolerated, Ben could never understand the motivation behind it.

Still didn't.

He wondered how Cec and Patrice were getting along? A very pretty but rather odd lady. Ben would have someone run a check on her. Ben had once prided himself on knowing everybody in the Rebel army. But it had grown so, become so diverse and complex, that it was now impossible.

His thoughts shifted to Denise Vista, the Indian woman they'd found enslaved in Kansas. Their affair had been very intense and, it appeared, very brief. That was fine with Ben. He really did not wish to become emotionally involved with another woman. He knew his faults only too well; knew that he was complex and not that easy to get along with.

He wondered how Gale was doing.*

He smiled at the thought of her. What a character she was.

He thought of Rani.**

*Anarchy in the Ashes—Zebra
**Alone in the Ashes—Zebra

He quickly put her out of his mind.

He wished to God he could find a woman who didn't want to tie him down. For Ben was not the tying-down sort.

The women he had known walked through his mental memory banks. He had, in his own way, loved them all. And yet, of them all, his thoughts always returned to Jerre. She had been so young, and yet so full of wisdom, realizing that Ben had a dream, a mission, and a woman forever by his side was not included. Salina had known that, too, but in quite a different way.

He knew that Jerre was still in the Rebel army, but he was damned if he knew where. Perhaps, he mused, that was best for all concerned.

And Rosita had borne him children. Little Short Stuff, he had called her. She had known, too, that no one woman would ever be able to hold him back. And she had, with a smile, stepped aside.*

And Cecil was about to get involved with Patrice; Ben knew all the signs. But for Cecil, that was good. The man had not found his mental mate since Lila.

Everything and everyone had changed, as was the nature of things. Even Ben's outlook toward 'necks had changed. Because they had changed. And that puzzled Ben. He did not understand why that particular group had changed from Good Ol' Boy to savage, and in such a short time.

Dawn came walking and smiling into Ben's mind. The mother of his twins.

Jesus Christ, Raines! he mentally berated himself.

*Fire in the Ashes—Zebra

What are you trying to do, repopulate the earth singlehandedly?

He'd been accused of that, he recalled.

He checked his watch. An hour until he would meet with Cecil. He wondered how Ike and Tina were doing.

They had hit an ambush on old highway 96. For once, Tina had not been leading her Scouts; the two Scouts who had been at point were killed when automatic weapons fire raked their Jeep. The Jeep had slewed off the road and nosed into a ditch.

Ike and his people had gone on into Murfreesboro to check out the town, letting Tina and her Scouts go ahead and cut east, in order to clear any obstacles they might encounter.

"Well, we sure encountered one," she muttered. "Ham? Have you spotted them?"

"Just across that little bridge," Ham called. "I'm setting up mortars now. But I'm going to have to walk them in from the east. If we blow that bridge, we're screwed!"

Tina waved most of her team left and right, to protect their flanks, and sent the rest back to protect the rear. "Walk them in when you're ready, Ham!" She called. "Hal! Set up that recoilless rifle right over there. Bernie! Can you back that Jeep over there and use the .50? Good. Go!"

Ham began dropping rockets down the tube, deliberately aiming long so he could walk the rounds in. After three adjustments, he hit pay dirt . . . or raw meat, as the case was. The high-explosive round

128

landed right on the mark and sent two once-living bodies several feet into the air; one of the men was minus half his head.

"Every other round WP!" Ham ordered his two mortar crews. "Do it!"

The .50 caliber began chugging and Hal began working the recoilless rifle, the gun hammering, tossing out the six-pound rounds that destroyed nearly anything they came in contact with.

Then the Scouts came in for a rude surprise: the enemy they were engaging was just as well armed as they. Mortar rounds began dropping in on the Scouts' position. And a heavy machine gun began belching. But before the mortarmen could get their range, Tina was shouting her team back.

"Bug out!" she shouted. "Fall back. Move!"

The Scouts fell back a good mile from the combat zone and regrouped while Tina called Ike.

"What the hell's goin' on over there?" Ike's voice came through the walkie talkie.

"We've hit a solid pocket of resistance. And they're well armed."

"Hang tough, kid. We're rolling." Ike waved his columns forward. He muttered, "Knew I should have brought some artillery."

The two teams of Rebels rendezvoused in fifteen minutes.

"Lose any people?"

"Two," Tina told him. "They were killed instantly."

"Have you tried radio contact with the hostiles?"

"Negative. I don't even know who they are."

"Let's give it a whirl. We'll try them on the CB. That's probably what they're using."

He was right; they were on channel 25. They listened.

"We shore kicked their ass, didn't we, Butch?"

"Yeah. By God, people's gonna learn that this is our territory."

"Two-bit warlords," Ike muttered. "Punks, by the sounds of them. But smart punks . . . if there is such a thing."

"How do you mean, Ike?"

"They knew enough to teach themselves the nomenclature of machine guns and mortars and reloading equipment. They gotta have a smelter for the heavy stuff. They may be assholes, but they ain't stupid."

He waited until all traffic was gone on the channel and keyed the mic. "This is Ike McGowan of Raines Rebels. We're not here to claim any of your territory. All we want is safe passage through and then we'll be gone. How about it, boys?"

"Fuck you, McGoo!"

Tina almost laughed at the expression on Ike's face. "Boy," he muttered, "if I had the time, I'd kick your punk ass all over this area."

"Did you hear me, McGoo?" the voice popped out of the speaker.

"Yeah, I heard it. And the name is McGowan."

"I'll just call you fuck-head!"

"That does it. Major Broadhurst?"

"Yes, sir?"

"First platoon left, second platoon right. You stay with the third platoon in reserve, I'll take the Scouts and the fourth platoon and go nose-to-nose with the punks."

"Yes, sir."

"Radio when all platoons are in position. Pass the word."

"Yes, sir."

Ham handed Ike a slip of paper. "Coordinates, sir."

"Thank you, Ham." He turned to a sergeant. "Get the 81s set up. I want twelve-pounders, every other round WP. When I tell you, you pound the everloving shit out of that area."

"Yes, sir."

"Ah, sir," Ham said. "The bridge? . . ."

"I don't give a damn about the bridge. Should have just hooked up with Seventy back yonder and to hell with this."

"Yes, sir."

Ike laughed and slapped Ham on the back. "Didn't mean to snap at you, Ham. But I never did like punks."

"I never would have guessed, sir."

Fifteen minutes passed before the first reports came in by radio. "First platoon in position, sir. Have the enemy in sight. About a hundred of them, give or take twenty-five."

"Second platoon in position, sir. That estimate is just about right."

Ike acknowledged the reports and told them to sit tight. He glanced at Tina. "We're going to have to be resupplied at Crossville. We're burning a lot of ammo."

"My thoughts, too, Ike."

Ike lifted his walkie talkie. "Mortar crews commence firing for range. Forward platoons call in

131

adjustments."

The twelve-pounders began fluttering out of the tubes, humming their dirges. Ike received and relayed adjustments and the gunners went to work with a vengeance.

"Let's go!" he ordered.

The Scouts and the fourth platoon moved out under the umbrella of mortar rounds. When the battle area was in smoky sight, Ike ordered the mortars to cease.

"First and second platoons in! Let's go, people!"

The Rebels were all over the followers of the unknown warlord, and the Rebels fought with a savagery the undisciplined thugs and punks and creeps had never known and most would never live to see again.

And it came as quite a surprise for the outlaws, for a very brief time, to learn that the Rebels did not believe in taking prisoners.

Ike walked through the bloody carnage, his CAR-15 cradled at the ready. "Take all weapons and ammo," he ordered. "Pile the bodies and burn them."

"What about the wounded, general?"

"Treat those you think have a chance of making it. Hell with the rest."

Dr. Ling opened his mouth to protest.

Ike quickly closed it. "That's an order, doctor. Carry it out."

"Yes, sir."

To say that the Rebels were hard-nosed would be like saying a wasp stings. No need to belabor the obvious.

The Rebels were not always this harsh. This approach had been adopted only after one hard lesson followed another. Ben had finally ordered the rules of the Geneva Convention to be tossed aside.

Ike stood over a punk who'd been shot in both legs. "Who's in charge of this shit-outfit, boy?"

"Butch." The young man groaned his reply.

"Where is he?"

"Over yonder." The young man cut his eyes. "Propped up agin that tree. He's gut-shot."

Butch turned frightened eyes up at the stocky man with the black beret covering his salt-and-pepper hair. "I'm McGowan, punk. You got anything you want to say to me you better say it quick. 'Cause you don't have much time left you."

"Help me!"

"Sorry, boy, I'm not the Red Cross."

"You a damned . . . hard ol' fucker, ain't you?" Butch managed to gasp.

"That's right, boy."

"It hurts!"

"That's your problem. You started this dance, not us."

"Ain't you got no pity a-tall for me?"

"Do I look like the ACLU, boy?"

"The whut?"

"Never mind." Before he could say anything else, Butch had closed his eyes and had slipped into unconsciousness.

Ike turned away and found Ham. "Send some people under the bridge, Ham. Inspect it for damages. I want us to be at the Crossville airport by nightfall."

"Yes, sir."

Tina walked up. "We've got about twenty-odd who just threw down their weapons and started squalling and blubbering. Couldn't shoot them. Now what the hell do we do with them?"

"Line them up."

"General Ike. . . ."

"Line . . . them . . . up!"

"Yes, sir."

All looked to be in their early to mid-twenties, and they were a sorry-looking bunch. Some of them looked like throwbacks to the Peace and Love days, with some of the wildest looking hairstyles and manner of dress any of the Rebels had ever seen.

"I ought to shoot every goddamn one of you!" Ike yelled at them.

"Oh, Lard, Lard!" one young man squalled, falling to his knees, hands clasped. "Oh, Sweet Jesus!"

"You're calling on Jesus, punk?" Ike asked him. "You ambushed us, murdered two of my people — good people, not scum like you — and you have the nerve to call for divine help? Boy, you're nuts!"

Ham ran up to him. "Get up on your goddamn feet, asshole! Nobody told you to rest. Getup-GetupGetup!"

The young man scrambled to his feet, eyes wide and frightened.

Ham turned and winked at Ike. Ike fought to contain his smile. Little military indoctrination never hurt anybody.

"Now you hear me," Ike shouted. "Listen up, meatheads. I'm taking your weapons. All of them. And I don't ever want to see any of your ugly faces again. For if I do, I'm going to kill you. I will not hesitate; I'll just shoot you. I want you headed that way." He pointed west. "Straight down this highway. About a mile back, you'll find another contingent of Rebels. Don't fuck with them. Just keep marching and don't you ever come back. Now, move!"

They left, carrying their wounded, moving as swiftly as possible.

Only the moaning of the badly wounded could be heard.

Ike shook his head and looked at Dr. Ling. "Oh, hell, Doc. Give them something to ease the pain."

Ling turned away so Ike could not see his smile. Nobody is ever as hard as they claim to be.

"Are you ready for this, Cec?" Ben asked.

"Hell, no. But we may as well get it over with." They had stalled as long as they could.

"Get in the back, Captain Dubois," Ben said.

She scrambled in.

"Do you know where the headquarters of this movement is, Cec?"

"Yes. In the boat factory building. John Simmons and Richmond Harris will meet us there."

"That's a good idea. Since they'll be running this place when we pull out."

"Believe me, that day cannot come too quickly to suit me."

Ben laughed at the dour expression on the man's face.

"Permission to speak," Patrice said.

"Go ahead."

"Why all the flap about these people? What have they done?"

"Nothing yet," Ben told her. "But they're talking about killing all the honkys and taking over. Patrice, if this country is ever to pull itself out of the ashes, it will be only when people of all races work together. Can you see that?"

"Yes, sir. But is that plan feasible?"

"We think so," Cecil said. "One way or the other," he added grimly.

"You want black people to be like white people," Patrice blurted, then braced herself.

"That's horseshit, captain!" Cecil fired back. "You don't know what in the hell you're talking about. And until you do, I would suggest you keep your mouth closed."

Hell of a way to start a love affair, Ben thought, hiding his smile. But he and Gale had started out just about the same way.

"Would the generals prefer I not accompany them?" Patrice asked tightly.

"No, the generals would not prefer that." Cecil did not look around. "You might learn something by staying."

"Yes, sir."

They were silent as Ben drove the rest of the way, pulling in at a huge building that bore a sign reading: NEW AFRICA MOVEMENT.

"Wonderful," Cecil muttered, as his eyes found several men, all dressed in robes and turbans. "Instead of moving forward, they're regressing."

"What a racist remark!" Patrice said.

Ben got out of the Jeep and walked toward John

136

and Richmond before Cec and Patrice started slugging each other. Unlike Cec, Ben didn't mind robes and turbans. Dress had never been that important to him. But he did understand Cecil's resentment.

Cecil had once remarked, only half jokingly, that he had too much education for his own good. He said that because whites accepted him much more easily than did blacks.

It had surprised Ben to learn that back before the Great War, there had been a lot of prejudice among blacks against other blacks. A lot of blacks who were truly black in color distrusted many blacks of lighter color, equating a lighter color with easier access to success.

Black people, Ben had realized, had a hard row to hoe.

And there was no greater insult among the black race than for one black to call another a nigger.

And John Simmons, Ben recalled, had a dim view of many of his own people. But, hell! Ben thought. Don't I have a dim view of many of *my* own people?

"I am not a racist, captain!" Ben heard Cecil say, considerable heat in his tone. "And I resent the hell out of your implying that I am."

Ben tuned them out, greeting John and Richmond.

"Who's the fine-looking lady, Ben?" John asked.

"That's Cecil's new girlfriend."

John looked dubious. "What do they do for an encore? Back off ten paces and start shooting at each other?"

"They're just having a little spat."

"Halt!" one of the robed and turbaned men

137

shouted. "You are on the sacred land of Islam. Come no further."

Ben ignored him. "Who the hell is that?" he asked John.

"His name is Randy Jones. But he calls himself Duju Kokuma."

"Randy Jones. Why is that name familiar?"

"Oh, hell, Ben. You remember him. He's spent more time in jail than out. Burglary, assault, car stealin'. You remember him."

"Ah, yes."

"Leave our temple area immediately!" Randy/Duju shouted.

"Shut up, fool!" John told him.

"Are they sincere in their conversion to Islam?" Ben asked.

"Why, hell no! Not this bunch. I know some who are, but they won't have anything to do with Randy and Lumumba. They farm out in the parish. Get along with everybody. They're glad to see you come in. You have Muslims in your ranks, don't you, Ben?"

"Oh, yes. Hell, John, I've got a little bit of everything in this army." He looked at Randy/Duju. "My name is Ben Raines. I would like to speak with Lamumba."

"He does not wish to speak with you. He has nothing to say to white devils."

"If they all hate whites so much," John whispered, "ask Randy why he's always running around trying to put the hustle on white girls."

"I heard that, Simmons. Nothing out of your mouth is to be taken seriously. You are now and

138

always have been a white man's nigger."

"I think I'll just kick his ass."

Ben physically restrained the man. "Easy, John. Let's try to get along here."

"That, Ben, is going to be impossible. I'm telling you flat-out."

Ben looked back at Cecil. He and Patrice were busy standing by the Jeep, in a quiet but intense argument. "I knew I'd end up doing this myself," Ben muttered. He pointed a finger at Randy/Duju. "Get Lamumba out here. Right now!"

"And if I don't?"

"I can have about five thousand combat-ready troops in here in twenty minutes. And there is a fully prepared Rebel platoon right there!" He pointed to the end of the street. And the troops were there. Waiting. "Your move, Randy."

The front door to the building opened, another robed and turbaned man stepping out. "My name is Lamumba," he called. "What do you want?"

"I would like to speak with you."

"About living under your rules, Ben Raines?"

"About living and working together in peace."

"Pretty words."

"I am not a patient man, Lamumba. We can do this easy or hard, it's all up to you. Do we talk here or inside?"

"Infidels are not permitted inside the temple."

"Wonderful. Would you like to come over to my office?"

"No."

"We're here to stay, Lamumba. Get used to the idea."

"That sounds like a threat to me, Ben Raines. I do not like threats."

"Take it any way you want to take it."

The two men stared at each other.

Lamumba broke the silence. "I shall be at your offices just after noon."

"Fine."

He stepped back into the building and closed the door.

Ben walked over to Cecil and Patrice. "Thanks, Cec. I couldn't have done it without you."

Eleven

Buddy and his platoon stopped at the edge of the small city, just outside of a shopping center.

"Five teams of ten," Buddy said. "One team of twelve. That will be you and I, James."

The big sergeant major nodded his head.

"Stay in radio contact at all times. We'll clean out this place first, then use it for our base and HQ. Pull the vehicles inside at dark. It will probably take us the rest of the day to secure this place. So let's do it."

Buddy left one team with the vehicles, to guard not only the Jeeps and trucks, but their supplies. He ordered two teams to split up and mount machine gun emplacements at staggered intervals around the huge complex.

"When we go in, and the Night People see what we're doing, I think they'd rather brave the light than face us. Don't allow any to escape." He looked at his people, men and women. "It isn't going to be pleasant. But it's something that has to be done. And I suspect Father is going to assign this job to me permanently." He smiled grimly. "His way of keeping me out of trouble."

The Rebels laughed at that.

"Let's go."

And the grisly job began.

"That is the most infuriating and stubborn woman I have ever encountered!" Cec told Ben.

Ben smiled and let him rant.

"She has a head like a rock."

"Uh-huh."

"But she's done a marvelous job of educating herself."

"That's good."

"But I believe she is totally loyal to us."

"That's nice."

"A person does have a right to hold differing opinions, you know."

"Absolutely. No doubt about it."

"But I believe she's wasting her time on the close-combat range."

"Oh?"

"Yes. I'm going to pull her in and introduce her to the problems of logistics."

"You do need an assistant."

"I'm glad you agree, Ben."

"Oh, absolutely."

"What the hell is the matter with you, Ben?"

"Me? Nothing is the matter with me. I'm just agreeing with you, that's all."

"Maybe that's what's wrong."

"You need an assistant. I've told you that for months. So have an assistant."

"You're sure?"

"I'm sure! I'm sure!"

"Well, I'm glad you see my point."

"Are you going to be here when I meet with Lamumba?"

"Ah . . . no! I thought it best if Patrice and I got right down to work; start right after lunch."

"Old nose to the grindstone, hey?"

"Absolutely, Ben."

"Well, don't work too hard, Cec."

"See you, Ben."

Cec ran into the door facing on his way out.

Ben sat down and laughed until tears were running out of his eyes. "I don't believe it!" he said. "The man's in love!"

Hiram was strangely silent after the services. But all that knew him could see the raw hate shining out of his eyes. The hate directed at Ben Raines.

Most wanted to tell him that they believed Ben's story; that Harry had tried to ambush the man. But all knew better than to try.

At least half of the men and nearly all of the women had agreed to work with Ben and the Rebels. They could see that their quality of life with the Rebels in the area was going to improve vastly. It already had.

To make matters worse, Billy Bob had refused to come to his brother's funeral . . . and that really had set Hiram off. Billy Bob had said that his brother had acted like an ignorant fool, and was probably goin' to Hell for what he done. Hiram had then slapped him, and Billy Bob was in the house right now, packing to leave; to move close to Morrison.

And to make matters even worser, Billy Bob's snippy little wife had run to Hiram agin, with news that Billy Bob was talkin' up Ben Raines agin . . . and Hiram had said The Code was gonna be done this night. This very night.

Hiram had decreed it, and that was that.

Nobody among them that believed that Ben Raines was gonna make life easier around here liked Hiram's decree . . . but he done it, and The Code demanded that all witness.

And just a whole bunch of them wondered what Ben Raines was gonna do when he learned of it.

"It seems appropriate that you would take over a bank building, general," Lamumba said, a smirk on his face.

This one, Ben thought, is going to be easy to hate, so just take it slow and easy. "Why do you say that?"

"To house the great wealth you stole after the Great War."

Ben was startled and made no attempt to hide that fact. "What wealth are you talking about?"

"Oh, come, come, general! It's common knowledge that the Rebels, following the bombings, took thousands of pounds of gold from every possible repository."

"Yes, that's fact. And that gold is still stored where we put it, years ago. It will be used to back our currency if and when we ever get a stable government going again."

144

"And you kept none for your own use, I suppose?"

Ben laughed at the man. "What the hell do I need gold for? What could I buy with it? You're talking nonsense, man."

Lamumba narrowed his eyes in suspicion. He didn't believe a damn word Ben Raines had said. He didn't believe a word any white man said, so great was his hate.

"What did you wish to discuss, General Raines?"

"Law and order and working together."

The man said nothing.

"School starts Monday morning, Lamumba. Have any kids of your followers there." The man opened his mouth to protest but Ben cut him off. "And have all your people at the hospital tomorrow for physicals and shots."

"You go right straight to Hell, Raines!" Lamumba shouted the words.

Ben smiled easily. "I sent troops in to escort the rednecks over here. You want me to do the same with you and your people?"

"We'll leave first!"

"That is your option. But when you leave, get the hell gone far, buddy-boy. . . ."

"Don't call me boy!"

"Oh, hell, man! That's an expression. Not a racial slur. Get the chip off your shoulder and come down to earth, will you?"

"I accept your apology."

"I didn't apologize. And won't."

Lamumba tried to stare Ben down. He could not. "First time some white man calls me a nigger,

145

general, I'm going to kill him."

"That's fair," Ben said mildly. "But only if you bear this in mind: the first time you call some white man a honky or white bread or an ofay, I'm going to kill you."

"I don't believe that!"

"Don't ever push me to the wall on it, Lamumba. 'Cause when you do, somebody is going to be shoveling dirt in your face."

Lamumba sat very still in his chair. Very slowly, he nodded his head. "I do believe you would, general."

"I will do whatever is necessary to bring order back to this land. Now, are you interested in hearing my ideas, or would you rather leave — and I mean, *leave* — and continue spewing your mindless hatred for all those not of your color?"

"My people have been oppressed for thousands of years. We. . . ."

"Shut your fucking mouth!" Ben roared.

Lamumba fell silent, more shocked than anything else.

"Yes, Lamumba, your people were oppressed. Nobody with a modicum of intelligence would ever deny that. But a new day has dawned. Out of the ashes we can all rebuild a far better society. But we can't do it by working apart. We're all going to have to pull together. Now you can do one of two things: you can stay and work with me, or you can leave. You and your followers can go away and build your separate little hate-filled communities, preaching revolution and what-have-you, and then, sooner or later, as my plans take seed and grow, I'll have to come wherever you are and kick your ass all over the place. Now, then, what's it going to be?"

"By all that is holy, Raines, you are the most arrogant man I have ever seen! What god stepped down and tapped you on the shoulder?"

Ben sat and stared at him, meeting him look for look.

"I shall worship in the manner of Islam."

"I don't care. I don't care if you bow down to a kumquat. That's none of my business. But your kids are going to school. And we, that includes you and your followers, are going to work to make this place a better place."

"Better . . . as defined by who?"

"The people. Oh, I see what you're getting at. No, Lamumba, not by me. For as soon as we've set up this post, we'll be leaving to set up more just like it. You'll be given a basic set of laws to follow. Very simple, quite unlike the laws that you and I grew up with. You want to add more to it, call a town meeting and vote. Majority rule."

"And the black people get shafted again," Lamumba said scornfully.

Ben sighed. He summoned up strength from his rapidly emptying well of patience and said, "Lamumba, half of my troops are minorities. Or what used to be called minorities. We all work quite well together. There are whites taking orders from blacks, from Asians, from Hispanics, you name it. How is it, Lamumba, that we can do that, but you can't?"

Ben did not really expect any answer, and he did not get any.

"Have your people at the hospital tomorrow morning for physicals and inoculations. Have your kids in school at eight o'clock Monday morning. That's it."

Lamumba stood up. "And how about the Hiram Rockinghams of this world, Ben Raines? What about them? Where do they fit in among all your grand plans?"

"They don't, Lamumba. And I'm not so sure you do, either."

Tina and Ike had pushed hard, making the run to Crossville in quick time, arriving at the airport hours before even the most optimistic among them had even dreamed they would.

The place was a mess.

While a small team went into the once thriving little town, the others set about cleaning up and clearing the landing strip. Ike got on the horn to the new Base Camp One.

"What's your location, Ike?" Ben asked, after a runner had notified him that Ike was on the horn.

"Crossville, Tennessee, Ben. We've had some trouble." He brought Ben up to date.

"When can you have the landing strip cleared for planes, Ike?"

"Two-engine jobs only, Ben. We should have it ready by noon tomorrow; maybe a little sooner than that."

"You want some more people, Ike?"

"Ben . . . it wouldn't hurt. And lots of ammo. Ben, do you want us to clean out the cities as we go?"

"Ten-fifty on that. I've just got a hunch that if

148

New York City is standing, we'll cordon off the island and starve them out . . . that's providing there aren't any innocents trapped in there."

"If anyone is in there, their mental condition is gonna be next to lousy."

"Ten-four to that. I'll have the birds up and flying at first light, Ike. Start scrambling around for fuel."

"Will do, Ben."

"Luck to you, Ike. Ike? I think the lady with the torch is still standing."

"So do I, Ben. And I get to see it first! Nan-na-nan-a-nan-uh!" He laughed and broke it off.

Laughing, Ben left the building housing the main communications equipment. Then he remembered Patrice. He went back into the building and looked up the intelligence officer.

"Run me a check on a Captain Patrice Dubois. I want a vocal from every commander she's served under."

"Yes, sir."

Again leaving the building, Ben wondered how Buddy and his team were doing.

It had taken the teams more than five hours to clear the old shopping center of Night People. And to a person, the Rebels were blood-splattered and stinking with sweat.

They had dragged the stinking, deformed bodies out into a far corner of the huge parking area and doused them with flammable liquid, setting the pyre on fire.

"Let's take a break," Buddy said, sitting down

wearily on a curb and pulling out his canteen. Even the water tasted of death.

"Maybe this place was the main headquarters for them?" a Rebel asked hopefully.

"Don't bet on it." James Riverson dashed that glint of hope.

"After we've rested," Buddy said, "we find brooms and soap and clean up that filthy place in there." He saw their shocked looks. "Not the entire place! Good God. Just an area for us to live in."

Relieved laughter followed that.

Buddy looked at the huge shopping center. "Does anybody remember them when they were open and doing business?" There was a wistful note to his voice.

"Sure," James said. "Lots of us. I used to take the wife and kids and spend the entire day in a big shopping center."

"You must have been rich."

James laughed. "No. We just window-shopped." He saw Buddy's puzzled expression. "We just looked at all the things in the windows, then went on to the next shop."

"Ahh! I have . . . a vague memory of them. But it's all jumbled up with . . . what happened after the bombings. The fear and the crowds and the screaming of people."

"I used to take my wife into a shopping center about this size," a man said softly. "We hadn't been married but a couple of years. Matter of fact, we were in a shopping center when the first bombs came in."

"Warheads?"

"Germ. We were awful sick for a time. Went two, maybe three days not able to leave that place. Watching the rats chew on the dead."

"Your wife?" Buddy asked.

"She never recovered from the . . . poison; whatever it was. She lived about six months."

James Riverson stood up. "We don't dwell too much on those times, Buddy. It doesn't do a bit of good."

And most of them knew he was thinking of his own dead wife, killed back in the Tri-States.

Hiram sat on his front porch. It was quiet around the place; had been ever since those goddamned Rebels had taken the kids into town. Hiram wasn't used to all the quiet. He wondered if they'd ever get the kids back.

He doubted it.

He put the youngsters out of his mind and concentrated on Billy Bob. He'd sent men to block the old roads leading out of the area, so Billy Bob couldn't get away this time. Hiram hated to do it to his own flesh and blood, but his role as leader had to be reestablished. Besides, The Code demanded action. And as leader, it was up to Hiram to see that it got done.

Most of those damned Rebels had pulled out of the area, back to town. Only a few patrols still ran the roads. But the bastards didn't run on any schedule, so you couldn't tell when they might pop up. No matter. What was to be done could be done far from any road, and it would be over before the Rebels could stop them.

Hiram walked to the barn and got his horsewhip. He took the braided popper off the end. Wouldn't need it this night; be poppin' on flesh.

He looked around as a rattletrap pickup came smoking and banging into his drive. G.B. Hiram waved for him to come to the barn.

"Got the tar bubblin', Hiram," G.B. said.

"Good. I want it hot when we smear him."

"Boy of yourn needs to be taught a good, hard lesson, Hiram. And this here ought to do 'er."

"I reckon so. Hard thang for a man to have to do, though."

"You doin' rat, Hiram. Hit's the onliest way to restore power."

"Ten o'clock, G.B. 'At's when we do the deed."

"I'll be shore to have the folks there." He touched Hiram's shoulder. "Jist remember, Hiram: U-nited we stand." He smiled, knowing he'd said something quite profound. Not terribly original, but profound. G.B. prided himself on being able to wax sagaciously when the need called for it.

After all, he'd been named Grand Klackton of the local KKK, hadn't he? And that took brains, boy!

The team had returned from their inspection of the town, reporting to Ike.

"No sign of life, general."

"Nothing? Not a soul?"

"No, sir. There is not one living being in this town."

"Odd," Ike muttered. He shook that away. "OK,

thanks. Let's get this old runway patched up. We've got birds coming in about noon tomorrow."

"Yes, sir."

He found Tina and informed her of the deserted town.

"Town this size should have fifty to a hundred survivors in it, at least. I wonder where they went?"

Ike shrugged. "There was some pretty heavy fighting around this area last couple of years. Maybe they got killed; pulled out? Who knows? But at least there aren't any of those damnable Night People."

"Ike? Do you believe New York City is still standing?"

"Yeah, I do, Tina. I believe the lady with the torch is still there. And I believe the city is the headquarters, for want of a better word, of these Night People. I think they put out false information about the city being destroyed; false information about the eastern corridor being hot with radiation. And I think we're looking at the biggest fight we've ever faced."

"I am not looking forward to it, Ike."

"Nor I, kid. And I'd be willing to bet you we've got two, at least two, societies living there. One that tries to live normally by day, and the other that prowls by night."

"You ever been to New York City, Ike?"

"Oh, yeah. Used to go on liberty there. Big place, Tina. Buildings so tall they blot out the sun. And we're going to have to search every damn room of every damn one of them."

"I've seen pictures of the city, Ike. I can't even envision the task of doing that."

"It'll take months."

"Is it worth it, Ike?"

Ike thought about that for a moment. "Yes, it is. They'll be treasures in that city, Tina. Priceless art. Recordings of music that you and a lot of people your age have never heard. The information stored there on computer tapes would be worth it alone."

She smiled. "You'll never keep Dad out of this, Ike."

"I sure wouldn't want to try. No, he'll be right in there, leading the charge across the bridges or through the tunnels."

"The tunnels?"

"Under the river."

She shuddered. "They'll be dark."

"As midnight."

"And filled with you-know-what."

"Yeah. Don't worry. Ben will figure something out."

Twelve

Ben had his left boot and sock off, rubbing an aching corn on the side of his big toe . . . and muttering curses under his breath. Chase walked in and sat down.

"I could take that off for you," he suggested. " 'Course you'd have to hobble around for a few days."

"Later."

"You've been saying that for two years, Raines. What's the matter, don't you trust me?"

"I think you've dug enough lead out of me to answer that, Lamar."

"Ummp. You wanted to see me?"

"Tell your people to gear up for more inoculations, first thing in the morning." He told him of his meeting with Lamumba.

"Sounds like a charming fellow. Where is Cecil? I haven't seen him in hours."

"He's in love. Or in heat. One of the two. Walked into that door-facing a few hours ago."

After Chase finished laughing, he wiped his eyes and poured two fingers of whiskey. "Well, he won't be worth a damn for anything for a week, or more. Who's the lucky lady?"

Before Ben could reply, his door opened, an aide sticking his head inside. "Buddy just radioed in, general. They've cleared the big shopping center and will use that as CP." Ben nodded. "The pilots say they're ready to go, and two platoons are gearing up to fly up to General McGowan's position at first light."

"Very good. Thank you. What do the patrols report from the Stanford Community?"

"Nothing, sir. They say it's all quiet."

"Thank you." The aide closed the door.

"You expecting trouble from Hiram, Ben?"

"Yes. Problem is, I don't have any idea how it's going to come."

"Those children are pathetic, Ben. They don't even know their ABCs."

"You probably couldn't get them lost in the woods, though."

"What?"

"I bet you they'd survive on their own."

"Oh, all right. I see."

"That's a tough breed of people. If they weren't so damned ignorant."

Chase knocked back his drink and stood up. "Well, if your aunt had balls and all that, Ben. I'll be at the hospital if you need me." He left the office.

A runner from communications came in and laid a folder on Ben's desk. "The report you requested, sir."

"Thank you." When the runner had left, Ben

opened the folder and began to read about Patrice Dubois.

A good soldier. But distant. She got along well with others, but had not been assigned positions of any real importance because the various COs she'd served under didn't quite trust her.

Claimed to be from the South Louisiana area, but when casually questioned about it, knew practically nothing of the area. And the accent was not quite right. Spoke French fluently, but with a European accent. Highly intelligent.

She had joined in North Carolina.

"How the hell did she get from South Louisiana to North Carolina?" Ben muttered.

Cec had said she was self-educated. For some reason he could not quite pinpoint, Ben just didn't believe that.

Ben flipped through the papers until he found her enlistment date.

She had joined just about the time Khansim's people landed in South Carolina, give or take a couple of months, since Ben wasn't sure of the exact landing date.

"Cute, Khansim," Ben muttered. "I didn't give you credit for this much sense."

Patrice wasn't Creole. She was Libyan. A plant.

He read the entire report, then laid it aside in disgust. Hell, there it was. She'd been trying to get transferred to the main body of Rebels since the day she first joined.

Ben leaned back in his chair, deep in thought. If he was right — and he trusted his hunches, they'd saved his life more than once — what to do about it?

157

Should he tell Cecil? Yes. Yes, of course. His life might be in danger. But would he believe him?

One way to find out.

"Sit down, Cec. Have a drink. I found a bottle of good brandy." Ben poured them both snifters of brandy.

"I saw Dr. Chase a few minutes ago. He was laughing, or at least started laughing as soon as he saw me. What's wrong with that old goat?"

"Oh, really not much. We were discussing love a little while ago."

"Love?"

"Yeah. You know. Boy meets girl, and so forth?"

"I get the picture."

"How are you and Patrice doing?"

"Fine." Cec had a puzzled look on his face.

"I got a problem, Cec. I want your opinions on it, OK?"

"Sure, Ben."

"I want to run a scenario by you. Then you give me your thoughts on what to do about it."

"Fine, Ben." Cecil relaxed and sipped his brandy.

"Approximately a month before we learned of Khansim's arrival in South Carolina, a person shows up at our small outpost in North Carolina."

Cec held up his hand. "How did this person find the outpost? None of the mountain people in that area would have told him about it. A lot of our own Rebels don't even know where it is."

"That's a good point, Cec. One I also pondered. A very inexpensive homing device would do it, wouldn't it?"

"Yes. We have some powerful radio equipment up on that mountain. Had, I should say."

"That's right. Anyway, this person joined the Rebel Army. Right there. And this person immediately starts requesting a transfer to Base Camp One. With me so far?"

"It stinks so far!"

"I agree. It damn sure does."

"Go on."

"This person is transferred around, you know the training procedures; you set them up. Florida and North Georgia. But is still very persistent about joining up with the main force. This person claimed to be from a certain part of the country, but when questioned, knows a little about it. Give them the benefit of the doubt; maybe they moved away at an early age. This person claimed to be fluent in a foreign language peculiar to a section of the United States; but when they speak the language, it's with a European accent. And, as soon as this person does wrangle a transfer to Base Camp One, this person immediately seeks out a very high ranking officer and gets buddy-buddy with him. Now give me your thoughts on it, Cec."

"Why, hell, Ben! My first thoughts would be that the person is a plant; a spy. What's this person's coloring?"

"Dark-skinned but not negroid."

"Libyan?"

"Possibly."

"I'd pull this person in and interrogate the living hell of him."

"It isn't a him; it's a her."

"Well, her, then. She's here, in camp?"

"Oh, yes."

"Have you questioned her?"

"No. I don't know what I'm going to do about it, yet, Cec."

"I can't imagine who it is. Well, we're certainly going to have to warn this officer that he may be in danger."

"I agree. I thought I'd let you take care of that."

"I certainly will. Do I know this suspect female?"

"Yes. Captain Patrice Dubois."

"They're out there, Buddy," James Riverson spoke softly. "Gathering, but well out of range."

"Sergeant major?" a Rebel who was looking through night binoculars called.

"Yes?"

"Bunch of them gathering around the ashes where we burned those creeps."

"What are they doing?"

"Eating."

"Look at those torches in the hills around town." Ike pointed, turning in a slow circle.

"The Night People?" Tina questioned.

"I don't think so. I don't have that feeling in my guts. I don't think they'd deliberately expose themselves to an armed force this large."

"Then? . . ."

"You got me, kid. It could be a bunch of the

Underground People, letting us know they're there and friendly. Or a group of Woods Children, doing the same."

"At first light, I'll send some Scouts up there to check around."

"Good deal." Ike looked around, as if attempting to see through the night.

"You get the same eerie feeling that I do, Ike?"

"I bet so. I went into town myself this afternoon. Prowled around. Place has been deserted for a long time. No human skeletons, no fresh graves. Nothing. It's like they just vanished into the air."

"Maybe they did," Tina suggested, doing her best to put a grin with it. The grin didn't quite come off.

"Don't start that, kid. I'm spooky enough as it is."

And from back in the timber, a wolf or wild dog howled, the quavering notes lonely.

Tina shivered.

"You boys ready?" Hiram asked the gathering.

The crowd mumbled low in the night.

"Got your women movin' towards the meetin' spot?"

The crowd muttered low.

"G.B. and his boys done got Billy. He's ready for his punishment. Ready, but not too willin'. Let's go."

The men walked through the night, feet on familiar paths. They came to a gathering; a circle in the middle of deep timber. Billy Bob Rockingham was naked, hanging from a tree limb, tied by his wrists, his feet just barely touching the ground.

161

Hiram flipped out his long blacksnake whip.

Billy remained silent.

"Hit pains me to do this to you, boy," Hiram said. "But you broke The Code. And you know you got punishment comin'.'."

"I broke no code," Billy told his father and the gathering. "I never once spoke agin none of you."

"Liar!" Hiram screamed, and swung the whip. The leather cut into Billy's naked back.

"Now whut you got to say, boy?" Hiram challenged him.

"I broke no code. I . . ."

His words were cut off as the whip whistled through the night air. Hiram beat his son until he was arm-weary and Billy's back and legs were dripping blood, oozing out of dozens of raw cuts. Billy hung almost unconscious.

"Git the tar," Hiram panted the order. "And the feathers."

Billy screamed as the hot tar struck the open cuts. Then, mercifully, he dropped into a darkness where he could feel no pain.

"Feather 'im good," Hiram ordered. "Then take the traitor into town and dump him. He wants to kiss Ben Raines's ass . . . let 'im. I don't never want to see his face agin."

Cecil had risen from his chair and walked to the window, to stand for a long time gazing out into the darkness. After what seemed to Ben to be a half an hour, Cec returned to his seat, a grim look on his face.

"No fool like an old fool, is there, Ben?"

"She's a lovely girl, Cec."

"But therein lies the problem, Ben. She is a girl. I'm a middle-aged man with gray in my hair."

"And as horny as any twenty-year-old. Believe me, Cec, I know the feeling. I don't think age has a damn thing to do with the feelings between a man and a woman. Cec, forgive me, but I have to ask this of you. . . ."

"Did I tell her anything of importance? Yes, yes, I did, Ben. We spent the entire afternoon going over many things."

Ben jerked up a field phone. "Security." He waited for a moment. "Put guards around the quarters of Captain Dubois. Make certain she does not leave the area and under no circumstances is she to be allowed near any communications equipment, got that? Good." He shoved the phone back into the pouch.

Ben looked at Cecil. "What does she know, Cec?"

"She knows of our plans to form outposts, and where. She knows all our caches around the nation. She knows everything that pertains to supply and logistics." Cecil rose from his chair and slammed one big hand against the wall. "Son of a motherfucking *bitch!*" he shouted.

Ben sat quietly, letting his friend get it all out of his system. Finally, Ben said, "You all through, Cec?"

"Yes. I apologize for the outburst. The unflappable ex-college professor just lost his cool momentarily."

Ben smiled and refilled their snifters. He tapped the folder. "Cec, it's all circumstantial. There isn't one hard fact in here. And you are well aware of how I feel concerning circumstantial evidence."

Cecil nodded. "She has to be questioned."

"Of course."

"Let's have some coffee and sandwiches sent in, Ben. It's going to be a very long night."

The sentry wasn't sure what it was lying by the side of the road. It damn sure didn't look human. But then, a lot of things the Rebels had encountered over the years hadn't looked human.

The sentry thought he'd heard some sort of vehicle a few moments past; but it had turned off long before it reached his post. He hesitated, then called in on his walkie talkie.

"This is fifteen. I'm leaving my post to check on an object by the side of the road."

"Go ahead, fifteen."

Kneeling down beside the object, the sentry softly cursed. "This is fifteen. Send an ambulance to my post, and make it quick."

"Ten-four."

Sirens cut the night.

The medic cussed. "This man's been tarred and feathered. What kind of assholes would do this to a person?"

John Simmons had left his house to see what was happening. "That's Hiram Rockingham's boy, Billy. That tell you anything?"

"I'd sure hate to be the one to tell the general about this."

"Where is Ben?" John asked. "I'll tell him."

164

"Probably still in his office. We'll call him from the hospital."

John stood, watching as the stretcher was placed into the back of the ambulance. "Goddamn a person who would do that to a man."

"Don't worry," the medic told him. "God don't have to damn him, 'cause Ben Raines will!"

"I resent being brought here under guard, General Raines!" Patrice bluntly and hotly told him.

"Sit down, captain. Here," he shoved a snifter of brandy toward her, "have a drink."

"My reli . . . I don't drink."

"You were about to say your religion forbids you to partake of alcohol, captain?"

"I don't drink."

"Cut the shit, Patrice!" Cecil broke in. His eyes looked furious. "Believe me when I say that Rebel questioning can become brutal."

"Torture? The great and fair General Raines uses torture?" She smiled; but it was not a nice smile.

"Drugs, captain." Ben took it. "I can assure you that we can jack you so full of drugs you will have absolutely no control over what you tell us. It isn't pleasant."

"I never denied I subscribe to the teachings of Mohammed. I was just never asked. That is why I became upset this morning; over your unfair treatment of those Muslims at their temple."

Ben stared at her. He had absolutely no hard evidence that the woman was anything other than what she claimed to be. "Captain, will you agree to take a PSE or polygraph test?"

"Yes." She spoke quickly. "If it will help clear up this matter."

"It's going to be a long night, captain. Because I am going to find out all about you. One way or the other."

Patrice waved her hand. "There is no need to go to such trouble, general. My stalling would only delay the inevitable. I came to this country with Khansim. I'm Libyan."

"Son of a bitch!" Cecil exploded just as the phone rang.

Ben jerked it up and listened for a moment, his face hardening, then flushing with fury. "All right, thanks."

"What's wrong, now, Ben?" Cecil asked.

"Billy Bob Rockingham. Hiram horsewhipped him and then tarred and feathered him. The tar was bubbling hot. Third degree burns over most of his body. Chase says he's not going to make it. But Billy wants to see all the kids; tell them what happened. He knows he's dying."

"His kids?"

"All the kids."

"What do you suppose he wants to tell them?"

"To stay with us."

Thirteen

It had been an emotional and draining experience for all who witnessed it. Billy, despite his hideous pain, had insisted upon being wheeled into the lobby to face the children. He had told them what had happened. And he had told them that Hiram Rockingham was a bigoted, ignorant fool. He told the kids to stay with the Rebels, please, stay and learn.

Billy Bob Rockingham had died about two hours after speaking with the children.

Ben had been the last person to speak with him, and it had torn him emotionally.

"Who was there during the beating, Billy?"

"Ever'body. The whole community."

"Women included?"

"Yes, sir."

"That was a fine and brave thing you did with the kids, Billy."

"I couldn't do no less. It ain't rat . . . right . . . for nobody to choose to grow up dumb. It wasn't no different down where I live 'fore the bombs come. Dumbness was the thing to be."

"Passed on from generation to generation."

"Yes, sir. Superstitious, clannish, ignorant people, and they knowed it, and enjoyed bein' what they was. Still do."

Billy had closed his eyes and was still for a long time. Finally, he opened his eyes for the last time to look at Ben. "What I'm about to say is hard, general. But it's true. You believe that. . . ."

He gritted his teeth and balled his hands into fists to fight the pain.

". . . there ain't none of them ever gonna change. I seed, seen, that tonight. They still gonna follow Hiram and his wild babblin's. I think you know what you have to do, General Raines."

He closed his eyes and did not reopen them. Not in this life.

Long after Billy Bob had been body-bagged and made ready for burial, Ben still sat on the steps of the two-story hospital. He glanced at his watch. Three o'clock. He was tired, but not a bit sleepy.

A sentry who had been walking her lonely rounds stopped by Ben's position.

"Begging your pardon, sir. But you need to get some sleep. It'll be dawn in two hours."

"Yes, I know. Thank you for your concern. Did you just come on?"

"Yes, sir. The dog watch."

"Lonely watch."

The sentry agreed. "Hiram Rockingham and his bunch need to be wiped from the face of the earth," she blurted.

Ben smiled. "I agree. Do I detect a southern

accent in your voice?"

"Yes, sir. Alabama."

"You couldn't have been very old when the bombs came."

"No, sir. I just barely remember all the confusion of it. But I've been with you for almost five years."

Ben looked at her in the night. "Why?" he asked softly.

She didn't hesitate. "Because of what you stand for, general. You and General Ike and General Jefferys, and everybody. What are you going to do about Hiram Rockingham and that bunch of trash?"

"I don't know. We have the children; that's what's important. As for Hiram and the others, I just don't know."

"See you around, sir."

"Yes." Ben watched as she resumed her rounds, watching until she was out of sight.

He didn't feel like going to his quarters, so he reentered the hospital and ran into Chase.

"You better go to bed, you old goat," Ben told him.

"I might say the same to you, Raines. What the hell are you doing lurking around here?"

"I didn't feel like going back to my quarters, that's why. You have an extra bed I can use for a few hours?"

Chase smiled, sort of strangely, Ben thought.

"Why . . . sure, Ben. I sure do. Come on down to my office for a minute."

Chase walked a half step behind Ben, noticing the man's pronounced limp. Corns on both feet, the doctor thought, then grinned wickedly.

169

In his office, the doctor poured them both a double whammy of bourbon — homemade — and jiggled two pills out of a bottle. Ben watched him warily.

"Been a long day, Ben. You're all wound up. That affair with Dubois, now Billy Bob's dying. These are muscle relaxers. Not dope, so don't look so skittish. I wouldn't give you anything that I wouldn't take."

Ben sighed and took the offered pills. "You're right, Lamar. It's been a trying day." He swallowed the pills and knocked back the bourbon.

Chase refilled his glass. He had but sipped at his drink. "Hiram Rockingham, Ben?"

"I don't know. I wish I could just sleep for a few days; get over my rage. The way I'm feeling now, I just might take a company down there in a few hours and wipe out the whole goddamned mess of them."

"Uummm. Well, you're going to get a good rest, Ben. And you need it. No doubt about it. And I think that when you wake up, you'll have a better insight into the problem."

"I hope you're right."

"Oh, I am, Ben. Rest assured of that."

Ben yawned hugely. "Guess I was tired; more so than I thought."

"Come on. Let's find you a bed."

Ben balked at putting on the hospital gown. "I'll sleep in my shorts."

"Oh, come on, Raines. Stop being such a baby!"

Reluctantly, Ben got into the backless gown and stretched out on the bed. In two minutes, he was sleeping peacefully.

Chase waved at a floor nurse. "Schedule Ben Raines for surgery at ten o'clock. Work on his feet. And while we've got him, I want to dig that old lead out of his right leg. Knock him down at six and again at eight."

"That's a lot of Demerol, doctor."

"You don't know Ben Raines the way I do."

"Yes, sir."

Lamar Chase walked away, to his hospital quarters. He'd get a few hours sleep. He was still chuckling as he drifted off into sleep.

When Ben woke up at one o'clock that afternoon, both feet were bandaged and there was a bandage on his right leg.

He lay in the hospital bed and cussed, loudly, sending nurses and orderlies running in all directions.

Then he lay back and grinned. "The old son of a bitch did it to me again!"

Book Two

We think our civilization near its meridian, but we are yet only at the cock-crowing and the morning star. In our barbarous society the influence of character is in its infancy.

Emerson

Fourteen

"I love it!" Tina yelled, when the pilots told her what Dr. Chase had done. Ike came running over and began whooping with laughter.

"I bet you Ben is so mad he's got every nurse and doctor in that place running for cover."

"Knowing Dad, he won't be down for very long. I'll bet you he's back at work, in house slippers, by late this afternoon."

"If they give him back his clothes!" Major Broadhurst doubled over with laughter.

Tina wiped her eyes. "Those two have been doing stuff like this ever since I can remember. Chase better watch out, or Dad will slip a whoopee cushion in his chair."

The platoon of Rebels just flown in with the additional supplies brought the complement to over three hundred. Rebel mechanics had been working fast and furiously on half a dozen trucks they'd found; the extra vehicles were needed because of the new platoon and all their equipment.

The chief mechanic walked up to Ike. "Sorry, sir. But it's going to take us at least another day to get these trucks running."

"Just do the best you can, Sid," Ike told him. He turned to Tina. "Beef up your Scouts, Tina. Pick whoever you like. Then shove off. Start clearing any blockades you find around Knoxville; I'm pretty sure you're going to find a lot of them. Get movin', kid. We'll see you in a couple of days."

Tina trotted off, shouting for her team.

They pulled out within the hour, heading eastward . . . into the unknown.

The pilots brought Ike up to date on the Patrice Dubois affair, and about the rednecks.

"Ben won't tolerate that," Ike summed it up. "He'll brood about it for a few days, and then he'll take a team in and clean out that nest of rattle-snakes. Bet on it."

"Well, Raines!" Chase said cheerfully. "How are we feeling this afternoon?"

"If you think I'm going to respond to that old joke, Lamar, you're nuts. You tricked me, you old bastard."

"In a few days, you'll be thanking me." Chase thought about that for a few seconds. "Well . . . no, you won't thank me. But you will feel better." He tossed a chunk of lead onto Ben's chest. "That's what's been causing your leg pains. I told you to let me dig that out years ago."

"*You* did the surgery? Jesus! I'll probably never walk again!"

"Actually, no, I didn't do the surgery. I let a young lady do it. You haven't met her. She's been working up in North Carolina for the past year." He turned and called out the door. "Dr. Allardt? Would you come in here, please."

Ben looked up as she walked into the room. He sure hadn't met her! He would have remembered that.

"Dr. Holly Allardt," Chase said, "I believe you've met Ben Raines . . . informally. Ben, this is the newest addition to my staff."

Ben's eyes drifted over her. From head to knees. Since that was as far as he could see from flat on his back.

About five-five. Honey-colored hair. Blue eyes. Very fair complexion, but touched with a summer's tan. Shapely.

"Dr. Allardt. Welcome to camp."

"Thank you, general." Her voice had a husky quality. Very sexy-sounding, Ben thought. Hell, everything about her was sexy.

"I'll just leave you two alone to get acquainted," Chase said.

"You wait just a damn minute!" Ben stopped him. "When the hell do I get out of this dump? I've got a lot to do."

"I have no idea, Raines. You're not my patient. Ask Dr. Allardt. 'Bye, all." He left the room.

"We'll keep you for twenty-four hours, general," Holly told him. "That's SOP. Probably discharge you at noon tomorrow."

Ben began bitching. Holly folded her arms under her breasts and calmly waited until he was finished cussing. "That won't do you a bit of good, general. You'll be discharged when I say so. The surgery was

177

really very minor, so you should be back to full-throttle in a couple of days."

"Good. I've got a nest of crap to clean out."

"Violence is not always the best way in dealing with the uneducated, general."

"It is with this bunch of trash. They've had a hundred years to clean up their act. And made no progress on it."

It was obvious that she did not agree with him. But from the expression on her face it was clear that she also realized that he was the Supreme Commander of all Rebel forces. But Ben, loving a good debate, wasn't about to let this one pass.

"If you don't agree with the Rebel philosophy, doctor, then why did you join?"

"I didn't join the Rebels, general. I am a doctor, practicing with this unit. I can practice better medicine here than anywhere else in the nation. And learn a lot as well."

"I see. And you just happened to be in North Carolina?"

"Actually, no. I was in West Virginia. I'm from Virginia."

"You say that, announce it, really, like it's supposed to impress me."

Her eyes flashed Danger! Ben saw it, liked it, and grinned at her.

When she would not speak, Ben said, "First family and all that, huh?"

"Among the first to settle there, yes."

"My goodness! I'm among royalty and didn't even realize it. Do I salute or bow or what? I better salute. If I bent over, I'd be letting it all hang out."

"Are you deliberately trying to provoke a quarrel, general?"

"Why not? Nothing else to do in this place."

"Oh, yes, there is, General Raines."

"What?"

She walked to the door and turned, smiling sweetly. "Get better." She walked out the door, closing it.

But she smiled as she heard Ben's laughter following her up the hall.

Cecil pushed open the door and stepped inside the room just as Holly was rounding a corner, disappearing from view.

"What's so funny, Ben?"

"Did you see that class act that just left?"

"That's funny?"

"Never mind. Cec, pull all Rebel patrols out of the Stanford Community."

"All of them?"

"All of them. Stop patrolling at once."

"All right, Ben. Would you mind telling me why you're doing this?"

"Hiram wants a fight."

Cecil looked at him. "That's it? I'm supposed to make sense out of that?"

"You didn't let me finish. Give me a piece of paper and a pencil. Thanks." He drew a ragged circle. "This parish is roughly seven hundred square miles. One of the biggest in the state. On the west side of this circle—which represents the Stanford Community—is a series of interconnecting bayous. From about here to here. On the east side is a river. The bayou joins the river here, right down here at the bottom. The Stanford Community comprises roughly two hundred square miles. You with me?"

"Yes. Thank you for the geography lesson, professor."

"You're welcome. Now pay attention," Ben said, chuckling.

"I shall. You should go into the hospital more often, Ben. It improves your disposition."

"It isn't the hospital, it's the help."

"You're speaking, of course, of Dr. Chase."

"Oh, of course, of course! Pay attention. The bayous meander throughout the area, but there are six main bridges connecting this den of abysmal heathenism with the outside world." He looked up at Cecil and smiled.

"You wouldn't!"

"Oh, yes, I would! They wish to be left alone. I am going to see that they get their chance."

"You're an asshole, Raines!"

"Oh, nay, nay, old friend. I am a wonderful person to have as a friend and ally. But I'm a motherfucker for an enemy."

Cecil leaned back in his chair. "Well, we got the kids out, anyway."

"Be damn sure that we did."

"I checked with some of the older children. We got them all. Half a dozen walked out of their own accord, just to join the others. What's this going to accomplish, Ben?"

"For one thing, it's going to force Hiram's hand. He'll sit back for a couple of weeks and be content. Then somebody will have to go scrounging for a part. They won't be able to get out. They may want to go visiting somewhere, but they won't be able to do that. That's going to put Hiram between that rock and the hard place."

"And? . . ."

"He's going to try to lead some people out. But when he does, he's going to run into Rebels, patrolling outside his perimeter, and they'll turn him back."

"And? . . ."

"I've got to whip them all, Cec. Everyone of them. Men and women. But this way is the most bloodless. They understand force, Cec. That is the one thing a redneck does understand. Force. I've got to make them understand that the Rebels control every facet of their lives. I've got to beat them down to their knees; fighting lawlessness with lawlessness. Cec, it's a hell of a lot better than going in there and bombing the place."

"Yes. I'll give you that much. But many of them will hate you for the rest of their lives."

"Yes, they will, Cec. But they'll experience one other emotion that will override that."

"What?"

"Total blind fear."

"How much of this is personal, Ben?"

"On a scale of one to ten, with ten being the highest?"

"That'll do."

"One. Maybe half of one. Cec, get ready for it. We're going to be doing this all over the nation as we push our outposts in all directions. Cec, Billy Bob told me something just before he died. He said that it wasn't right for anyone to choose to grow up dumb, knowing it, and enjoying being what they were."

"He was probably the best one of the lot."

"Yes, I think. And they killed him for it. Billy said the entire community turned out for the whipping and the tarring. Men and women."

"That's disgusting!"

"Yes. Start blowing the main bridges at dawn tomorrow. No one goes in, no one comes out."

Cecil nodded. "I'll get the demo crews working on the charges now. Can I get you anything to read, Ben?"

"How about that copy of *A Gathering of Old Men* you mentioned."

"Well, ah, it's this way. . . ."

Ben laughed and waved him silent. "I know, I know. You gave it to Patrice." Ben peered closely at his friend. "It's damned hard to tell, but I do believe you're blushing!"

Cecil gave him the finger and left, smiling.

Tina and her scouts had to pick their way toward Knoxville, the Interstate being littered with rusting and broken-down vehicles of all shapes and sizes. Many had to be wrenched out of the way. And a whole lot of them, as one Rebel observed, had been deliberately placed in the roadway, and not too long ago, either.

They were still about twenty miles from the Knoxville loop when Tina called a halt and ordered camp set up.

The Rebels worked very quickly in securing their

camp, setting up Claymores around the outer perimeters and digging machine gun pits. They could all smell trouble in the air, and the smell was of fetid, unwashed bodies. None of them had to be told what that meant.

Buddy had halted his team's bloody work two hours before dusk; all wanted plenty of time to bathe and eat while there was still light. For the Night People would gather around the shopping center as soon as full darkness came, chanting and humming and shouting filth at the Rebels. They hurled stones and spears and fired arrows at the shopping center. But Buddy had noticed something during the night's barrage; something he had not mentioned to any of the others.

Until now.

"They're going to try to infiltrate the complex tonight," he told James.

"How do you figure, Buddy?"

"I was watching the way they operated last night. They wanted all our attention on this end. If they do the same tonight, we'll know they've found a way in that we don't know about."

Buddy pointed upward.

"The roof," James said softly. "Sure. With dust a foot deep in the other shops and stores; all the old rags of clothing and boxes and crap piled everywhere, one firebomb could destroy us all."

"That's the way I think."

"So let's have a little surprise waiting for them when they try it."

"Claymores?"

"Oh, yeah!"

"Have the people prepare the charges now. At dusk, get up on the roof quickly and place the Claymores. In the meantime, have teams setting up machine guns on the left side of the inside mall. When they rush us, if they rush us, they'll be coming from the inside as well. If it works, it will make our job tomorrow ever so much easier."

"Yeah," Riverson grunted. "A whole hell of lot less of them."

"Do you mind if I have dinner with you, General Raines?" Holly asked.

"Not at all. I'd enjoy the company."

She waved a cart in and set two trays on a table. "Are you experiencing any discomfort, general?"

"No. Just a little ache in my leg. I just took two aspirin. I'm fine."

He noticed she had changed out of her hospital clothes and into jeans and T-shirt. He was amused at the logo on the T-shirt.

WOODSTOCK

"Where in the world did you find that shirt, Holly?"

She smiled as she placed the tray on his table and adjusted it. "In a deserted shop in Charleston. I wish I knew what it meant."

"Peace and love, baby."

She cut her eyes to him. "I beg your pardon, general?"

"Peace and love and music . . . more or less. A

184

big bash in Woodstock, New York."

"Did you attend?"

"Hell, no!"

She smiled at his expression. "It couldn't have been *that* bad, general."

"It probably wasn't. If you like the kind of music played there. I don't. Call me Ben, please."

"All right, Ben. What kind of music do you like?"

"Serious music, mostly. But I also enjoy a lot of the other types, as well."

"What is your objection to rock and roll?"

"Too damn loud!"

She laughed out loud at him. "Well, I suppose it's all moot, now, isn't it?"

"Yes. And I hope it stays that way."

"Eat your dinner, Ben."

"Yes, doctor."

They smiled at each other, eyes meeting. Something silent passed between them, invisibly touching them both.

"My father and brother were great fans of yours, Ben."

"Oh?"

"I did not share their enthusiasm."

He smiled at her honesty. "Well, not everyone can appreciate genius, Holly."

She looked up to see if he was kidding, and visibly relaxed when she saw he was. "You must know, Ben, that you are, simultaneously, the most loved and the most hated man in the world."

"Yes, I know."

"The hatred doesn't bother you?"

"Not really. I got used to that as a writer of many

controversial novels. You should have seen some of the hate mail I received."

"When you were a writer, did anyone actually try to kill you?"

"Oh, yes. Fortunately for me, they didn't succeed."

"The people of the Stanford Community . . . were some of them involved in the attempts on your life?"

"Oh, yes."

"You certainly have the troops to just go in there and wipe them out."

"Yes. But that isn't what I want to do." He thought about that for a moment. "That's not true. That is what I want to do. But I'm not going to. I hope not, anyway."

"But if it came to that? . . ."

"I would."

"You're a strange man, Ben Raines. You're a curious mixture of compassion and brutality. Killing does not seem to bother you."

"It all depends on who I'm killing. Or whom I'm killing."

Again, Holly noted the almost-sarcastic grin on Ben's face. "I don't know whether I like you, or not."

"Yes," Ben said softly. "You know."

Fifteen

When the dusk had spread itself over the land, a team of Rebels quietly slipped onto the roof of the shopping center and set up the lethal Claymores, then backed away, stringing the lead wires back.

Since no Claymores had been produced for years, the Rebels made their own, and they were quite inventive with it, manufacturing several types of the deadly antipersonnel mine.

The type the Rebels were using this night at the shopping center each held eight hundred small steel ball bearings. The ball bearings were propelled out the front of the mine, pushed by two pounds of composition C-4 plastic explosive. The efficient killing zone, or K-Z, was seventy-five yards, with some lethal fragments traveling as much as three hundred yards. The side and rear back-blast concussion area had also been extended with the additional front range. This night, the integral sights on the mine were set to strike the enemy hip to chest high.

Their jobs done, the Rebels slipped quietly from the roof, trailing the lead wires.

Inside the darkened mall, M-60 machine guns had

been set up according to Buddy's directions. The gunners lay quietly behind and beside their weapons, waiting.

Outside, ringing the shopping center, the Night People began to gather and chant and shout and hurl objects at the small force of Rebels holed up inside.

"Hold your fire," Buddy ordered. "No one fires until I give the word. Pass it along."

The Rebels wiped sweaty palms on their field pants and tiger-stripe field shirts and waited.

The first Claymore mine that was detonated on the Rebel camp's outer perimeter brought shrieks and howls and screams of pain from the still-unseen intruders. Grenades were tossed from the Rebel camp, the explosions rocking the night and bringing more wails of agony; those intensified as WP was added to HE and Fire-frag grenades. And as brush fires sprang up from the grenades, the Rebels could see that the enemy was not Night People.

"Hold your fire!" Tina yelled above the din of battle. "Hold your fire!"

When the weapons' fire had ceased, Tina yelled into the darkness, "Who are you and what do you want?"

"This is our territory," a woman's voice called. "Get out or die. The choice is yours."

"We're a contingent of Raines Rebels!" Tina shouted. "We're just passing through this part of the country. We don't mean you any harm."

"You'll all die if you don't leave. Just like the

people did in the town where your planes landed."

"Well, now we know what happened," Ham whispered. "But who the hell are these people?"

"One way to find out." Tina shouted: "Who are you?"

"The Sisters of Zenana."

"That doesn't tell me a goddamn thing!" Ham whispered.

"Me, either," Tina returned the whisper. Taking a deep breath, she called, "What the hell is that?"

"Are you in charge, sister?"

"I'm not your sister. Yes, I'm in charge."

"Sisters may leave. The men must stay."

"I told you, I'm not your sister. Why should we leave the men?"

"For breeding purposes."

"If they just want to fuck," a Rebel called out from the darkness, "tell 'em to come on. Let's have a party."

"Shut up, Gary," Tina said, glad that Gary could not see her grin.

"Pigs!" the woman's voice was shrill. "Filthy male pigs."

"Uh-huh," Gary said. "Now I get the picture."

"Carry your asses on, girls," Ham called. "Go do your things somewhere else."

"You'd better think about it, sister," the voice called. "We are many and you are few."

"If you don't like men, why do you want to breed with them?" Tina called.

"To produce more Sisters of Zenana."

"Something tells me that they kill any boy babies," Ham said.

"We run into the most interestin' folks," Gary said.

Tina didn't tell him to shut up. As the camp clown, Gary could be counted on to act the fool even under the most harrowing of conditions.

"How much area do you control?" Tina called.

"Why do you want to know?"

"So we can avoid it the next time."

"There will be no next time, sister."

"Get ready," Ham called hoarsely. "They're coming."

"That's one way to put it," Gary said.

Screaming, the Sisters of Zenana charged. And ran headfirst into death. The Rebel Scouts opened up with everything they had, throwing up a solid wall of firepower. The Claymores were electronically fired, the ball bearings ripping the life out of anyone in their K-Z.

A big .50 caliber added its chugging to the melee, the thumb-sized slugs knocking the Sisters spinning and screaming to the ground.

But even with the firepower, several Sisters managed to breach the camp's inner perimeters, and the weapons changed from guns to knives and hand-axes and entrenching tools.

Tina was knocked down by a charging Sister, losing her M-16 as she fell. Tina fumbled for her sidearm just as a fist slammed into her jaw.

"Don't kill this one," she dimly heard a woman's voice say. "She's prime." Hands roamed her body.

Screw you! Tina thought, as her hand closed on the handle of her knife. She drove the blade to the hilt in the woman's belly. Blood oozed onto her hand as she pulled the blade free and drove it in again.

The Sister screamed and fell to one side. Tina jumped to her feet, the big knife at the ready. She looked around her. The fight was over.

From deep in the brush and timber, the voice called, "You are marked for death, Sister. Beware, Beware!"

"Fuck you!" Tina yelled. "That's probably what you need."

"Will somebody come get this broad off me!" Gary yelled. "Damned heifer must weigh three hundred pounds!"

The Rebels all heard the faint sounds of feet on the roof. Faint, but very real.

Outside, the shouting and the hurling of stones had increased.

"Whenever you're ready," Buddy called to the men with the lead wires in their hands.

The huge complex trembled as the Claymores were fired, the back-blast sending shock waves through the roof-entrance. The bodies, intact and in bits and chunks, were actually hurled from the roof.

The floor of the littered and darkened inner mall was suddenly filled with robed men and women.

"Fire!" Buddy shouted.

The machine guns began yammering, the noise deafening in the closed complex.

Riverson stood at the store's open end, holding an M-60 in his big hands, the belt working, spitting out death.

A piece of the roof collapsed, caused in part by the explosions from the Claymores, the debris trapping those remaining Night People in the closed mall.

From that point on, it was carnage, as the Rebels finished their work.

Buddy chanced a look outside. The parking area was empty of Night People.

When the last shot had echoed away into stillness, Buddy said, "It's over. This town is cleared. They've had enough. They've pulled out."

Ben was up early, found his clothing, and dressed, shoving his sore feet into house slippers. He walked out into the hall, startling a floor nurse.

"Sir! You shouldn't be out of bed!"

"I'm fine. Where is Dr. Allardt?"

"Ah . . . having breakfast in the dining area, general."

"Fine, I'll join her."

He walked toward up the hall, then paused. Hell, he didn't know where the dining area was.

He asked the nurse, thanked her, and walked on. He got a dirty look from Holly when he stepped into the dining room.

Smiling, he walked over to her table and sat down. "What are you having?" he asked pleasantly.

"You are a bullheaded man, General. You should not be on that leg."

"It wasn't a long walk, and I don't intend to do much walking. Can you drive a Jeep?"

"I . . . of course, I can drive a Jeep! Why?"

192

"I thought you might like to take a ride around the town . . . after you've finished your rounds, of course."

"I have no rounds. You were my only patient. The Rebels are the healthiest bunch of people I have ever encountered."

"Clean living and good exercise, Holly." He was straight-faced as he said it.

"Right," she said drily.

"Is that your answer, Holly?"

"If that is the only way to keep you off your feet, yes, we'll take a drive."

"Good!"

Then she watched in astonishment as Ben ordered bacon and eggs and fried potatoes and biscuits and milk.

"Is that all for you?"

"I'm a healthy eater. And where is my Thompson?"

"Your what?"

"My weapon."

"I haven't the foggiest. I hope you didn't leave it in your Jeep."

"Why?"

"Because it might get stolen."

Ben smiled at her. "Did you hear any gunshots last night or this morning, Holly?"

"Why . . no."

"Then no one stole it."

"What are you saying?"

"We don't tolerate crime in a Rebel community, Holly. No one has to steal, and we won't tolerate it."

She stared at him, her blue eyes serious. "What

happens to the people who steal?"

"That depends on whether or not they're shot dead on the spot."

"I don't believe I'm hearing this."

"Believe it. Our schools teach much more than the ABCs, Holly. Our schools teach honesty and values and the work ethic."

"Then it's all true; everything I've heard. That's why I've been avoiding locations where the Rebels might be."

"What have you heard?"

"That your society is a very rigid one. . . ."

"It is, to an extent."

". . . and that it is a dictatorship. With you the director."

Ben thought that was funny. He was still laughing as his breakfast was placed in front of him. And Holly was getting angry.

"Holly, there are few written laws in any Rebel settlement. And those laws are agreed upon by all who join us. They were not written by me alone; they were voted on, years ago. Back when we formed the Tri-States. A person does not steal, cheat, lie, misrepresent the truth . . . it's a common-sense form of government, Holly. All we did was go back to the basics."

"But you'll shoot someone for stealing a . . . a, anything!"

"Most of the time, no."

"What do you mean?"

"Our reputation goes back years, Holly. People know we're a bunch of hard-asses . . . that's on one hand. On the other hand, they know that if they need food, we'll share with them. If they're sick, we'll help them. They also know that if they try to steal from us, we'll shoot them on the spot. And that's the way it is. Are you going to eat that toast?"

"What . . . what? Ah, no."

"Thanks." He speared it with his fork and spread blackberry jam on it.

"When was the last time you shot someone for stealing, Ben?"

Ben chewed reflectively. "Oh . . . years ago. I told you. No one steals in a Rebel community."

"Incredible! And people actually flock to join you people. I don't understand it."

"Do you have a sister?"

"What? Ah, as a matter of fact, I do."

"Her name wouldn't be Gale, would it?"

"No. It's Nancy. I don't know where she is. We became separated just after the bombings. Who is Gale?"

"A lady I used to know. You'd like her. She was a liberal in the midst of war."

"If the world had had more liberals, we wouldn't have had a war."

"Probably not. It would all be under communist rule. Let's go."

"Daddy," Grover Neal said. "Them Rebels is a-blowin' up all the bridges."

"Why you reckon they'd do a damn fool thang lak 'at?"

"Don't know, Daddy." Which accurately summed up Grover Neal's understanding of just about any-

195

thing one might wish to mention.

"Wal," Hiram picked up his rifle, "le's us jus' go see these soldier-boys."

Hiram gathered up all of his sons he could find, and several of his neighbors, all armed, and went to see the soldier-boys.

"Why for y'all blowin' up our bridges?" Hiram called across the space where a bridge had once stood.

The Rebels ignored him, as they had been ordered to do. And they also had a few other orders that would soon have to be followed.

"Hey, boy!" Hiram called to the Rebel who was busy planting charges that would blow out the concrete stanchions. "Ah'm a-talkin' to you, goddamn-it!"

The Rebels ignored him.

Hiram and his crew did not notice as the Rebels in the Jeeps swung the .50 calibers in their direction.

"Ah thank they's all deef, Hiram," one of the neighbors proclaimed, in what could loosely pass for the English language.

"Remember the orders," one of the Rebels behind a .50 whispered. "No killing if it can be avoided."

"Gottcha."

Flush with the thrill of victory after having witnessed his brother being flogged and then tarred and feathered, Efrom Silas said, "Ah thank ah can git they attention, Daddy."

"Go ahead, son," Hiram told him.

Efrom jacked back the hammer on his .30-30 and put a round near a Rebel.

About a half second after he did that, it seemed to

Hiram and Efrom and the others that the gates of Hell suddenly opened.

Both .50's opened up, as well as a squad of riflemen with M-16s, two M-60s, a mortar crew back in the timber, and a half a dozen Rebels with Uzis.

Hiram's pickup truck was knocked over by a mortar round. G.B.'s pickup exploded as .50 caliber rounds ignited the gas tank, and the air around the rednecks was literally filled with lead.

"Holy fuckin' shit!" Hiram hollered, and started pickin' 'em up and puttin' 'em down. Charlie Jimmy got so excited he jumped in the bayou and came up nose to snout with a 'gator; it was a toss-up as to who scared whom the most. Charlie Jimmy went one way and the 'gator went another.

G.B., his big belly jumping with every step, allowed as to how this was plumb embarrassin' for a man who'd ris so high up in the Klan. But he put all those thoughts out of his head as a Rebel started pulling slugs around G.B.'s feet. G.B. decided he'd better get the lead out of his ass before he got some lead in his ass. "Gawddamnit, Hiram!" he squalled. "Wait up for me!"

The crew of marshmallow brains rounded a curve in the old road and disappeared from sight, leaving a bunch of Rebels laughing so hard they could hardly see.

"That'll give them something to think about," the Rebel in charge of the unit said. "Let's blow this thing and move on to the next one."

"Halp!" Charlie Jimmy hollered. He was in about a foot of water and was splashing like a beached whale. "Halp! I's a-gonna git drowned!"

"Stand up, and walk out of there, you silly fucker!" a Rebel yelled.

Charlie Jimmy stood up and with as much dignity as he could muster began the trek up the bank. He had lost his britches and was buck-assed naked from the waist down.

Charlie Jimmy did his best to ignore the wolf-whistles coming from the women Rebels on the other side of the bayou.

Sixteen

"Ah'm a-gonna kill that goddamned Ben Raines!" Hiram said. He was sitting on his front porch of the house that housed wife #2. He couldn't find his left shoe, having ran out of it about two miles back up the road. "That there was my bestest pickup."

"Well, now, Hiram!" #2 asked, her hands on her hips. "Jist how am I 'pposed to visit my sister acrost the bayou if Ben Raines has done blowed up all the bridges?"

"I don't know. . . ." Hiram couldn't remember her name. Lucy something-or-the-other, he thought. "And I don't much care. I never laked her nohow."

#2 glared at him. "Wal, you jist a-better come up with sumthang, Mr. Big-Shot. And I mean do hit quick!"

"Awrat, awrat!"

She stormed back into the house.

"Gawddamn agitatin' wimmin!" Hiram muttered.

One of his own kids started squallin' at the other end of the porch. Hiram picked up a chunk of wood and threw it at the boy, knocking him off the porch.

"Shut up, gawddamnit!"

Hiram had never heard of Dr. Spock. The only Spock he'd ever heard of was that one with the funny ears that used to be on the TV.

Hiram looked to see who he'd hit. Bubba Willie. Well, couldn't make him no goofier than he already was, he reckoned.

"I hate you, Ben Raines!"

"Why are you tearing down those buildings?" Holly asked, pointing to where a bulldozer was working.

"We don't have slums in Rebel communities, Holly. Not only are they eyesores, they're dangerous. So we tear them down and start over."

"And over there? What is that, slave labor?"

He laughed at her. "Those are people who want all that we can give them, but refuse to pitch in and work alongside us."

"So your troops come in with guns and force them to work." Not a question.

"No. They're given a choice. Work or get out. Obviously, those chose to work."

"With a little gentle persuasion," she said sarcastically.

"There are no free rides, Holly. The free rides ended when the bombs came. Look closely, Holly. Just stop the Jeep. Thank you. You see any handicapped or elderly people out there working? Huh? Do you?"

She did not.

"Those are all able-bodied men and women. You should know, Holly . . . you helped with their physical exams."

"But many of those women have children!"

"The kids are being cared for at a day center. They aren't home fending for themselves, Holly. Give us more credit than that."

"Ben Raines, I don't know if you are the total personification of evil or whether you are what this country needed thirty years ago."

"Thank you. Drive on, please."

She muttered under her breath, but put the Jeep in gear and drove on.

"What's that building over there?" she asked, pointing.

"Dr. Chase's lab and factory . . . soon to be. He might already have it running."

"For the manufacture of medicines?"

"Precisely."

"And that building 'way over there in the field?"

"Munitions. That's why it's set so far away from the other buildings."

"You ready to head back?"

"To my office."

"No, general. To the hospital. I want to change the dressing on your leg."

"All right. What are you doing for dinner this evening, Holly?"

"Why . . . nothing."

"Would you like to have dinner with me?"

"Is that wise?"

"What's unwise about it? You're not a member of the Rebel Army."

"That's not exactly what I meant."

"I know."

She refused to look at him. "Where will this dinner take place?"

"My quarters, I guess. Wherever you would like."

She hesitated for a few seconds. "All right. I'll meet you there." She glanced at him. "Where are your quarters?"

He told her. By that time, they had reached the hospital complex and she had pulled in and gotten out. "I'll see you about seven, Ben."

"Fine." She turned away. "Holly?" She turned around. Ben was smiling at her.

"What's so funny, Ben?"

He patted the leather boot holding his Thompson SMG.

She muttered something about barbarism and walked into the ground floor of the hospital. But she had to smile as Ben's laughter reached her.

Cecil looked up from his desk. "Should you be up, Ben?"

"I'm not doing much walking. What's the status on Patrice?"

Ben sat down.

Cecil poured them both coffee and sat back down. His offices were on the opposite end of town from Ben's HQ. That lessened the chances of both of them being killed in case of attack.

"She says that she came over with the terrorist and was sent to infiltrate our army. To get as close to the leaders as possible. But she claims that she has had no contact in any way with Khansim since she joined in North Carolina."

"Do you believe her?"

"She passed both a polygraph and a PSE test."

"Drugs?"

"Not yet. What do you think?"

Ben sighed heavily. "I hate to subject a person to drugs. It's a tough go. But if we're going to get to the truth . . . yes, Cec. Go ahead."

He nodded. "I'll contact Lamar. Have him set it up."

"The bridges blown?"

Cecil smiled. "Yes. Only one incident."

"Anybody killed?"

"No. Just a slight loss of dignity is the most anyone suffered."

"Dignity? Hell, those people can't even spell the word." He stood up. "Hold it down, Cec. I'll be at my quarters."

Ben paused at the door. "Any further word from the eastbound teams?"

"Not yet."

"Buddy?"

"Monroe is clean. They're burning the last of the bodies."

"Have him come back here and resupply before he pushes on."

"Will do, Ben."

Tina and her team had spent most of that day clearing the blockades from around Knoxville. Ham finally straightened up, easing his back, and said, "I don't understand these barricades, Tina. If these people thrive on human flesh, and we know that's true, why barricades? It seems to me they'd want to lure people into the cities, rather than keep them

203

out."

"I've been thinking about that, Ham. Remember what we found in Atlanta?"

He nodded.

"I think these Night People go out on forays and bring prisoners back, keep them locked down until they're . . . well, ready for them. If you know what I mean."

Ham knew. "General Raines will never permit that, Tina. And I think he should know for sure."

"Yes. And I've been thinking about that, too. I think I'll contact Ike. Give the people a break, Ham."

She walked to her jeep and got Ike on the horn, sharing Ham's and her theory with him.

She could practically hear Ike sigh over the miles. "You're right, Tina. I think Ben should be informed of your theory. Hold what you've got. I'll link up with you tomorrow. We'll go into the city and check this out. I'll notify Ben and tell him what we're doing."

"Ten-four, Ike."

Ike couldn't get Ben, but he got Cecil and brought him up to date.

"What'd you think about it, Cec?"

"If there are people being held prisoner, Ike, we've got to free them. Or at least try. Go ahead, I'll square it with Ben."

"Ten-four, Cec. I'll call in just before we enter the city. That will probably be around noon tomorrow. Shark out."

He radioed to Tina. "It's a go, Tina. Pull back off the loop and wait for us west of the city."

"Ten-four, Ike. Oh, Ike . . . watch out for the Sisters of Zenana."

"The *who*?"

"They kidnap males for breeding purposes."

"What happens after that?"

"They kill the men."

"Sound like nice people. Where'd you run into them?"

She gave him the twenty of the Sisters of Zenana.

"I will do my best to avoid that spot. Shark out."

"Pull them back, Ham!" Tina shouted. "We'll enter the city tomorrow."

"Dr. Chase has assigned a team to question this Patrice Dubois person," Holly told Ben. "I asked if I could be a part. He very flatly said no to that."

"And that offended you?" Ben handed her a drink.

"Thanks. As a matter of fact, it did."

"Why should it? You said it yourself: You are not a part of the Rebel Army."

She took a sip of her drink and coughed. "Good God! What is this stuff?"

"Homemade vodka. Would you prefer homemade gin or homemade whiskey?"

"One is probably as bad as the other."

"True."

"What happens during this questioning?"

"A team of doctors put the subject into drug-induced hypnosis. It's repeated several times over a period of several days, gradually breaking down the person's mental guards, to use laymen's terms. It's

205

effective."

"And dangerous."

"Not according to Chase. The subject is very carefully monitored. Whether you choose to believe it or not, Holly, we're not here to harm anyone who will just give us a chance."

She gave him a very dubious look. Almost painful. Of course, that might have been caused by the homemade hooch.

"You have yet to convince me of that, Ben."

"Holly . . ." Ben sat down in a chair opposite her. "Civilization, order, productivity, are based on rules. Laws, if you will. And laws are based on, steeped in, among other things, fear. And respect for a fellow human being."

"I will agree in part. But you're a fine one to be talking about respect. What respect have you shown this Rockingham person and his followers?"

"The same amount he's shown me."

She thought about that and slowly nodded her head in agreement . . . Ben hoped.

"But you force people to work."

"Oh, no, Holly. That's wrong. If people wish to share what the Rebels can offer them: medical help, schools, protection, any type of help that we can offer, then yes, we ask that they work . . . at whatever they are qualified to do. If they're not qualified to do anything, we'll train them. But if they choose not to work with us, that is their option, but they will receive nothing from us. Nothing."

She drained her glass and held it out for a refill. Ben obliged. "You're not going to lecture me on the potential of this stuff, Ben?"

"You're an adult, Holly. I'm not your keeper."

"Another Rebel philosophy?"

"A truism."

"Perhaps. When are we going to eat and what are we having?"

"Steaks, baked potato, and a salad. Is that all right with you?"

"Sounds good." Her words were already becoming a bit slurry.

Ben made a silent bet she'd be passed out in thirty minutes, and he hadn't even put the steaks on the grill.

Holly was already knocking back another half full glass of the home-brew. He smiled and adjusted the wick on a lamp, darkening the room. If Holly paid any attention to it, she didn't let on.

Ben got a blanket from a hall closet. When Holly passed out, she was going to just keel over right there on the couch. Might as well get ready for it.

"How do you like your steak, Holly?"

"Well dome . . . done."

"Right." He got the steaks out of the generator-powered fridge and held them for a moment. No point in wasting one. He started to put one back and thought, Oh, what the hell.

Then he heard a soft, thudding sound in the living room. He put her steak back and looked in on the doctor. She was asleep on the couch. She'd had about seven ounces of home-brew, on probably an empty stomach.

Ben straightened her out and covered her with a thin blanket. Then he went outside to cook his steak.

One thing for sure, and Ben knew from experience: Holly would have one hell of a hangover in the morning.

"Men catch us meetin', and we gonna be in big trouble, Jenny Sue."

"For what? It ain't agin no law for wimmin to git together and gossip."

"But that ain't why we're here and you know it."

"Did any of you like what we all seen the other night?"

None did.

"So what are we gonna do about it?"

No one said anything.

"Will somebody tell me what the hell The Code is?" Jenny Sue asked.

Nobody really knew. But Laura Jane said, "I think it means you ain't 'pposed to talk agin your neighbor."

"But what if your neighbor is wrong?"

"Daddy says that ain't for us to judge," Billie Jo spoke up.

"Well . . . who judges, then?"

Nobody knew.

"Well, I know one thing: I want my kids back," Jenny Sue stated. "And I'll do whatever it takes to git 'em back." And then she spoke the damning words. "And I want to git away from this place."

"Jenny Sue! You hush 'at kinda talk." The young woman looked around, fear in her eyes.

"Now this is pitiful!" Jenny's words were hard-spoken. "We're grown wimmin. All of us twenty or near there. And we have to sneak out into the bushes to talk. Girls, I thought the whole world lived lak we'uns; till I seen them Rebels other day. I bet ever'one of 'em can read and write and figure. I can't. Can any of you?"

No one could.

"And why cain't we read and write and figure?"

" 'Cause we ain't never been to school, Jenny Sue! You know that."

"Why ain't we?" Jenny pushed.

"Wal, hell, they ain't no schools, fool!"

"And why is that?"

"Whut you tryin' to get us to say, Jenny?" Misty asked.

"Why is we bein' held back from learnin'?"

"Them's blasphemous words, Jenny," she was cautioned. "You steppin' mighty clost to the line, girl."

"I'm fixin' to step over it, Carol Ann."

"Whut you mean?"

"I'm leavin'. I'm gonna go into town and be with my kids and git me some learnin'."

"Hit'll go turrible hard when Frank catches up with you, girl."

"No, it won't. 'Cause I'll be with the Rebels, and they ain't gonna let nothin' happen to me. And the same goes for the rest of you, too."

"Donnie ain't let me go to town in near 'bouts a year," Carol Ann said wistfully. "I never could figure out what he was so fearful of."

"Learnin'." Jenny put her finger on the mark. "He's stupid, jist lak Frank is stupid. Jist lak we're stupid for puttin' up with it."

Misty took a look around her and said, "Ah

thank Hiram's done gone around the bend. Nobody in his right mind would do what he done to his own flesh and blood. And I heared that Billy Bob was dead!"

"That don't surprise me," Jenny said. "Nobody could've lived through all that. I'm tarred of bein' ignorant. I'm tarred of workin' from can to cain't and don't have nothin' to show for it except a lazy-assed old man who don't want to do nothin' 'cept hunt and fish. He ain't even tried to put in no crop in two years. Won't work the garden. Won't help around the shack. I'm jist tarred of it!"

"Ah bet we could get fifteen-twenty others to go wif us," Laura June said. "I'm game! Let's git as many as we can, and meet back here," she looked up, "when the moon is there! Let's git gone, girls!"

Ben grilled his steak and baked his potato on the grill, then ate his dinner. He had ceased his looking in on Holly. She was out as surely as the lights were out around the world.

He cleaned up the small mess, turned out the lanterns, and went to bed.

Holly was in for a rougher time than she thought. For it would not go unnoticed that she had spent the night with Ben . . . or at least in his quarters.

Tomorrow, Ben mused, promised to be an interesting day.

Just how interesting, he really couldn't realize. Yet.

Seventeen

The banging on the door brought Hiram straight up in bed. "Alrat, alrat!" he yelled. "I'm a-comin'!"

He jerked open the door and faced a whole passel of armed and angry-faced men.

"Whut the hale-far is goin' on?"

"Our wimmin done took off, Hiram!" Jakey yelled. "Laura June's done packed her kit and git!"

"Gone? Where'd they go?"

"Hale, Hiram, we don't know!" B.M. hollered. No one really knew what B.M. stood for . . . but most could guess what it should stand for.

"You better check your own house, Hiram," Wilbur told him.

"Precious!" Hiram hollered. "Oh, Precious Thrill! You bes' answer me, gal."

But Precious had done taken her thrill and hauled ass. The girl had been living in absolute terror since witnessing her father beat and tar his son.

"Whut time is it?"

"Near 'bout one in the mornin', I reckon," Donnie Jeff said. "I figure they been gone three hours. I figure they waited till we was asleep and then tooken off."

211

"But where the hell did they go?" The question was shouted.

"Ben Raines." Hiram spoke softly. "Bet on it."

"Let's git the dogs and take out after 'em!"

"If they been gone three hours, boys, we'll never catch 'em now. They on the other side of the bayou and linked up with a Rebel patrol. Bet on that."

"Whut is we gonna do, Hiram?" The question was whined out. "Hit ain't rat to take no man's woman."

"Nobody took 'em. They lef on they own."

"I say we fight!" a man screamed.

"Fight?" Hiram's eyes found the man. "Wif what?" The words were bitter on his tongue. "Deer rifles and shotguns agin tanks and machine guns? Planes lak done come in here and des-stroyed a whole ten acres in ten seconds?"

"Then what is we gonna do?"

"Go see Ben Raines." Hiram's words were spoken wearily.

It was an hour before dawn as the men from the Stanford Community put their boats into the waters of the bayou. When they reached the other side, they found themselves looking down the barrels of automatic weapons, in the hands of grim-faced, tiger-striped Rebels.

"Get your asses back across the bayou," a man with captain's bars ordered.

"We come to fetch our wimmin back home," Hiram informed him.

"Your 'wimmin' don't want to be 'fetched' back home. We took them into Base Camp One about

212

midnight. Get back across the bayou."

"Hit's 'pposed to be a free country!" Hiram squalled.

"Yeah. If Ben Raines says it is. You told the general you wanted to be left alone. We're giving you that chance."

"Who's a-gonna cook and clean?" B.M. yelled. "I ain't got no clean drawers to put on."

The Rebels exchanged amused glances. "Well, partner," the captain said. "In about three weeks, we might let you see *your* women. I think you're gonna be surprised."

"Whut you mean?"

"They'll start five hours of classroom work daily, and five hours of Rebel training and indoctrination. The changes in them will not be subtle."

"Whut the hale did he said . . . subble? Whut's 'at mean?"

"Ah thank they gonna be made into doctors."

"In three weeks! Lard, Lard!"

The Rebels started laughing. "Why don't we just shoot them, captain?" a sergeant suggested. "Put them out of their misery."

"That's a damn good idea, sergeant."

"Now jist hold ever'thang!" Donnie Jeff hollered. "Cain't we jist talk this over some?"

"If you're not across the bayou in one minute, we start shooting."

The men returned to the other side much more quickly than they had originally crossed.

"Why is the gencral putting up with this crap, captain? Why doesn't he just let us run them off?"

"I think these people are a personal challenge to

213

the general."

Another Rebel laughed. "I want to be there in about a month when those 'necks try to take their wives back home. If two or three 'necks don't get butt-stroked or shot, it'll sure surprise me."

"I doubt if those guys will even recognize their wives in a month. I've seen it happen. In a month's time, those ladies won't be talking the same or looking the same. Let's get some breakfast."

"How about some breakfast?" Ben asked Holly.

"Ooohh!" was her reply.

"Bacon and eggs sound all right to you?"

A gagging sound came from the darkened room.

"Well, I'll just start cooking. You might change your mind." He walked into the kitchen, chuckling.

Holly lay on the couch. Her head felt like a gang of leprechauns was inside, banging little pots and pans.

She kicked off the light blanket and sat up. She lay back down. "Aspirin!" she croaked.

"On an empty stomach, doctor? That's not good for you."

"Get me some aspirin, Raines! You did this to me; you take care of me."

"I didn't do anything to you, Holly. You did it to yourself. And that is yet another Rebel truism."

She cursed under her breath. "You are the most . . . most *impossible* man I have ever met!"

Ben walked into the room and opened the drapes. Silver light flooded the room and Holly closed her eyes and moaned.

"First hangover for you?"

"Yes, and I can assure you, it will be my last one." She glanced at the vile-looking concoction in the glass he was holding. "What in God's name is that?"

"Come on, Holly. You're no spring chicken. You know what a Bloody Mary is." He laid two aspirin on the coffee table and set the drink down.

She took the aspirin and chased them down with the mixture. Then, quite unladylike, she belched.

"Of course, I know what a Bloody Mary is. I've just never had one. What's really in these things? And what do you mean, I'm no spring chicken?"

Ben grinned at her. "Well, in that particular drink . . . home-canned tomato juice, homemade hot sauce, salt, and a dash of the hair of the dog that bit you."

She smiled thinly and then confessed, "It isn't bad. I'll try a little breakfast, Ben. And for your information, I'm thirty."

"Like I said, no spring chicken."

"Where's the bathroom? Do you have a spare toothbrush . . . and some *real* toothpaste?"

"Right down that hall. And yes, real toothpaste. Homemade, of course."

She stood up and swayed for a moment. "You people really have one hell of an organization, don't you?"

"We try to live as normally as possible, Holly. I've got over a hundred people who don't do anything except research; another hundred who put that research into reality. I like to think that we bring some light into a postwar darkness."

"All right, Ben," she said very softly.

"All right, what, Holly?"

"I'll join the Rebels."

Ike and Tina and the Rebels entered the city of Knoxville on Interstate 40, exiting off into the city proper. No one had to tell them the Night People were here; the smell of death lingered over everything.

"Where to start," Ike muttered, looking around him at the ruins of the city.

"Let's try the university complex," Tina suggested.

"Yeah, we might learn something there."

Collective groans followed his statement. Ike did his best to look hurt. It didn't quite come off.

As they drove, weapons at the ready, all could see piles of human bones scattered about, some of them very fresh, scraps of meat still hanging to the bones.

Ike halted the army convoy and got out, inspecting the piles of bones. He shook his head and climbed back into his Jeep, telling his driver, "Men, women, and children." His face was hard and grim as he picked up the mic. "No mercy and no prisoners, people. Kill them all as we find them."

They drove slowly into the university complex.

The stench of unwashed bodies was almost overpowering. Ike shook his head and told his driver to lead the convoy out, back to the Interstate.

His radio crackled. Tina's voice. "What's wrong, Ike?"

"We're going to have to put it off, Tina. We're not equipped to cope with the health problem."

"I agree." Dr. Ling's voice was added. "God alone

knows how many diseases we might encounter in here. We're not properly suited for this type of situation. Ike? Get in touch with General Raines. Didn't you tell me he told you that Buddy was cleaning out Night People to the west?"

"That's what he said."

"Ask him to break if off, and have him advice Dr. Chase of this decision."

"Ten-four, Doc." When they were back on the Interstate, Ike halted the convoy and walked to the communications van. "Get Base Camp One on the horn."

Ben was not yet in his offices, but Cecil was.

"All right, Ike. I agree with Ling. I'm sure Ben will agree. Stay out of the cities and avoid contact with the Night People. Check back in when you make camp this evening."

Ike looked at Major Broadhurst. The major said, "We may be forced to destroy the cities, Ike."

"That thought has occurred to me, Tom. But I doubt that Ben will go along with it. I'd consider the use of poison gas, but damnit, we don't know how many innocent people might be held in the cities. I think, ol' buddy, we're going to have to do it house to house."

Tina had joined the men. "How did there get to be so many of them without our discovering it?"

"Well, Tina, they've had almost fifteen years to set this up. Hell, there might not be *any* major cities destroyed, with the exception of D.C. This could all be a hoax on the part of the Night People. I just don't know."

Tina glanced at her map and did some quick

figuring. "Only about seven hundred and fifty miles to go, Ike."

"With no idea of what is waiting for us after each mile," Ike said. "Scouts out, Tina. Let's go!"

"I can't go to work looking like this!" Holly bitched.

"Call the hospital and have somebody send over some clothes."

"Are you serious?"

"Holly, everybody knows you spent the night here. The entire base. And you're going to be treated a lot differently from now on. Get used to the idea."

"Then there is no point in my trying to say that nothing happened."

"Not a bit."

She walked to the window and stared out. The base was up and working. She turned to face him. "Well, if that's the case, I might as well just get my things and move in!"

"That wouldn't hurt my feelings."

"Don't you ever give me another damn drink of that homemade crap, Ben Raines!"

"Yes, ma'am."

The field phone rang. Ben picked it up and listened for a moment. "I'll be right there."

He turned to Holly. "Come on, I'll drop you off at the hospital and you can change. I want you with me on this one."

"What's going on?"

"Tell you on the way. We just scored a small, bloodless victory over Hiram and his crew."

She watched as Ben struggled into his jump boots and laced them up.

Finally she said, "Stupid!"

"They feel good," he lied.

"Uh-huh."

He waited at the hospital while she showered and changed. She dressed in jeans, but with a white smock over her casual wear, and climbed into the Jeep.

They drove to a holding area that had been set up on the football field of the local high school.

"What in the world? . . ." Holly muttered, upon sighting the women from the Stanford Community.

"Our newest converts to the Rebel Army, my dear. And you can bet they have left behind a lot of pissed-off husbands."

"Now I recognize some of them from the hospital. Yes, I gave several of them physicals."

Ben climbed out of the Jeep and walked toward the ladies. They ranged in age from fifteen to thirty, most of them, he guessed, in their twenties.

"Ladies," he greeted them. "I understand from Captain Gorzalka that you want to join us. Is that correct?"

"Yes, sir!" one young woman spoke up the loudest.

"And what's your name?"

"Jenny Sue, sir." Then she proceeded to introduce every woman in the ranks.

"Only a few of these had to be deloused," Holly whispered to him.

"That's gratifying to learn." He returned the whisper. He watched as Cecil drove up and got out, walking over to join them.

"What the hell! . . ." Cecil whispered. "Is that who I think it is?"

" 'Deed it is, my friend." Raising his voice, Ben said, "This gentleman, ladies, is General Cecil Jefferys. Do any of you have any objections to taking orders from a black person?"

"No, sir!" the group shouted.

"Amazing," Cecil muttered. "Are you sure they came from the Stanford Community, Ben?"

"Slipped across the bayou last night."

"All right, ladies. If you will follow that sergeant right there," Ben pointed, "she will take you to be outfitted."

"General, sir," Jenn said. "Can I ax a question, please?"

"Certainly."

"Can we get to see our kids sometimes?"

"Of course you can. They'll be returned to you just as soon as you fully understand what you're getting into here, and have taken the oath and signed up."

"There ain't but one problem with that, general."

"And what might that be?" Ben knew, but he wanted the ladies to say it aloud. He knew the first step toward education is for a person to admit he needs it.

"Cain't none of us read or write, sir."

"I guarantee you all that you will soon be able to read and write. And that's a promise."

" 'At's good enough for us, general," Jenny Sue told him. "Oh, and general? I feel it my bounden duty to tell you that y'all best brace for trouble.

220

'Cause Hiram and them ol' boys will shore be comin' in here after us."

"You left them, Jenny Sue. They are no longer a part of any of you ladies. Not unless they agree to come in and agree to obey the rules."

"I don't figure that very many of them is gonna do that, sir."

"Then if they come in, I assure you all that we will be able to take care of any trouble they might wish to start."

"Yes, sir," she said slowly. "I reckon y'all can, at that."

Eighteen

"How'd it go, son?" Ben asked Buddy.

"Grim, father. But Monroe is cleaned up. Or out. Why were we recalled to camp?"

"For medical reasons. I want you and your team to check into the hospital for some blood work. Do it right now, son."

"Yes, sir. Is there anything that I should know about?"

"Oh, no. I wouldn't hold back from any of you. This is just precautionary."

"What's the word from General Ike and Tina?"

Ben brought his son up to date on the Shark and the Big Apple Scouts, and why all felt the need for blood work.

"Ahh! Now I see. Father, the flesh-eaters must be destroyed. If we cannot go in and face them, then how?"

"I don't know, son. And don't discount us going nose-to-nose with them. Everything will depend on how your blood work turns out. So pull your team back together and get over to the hospital."

"Yes, sir. Do we report to Dr. Allardt, father?" There was a wicked glint in the young man's eyes.

"Now, how? . . ." Ben waved that off. "Get out of here!"

Laughing, the young man left the office. Ben had not stepped out from behind his desk when Buddy entered, nor had he stood up. He didn't want the boy to see that he was in his stocking feet. His feet were killing him!

Cecil was haggard-looking when he came into Ben's office. He poured a cup of coffee and sat down. "It looks like Patrice was telling the truth all the way around, Ben. Lamar says she isn't attempting to hold anything back or to fight the drugs. He thinks she's on the level."

"What's your next move?"

"Lamar has ordered the questioning stopped. Breaking off the drugs. We'll let her sleep tonight and then you and I will question her tomorrow. If that's OK?"

"Fine with me. I'm curious to know why she never made any attempt to contact Khansim after she linked up with us. If that's the case."

"We'll listen to the tape of the questioning tomorrow, before we talk with her. How are you feeling, Ben?"

"I'm a little bit sore where the lead was dug out of me . . . and my fucking feet are killing me!"

"I told you not to wear those boots today," Holly reminded him.

"Are you going to be one of those women who nag constantly?" Ben softened that with a smile.

"Only when I have to be. What's for dinner?"

Ben grinned at her. "Whatever you like. There is the kitchen. You told me to stay off my feet, remember?"

* * *

Ike and his teams spent the night along a barren stretch of Interstate about fifty miles outside of Knoxville. They had not seen one living soul, other than Rebels, all that day. Tina and her Scouts had pushed on, making camp just outside of Bristol.

At full dark, she was the first to see electric lights shining in the town.

She radioed in to Ike.

"What do you make of it, Tina?"

"I don't know. Might be a trap. You want me to check it out?"

"Negative. Let them approach you. Double your guards tonight. I'll push out of here at oh-three-hundred in the morning. I don't like the feel of it. Might prove to be a bunch of good folks; but let's check it out in strength."

"Ten-four." She turned to Ham. "Double the guards, Ham. Heads up and no one leaves the camp."

Tina and her Scouts settled in for a very long night, looking at the lights of the unknown shining out of the darkness.

Ike pushed his people hard the next morning, arriving at Tina's camp just after dawn; since the Scouts had cleared the Interstate, they could push their vehicles as hard as they dared.

"I gather there were no hostile moves against you last night, Tina?"

"None. But we were being watched. I warned the watchers about Claymores, and they knew what I was talking about. They—whoever they might be—said they'd see us in the morning. Then they left."

224

"That doesn't sound hostile."

"Not a bit."

"All right. Break camp and let's push on, see what's happening in Bristol."

The Rebels found, much to their delight, a clean, organized, and well-defended town. The townspeople had huge, well-cared-for gardens, had reopened a clothing factory and various other businesses, and the barter system was once more alive and well.

A Ricky Owens was the clear and undisputed leader of the several-hundred-strong community. Upon questioning, it was discovered that Ricky was an ex-AF fighter pilot, about the same age as Ike.

"Never seen it fail," Ike told the man. "We've never come up on any safe town where the leader didn't have some sort of military background. You folks have a great-looking place here."

"Thanks. We were going to invite your Forward Recon people up last night, but when I learned they were Rebels, we backed off. You folks have a reputation for shooting first and asking questions later."

"We've learned to do that over the years. Show me the town?"

"Sure. Use your Jeep?"

"Hop in."

As they toured the town, neat, clean, and secure, Ike said, "Tell me about the Night People."

Ricky's face hardened. "Cannibals. Most of them—and we figure they number in the thousands—twisted, mentally and physically. They hate anyone not like them. Whatever we do, we have to do it in the daylight. At dark, we secure the town."

"Solely because of the Night People?"

225

He shook his head. "No. 'Bout fifty miles east of here you've got a bunch of 'necks and trash that roam the countryside. Several hundred strong. Robbing, raping, killing. Man by the name of Finley is the warlord in charge."

"Khansim's people bothered you yet?"

"No. But we monitor a lot of their radio chatter. There's some pretty heavy fighting going on down in South Carolina, between the citizens and the IPA. From what we've been able to learn, the citizens are holding their own."

"Maybe that will keep them off our asses for a while. How do you fuel your power generator?"

"Coal."

"Thought that's what I smelled." Briefly, as they rode, Ike explained the outpost system they were setting up.

"Count us in." Ricky smiled grimly. "There aren't many liberals left around here, Ike. Finley and his trashy-assed bunch made short work of them—those the Night People didn't get."

"They approached them with the olive branch of peace?" the question was sour-sounding.

"Oh, sure. The same old tired line. 'Oh, you poor, poor unfortunate people. Here, let us help you.' After the women were raped and the men buggered and tortured—depending on which faction seized the people—they were either eaten or taken for slaves."

"Your people made any attempts at rescue?"

"No. I'm not about to fuck with anybody that damned stupid."

And Ike knew there and then, the Rebels had found a strong and loyal ally.

* * *

It was a tired and worn-looking Captain Patrice Dubois that faced Ben and Cecil in Ben's office. Battered, but not beaten.

"I should not like to go through that experience again," she told the men.

"Odds are, you won't," Ben replied. "Feel like answering a few more questions?"

"Do I have a choice?"

"No."

"Ask your questions."

"You claim to have made no contact with Khansim during your time with the Rebels. Why is that?"

"Because I was not sure, then, that what Khansim was doing was right."

"And now?"

"He's wrong. Wrong in the way he's going about things. Both of you are, but the Rebel way is a lot more just and bloodless than that of the Hot Wind."

"But you think we're still wrong to a degree?"

"Yes."

Cecil had not yet asked a question. But his eyes never left the woman.

"By imposing law and order on the people?"

"By imposing *your* concept of law and order, general."

"It's a dirty job, Patrice, but somebody has to do it."

His humor was lost on her. "What is to become of me, General Raines?"

"Do you want to stay here with us, Patrice; work with us?"

"Yes," she answered quickly.

227

"In what capacity?"

"Wherever you choose to put me."

Ben hesitated, then picked up her holstered .45 from his desk, still attacked to the web belt, and tossed it to her.

She caught it, a surprised look on her face.

"You'll act as liaison officer between Lamumba and his screwballs, and Cecil's office. In addition, you will act as peacemaker between Hiram Rockingham and his followers, and this office."

"Yes, sir."

"You may have a staff of five. You will work out of Cecil's office complex. Take this day off, rest and think about your staff." He looked at Cecil. "Cut orders for her so she can get past the patrols and into Hiram's territory." He looked back at Patrice. "That's all, captain. You may leave."

When she had left, Cecil smiled. "You know damn well that redneck will never accept anything Patrice has to say, Ben."

"That's Hiram's problem. I'm probably going to have to kill the son of a bitch anyway. But before I do, I'm going to give him and his ilk every opportunity to come around."

"She might be able to get through to Lamumba."

"You know better, Cec. His hate is just as strong and just as unreasonable as Hiram's. They've both hated too long to ever change. But Lamumba is your baby."

"Thanks ever so much. Can I just go shoot him now?"

Ben smiled. "Oh, by the way. I forgot to ask. Did Lamumba bring his people in for shots and physicals?"

"Yes. Reluctantly. And spouting the most absurd mouthings I have ever endured."

Ben laughed at the expression on his friend's face. "Worse than Hiram's?"

"Just as bad."

An aide stuck her head into the office. "Excuse me. General Ike just radioed in. There is a strong outpost at Bristol. About four hundred strong and growing. He reports they've lined up solidly behind us."

"Great! Thank you."

Ben rose and walked to a wall map, circling Bristol. "That makes three for sure. I think we're really going to do it, Cec."

Cecil rose and stood beside his friend, looking at the map. "But so much more to do."

Both men turned at the sound of the door opening. Lamar Chase, unannounced, as usual. He poured a cup of coffee and sat down.

"We won't know for sure until tomorrow, boys. But it looks like the Night People aren't carrying any type of infectious bugs. Buddy's team all got splattered pretty well. So it appears we've lucked out there. But!" he held up a warning finger. "I would suggest face masks at the very least. Long-sleeved shirts, secured at the wrists, and gloves. No one with any open wound should be a part of any clean-up. Any wounded Rebels should be evacked immediately."

"All right, Lamar. Thanks. You look glum. What else is on your mind?"

"You are aware of Emil Hite's presence up the road, are you not?"

"Sure. But he isn't bothering anyone."

"That's not the point. He and his followers of . . . nuts and bolts and goofballs need to be given physicals."

Ben smiled. "All right, Lamar. I need a good laugh. Cec, you want to come along?"

"I can't, Ben. I've got a stack of reports a foot high on my desk."

"Dr. Allardt is through," Chase suggested. "I'm sure she would enjoy a ride out into the country. Besides," he added dryly, "I'm sure she's never seen anything like Emil Hite."

"Oh, what a peaceful little commune," Holly sighed. "Ben, you haven't come out here to harm these peaceful people, have you?"

"No, Holly. I'm going to let Brother Emil continue running his little scam."

"Scam?"

"Brother Emil Hite, Holly, is a phony. We've been running into Brother Emil for several years now. Emil and his followers worship the Great God Blomm. . . ."

"Are you serious?"

"Yes. You'll see. There is Brother Emil now."

"Oh, Ben! He's harmless."

"Sure he is. If we didn't have people like Emil Hite, we'd have to build nut houses for all the people who flock to him."

"That's cruel, Ben!" But looking at Emil, she had to cover her mouth with a hand to keep from laughing.

"My dear, dear General Raines!" Emil said, running up, almost tripping over the hem of his robe.

"How wonderful it is to see you."

"Yeah, Emil. I know you're just overjoyed at the sight of me. Relax, I'm not here to bust up your little scam."

"Oh, thank you, Blomm!" Emil looked heavenward.

"Knock off the Blomm shit, Emil. You have any kids in this whacko encampment?"

"Kids? You mean, like babies?"

"Yes."

"*Hell*, no!" He looked at Ben suspiciously. "Why do you ask that?"

"Because if you had any, you wouldn't have them long. What adults do with their time is their business. But you won't raise kids believing in this hogwash. You got all that?"

"Oh, yes, sir, Great Supreme Commander of Forces on Earth General Raines!"

"Emil! . . ." Ben tried to cut him off.

"I heard you were back in the area, Great Good General Raines, and I've composed a new song in your honor."

"Emil! . . ."

Some of Emil's other followers had gathered around.

"I call this my Dance of Tribute."

"Jesus Christ!" Ben muttered.

"Him, too. Right!" Emil said. "Actually, it's more of a dance than a song. You wouldn't understand the words, general. They're in Blommers."

"They're in what?" Holly blurted.

"The language of Blomm."

"Oh!"

231

Emil started dancing in the dust. "Rockem, sockem, Go, Cat, Go. Lula boola and Lizzie Borden jumpa hoopa in the garden." Emil then proceeded to do a combination of the Twist, the Black-Bottom, and the Bunny Hop.

When he finally wound down, the entire camp had gathered around, applauding his efforts. Holly sat with head bowed, right hand over her face.

"See, see!" Emil shouted. "It even got to her, right, general?"

"It was a sight to behold, Emil," Ben admitted.

Emil then lifted his arms heavenward and began praying to Blomm. Ben turned him out.

When he finished, Ben said, "Thank you, Emil, I feel richly blessed."

Emil beamed. His beam changed to panic at Ben's next words.

"Be in town bright and early tomorrow morning. All of you. You're going to take physicals at the hospital."

"But, sir!" Emil protested. "We are all Blomm's children. In the best of health. We. . . ."

Ben stepped out of the Jeep, his Thompson in his right hand.

The crowd drew back in fear.

"Emil, I'm trying to help you and yours. Either come in on your own, or I'll send troops out here for you. The choice is yours."

Emil drew himself up to his full height. His head came to about Ben's chest. "I shall consult with Blomm on this matter, sir."

"Fine. Consult all you like. Just have your ass at the hospital at seven o'clock in the morning."

232

"Seven o'clock! Nobody but heathens gets up at seven o'clock!"

"I get up at five," Ben told him.

"Well, of course, I didn't mean to imply that you, sir, are a heathen! I mean. . . ."

"You want me to make it six o'clock in the morning, Emil?"

"Oh, nononono. Seven is perfect." He leaned close to Ben and whispered. "General, your medical people ain't come up with a cure for AIDS yet, have they?"

"No. The bombs came before anybody came up with a cure. So it's still around, Emil."

"One has to be so *careful*, general, you know?"

"I know, Emil." He looked at Holly, sitting in the jeep and winked. "I've found one way to avoid getting it, Emil. It works every time."

"Oh, tell me, tell me, tell me!"

Ben leaned close. "Spend a month among the natives of the Stanford Community."

"Ye Gods, general!" Emil shrieked. "I'd be a blithering idiot by that time."

"Works every time, Emil."

Holly sat in the Jeep and did her best to suppress her laughter.

"Well," Emil said. "I'll make a deal with you, general."

"It's your show, Emil."

"If you'll forget about the physicals — I *detest* physicals — I'll take my followers into that . . . that barbarous hinterland."

"You got a deal, Emil. Ah, Emil . . . you and your people do carry weapons, don't you?"

"Bet your ass! We are a peace-loving gathering,

233

general. In tune with nature and striving for the karma-smarma, reaching for the Om of earth, and the Ump of inter peace, we. . . ."

"Emil, knock off the shit!"

"Right, general."

"You are aware that the inhabitants of that particular locale are not always the most hospitable?"

"They're a bunch of redneck assholes, is what you're trying to say."

"I couldn't have said it better. So pack your pieces and carry lots of ammo."

"Gottcha, general! When is the best time to go in there? No, let me rephrase that; there is no best time. We'll make our move this afternoon."

"That's fine, Emil."

Emil stood and watched as Ben and that fine-lookin' piece drove away. He wondered if General Raines was putting him on about their arrangement? No! he shook his head. General Raines wouldn't do that.

"All right, followers of Blomm. Gird your loins and cock it back. We are going into the land that time forgot. General Raines has commissioned me to lead the expedition. Onward, soldiers, onward!"

Turning, Emil tripped over his robe and fell face-first into the dust.

Nineteen

"Ben Raines! You ought to be ashamed of yourself!"

"Why?" Ben said, reaching for the mic. "It'll be an experience for both sides." Lifting and keying the mic, he got his HQ and asked for Cecil. The operator patched him through. He told Cecil to clear the way through the Rebel patrols for Emil Hite.

They were going into Hiram's territory.

When Cecil stopped laughing, he said, "Ben, you may have hit upon the answer. Send nuts in to deal with nuts."

"I'd love to be there to witness it. Eagle out."

Ben started to hang the mic and then once more keyed it. "Captain Gorzalka, this is Eagle. Did you copy that transmission between Hawk and myself?"

"Ten-four, general." The captain was laughing.

"Make sure their weapons are all in good working order, give them plenty of ammo, and toss in several cases of grenades."

"Yes, sir!"

"Eagle out."

"Ben," Holly said. "Those . . . cretins might hurt Emil or his followers."

"Don't you bet on that, Holly. Emil is one tough little con artist. And most of those people with him, while a little bit off the wall, are just as tough. They didn't used to be, but over the past couple of years, they've learned to fight and to fight damn well."

They rode in silence for a mile before Holly again spoke. "Ben? What's the difference between Emil and his group and Hiram and his group?"

"Emil's followers all know that what he's doing is all bullshit. And they don't hurt anybody, Holly. It may be difficult for you to accept, but there isn't one illiterate person in Emil's group. And if they had kids, they'd send them in to be educated. Believe it. I don't particularly care for the little con artist, but I don't dislike him.

"Emil doesn't preach hate, Holly. You saw back there. People of all colors gathered around him. Emil is," and Ben laughed, "sort of like the old hippie movement . . . in a small way. You're too young to really remember that. But your true hippies, they weren't bad people. There's still a lot of them around, in the mountains, deep in the timber. They don't bother a soul, but they will knock your dick in the dirt if you mess with them. I leave them alone, and they don't fuck with me."

"I thought they were all dirty, smelly, worthless people. That's what I've read about them."

"Well, some of them might have been. But your true hippie, and I stress *true*, simply liked the laid-back lifestyle. They worked regular jobs like anybody else. If anybody would hire them.

"Hiram, on the other hand, is filled with hate. Hiram hates everybody. A hippie can look at a deer grazing in the woods and think what a thing of beauty it is. The Hirams of the world just want to kill it. The Hirams of the world are directly responsible for so many species' being extinct . . . not the Emils of the world."

"But what do the Emils of the world give back to it? What do they contribute?"

"Very little. But they don't take away from it, Holly. The people who drift into Emil's little scam will drift out of it in a year or two; right now, they're just looking to belong. Hiram, on the other hand, and those like him, will, for the most part, never change. They're takers, not givers. Anyway, it's going to be interesting to see what happens between Hiram and Emil."

"Whut the hale is 'at air?" Donnie Jeff said, sort of, as he lay on the bayou bank, watching Emil and his flock get into boats.

"Hit looks kinda lak Jesus and them Apissles to me," B.M. said, sort of.

"Jesus didn't tote no M-16, B.M. And He didn't have no fine-lookin' wimmin wif him, I don't believe."

" 'At air's a plumb fact, Donnie Jeff. Ah thank we best tell Hiram 'bout this here."

B.M. flogged his mule getting to Hiram. He found Hiram sitting on his front porch—at the home of wife #1—cussing Ben Raines.

"Strangers, Hiram! Look lak missionaries done come to spread the word."

"I done heard 'em, B.M. And they ain't no missionaries. That air's Emil Hite and his hippie-goofballs. Ah thank hit's time to put plan C into action."

Plan A was to take over the world; but Hiram

237

never could figure out just how to do that, so plan A was dropped. Plan B was to secede from the Union and restart the Civil War. But since there was no more Union, and Hiram never could get anybody all that worked up over it, plan B was also dropped.

Plan C was to take prisoners and force them to work the fields; but that plan also had its flaws. Since anyone with the intelligence quotient of an aardvark never went anywhere near the Stanford Community, plan C had had to be put on hold.

Until now.

" 'At air a rat good idee, Hiram!" B.M. shouted.

"Shore hit is. I thunk of hit, didn't I? Let's us let them queers and hippies git settled in and then we'll make our move. Tell G.B. to make us a cross. We'll have a meetin' tonight and bus' them hard at first light."

"Can we have us'uns a big cross, Hiram? Huh, huh?"

"Yeah. Jist don't build nothin' lak 'at one Johnny Edgar built. Damn thang fell over and almost squashed me. Caught my sheet on far. Flog your mule, B.M."

"Raines, you are incorrigible!" Lamar said, wiping his eyes exploding with laughter when Ben had told him about Emil Hite.

The shadows were gathering in dusty pockets around the new Base Camp One as darkness slipped in.

Ben moved restlessly in his chair. Lamar, Dan, and Cecil watched him.

Chase finally said, "You're getting itchy, aren't

you, Ben?"

Ben smiled. "Is it that obvious, Lamar?"

"To those who know you, yes. Just settle down, you old war horse. Be content for a few more weeks."

"Yes, general," Dan spoke. "Ike and his teams will be near New York City—if it's still there—in about a week. Then you can start making plans to go up there."

Ben laughed. "How do you know I want to go, Dan?"

"We all want to go, general."

"It's probably going to take all of us, too." Ben spoke softly. "And, to tell the truth, in quiet moments I've been thinking about whether it's worth the effort."

"It's worth it, Ben." Cecil sipped his drink. "If only to wipe out those damnable Night People." He glanced at his watch and stood up. "It's about time for Ike to call in. Think I'll wander over to the como building."

Nobody volunteered to accompany him; all knew he wanted to see Patrice. He closed the door behind him.

Lamar and Dan left, leaving Ben alone. Ben finished his drink and turned out the generator-powered lights, saying goodnight to those of his staff who still remained.

Standing on the concrete parking lot, Ben felt sweat trickle down his chest. The late-summer Louisiana night was hot and muggy. Ben remembered these hot nights well.

He looked up and down the almost empty street.

This will be the centerpiece of the outposts, he thought, his mind racing ahead. With shops and farms and schools and a fine medical center. The showpiece for others to be modeled after.

And racial harmony.

One way or the other.

"We were being paced on highway Eleven all the way up from Bristol," Tina radioed to Ike.

"Ten-four. I spotted them. What's your opinion of them?"

"They're pretty good, Ike. They're well disciplined and well trained. If that's a warlord bunch, they've had good training."

"That's what I think. I'm sending a platoon up to your location; beef you up. Whoever they are, they may try to hit you tonight. Stand ready."

"Ten-four, Ike. I figure there are at least a couple hundred of them. I'm the smaller force, so if they're hostile, they'll probably try me first."

"Watch your butt, kid."

Tina laughed. "Will do."

After talking with Ike, Cecil and Patrice sat in his office and talked.

"Bring me up to date, captain," Cecil said formally.

Patrice noted it, and smiled faintly. "I found my staff, briefed them, and then went to see Lamumba."

"And? . . ."

"He . . . well, has twisted the teachings. To say the least."

240

"Your opinion of him, now that you've spoken with him?"

She hesitated. "I think he's dangerous. Quite unlike the true believers in Islam out in the country."

"You spoke with them?"

"Yes. Briefly. They are going to work with us."

"What to do with Lamumba? . . ."

"General, it is unfair to force people to leave their homes simply because they do not agree with your philosophy."

"Philosophy has nothing to do with it, captain. Or very little. Emil Hite is so far off the wall he can't even see the paneling. But we allow him to stay because he doesn't preach hate. You had best advise Mr. Lamumba that if he doesn't toe the line, I'll step on him like a bug. Understood?"

"Yes, sir."

"Now then, about Hiram and his . . . crew."

"I was planning to go into that area tomorrow, sir."

"Cancel your plans. Concentrate on Lamumba. Hiram, ah, will probably be too busy trying to figure out what is happening to him to speak with you."

"Sir?"

"That will be all, captain."

"Yes, sir." She rose to leave. Looked at Cecil.

"Something on your mind, captain?"

"Could I, ah, get you some coffee or anything before I leave?"

Their eyes met. Both struggled with inner feelings. "Yes, captain. That would be nice. If you would join me."

Again, eyes met. The independence within her rose to the fore. "Is that an order, sir?"

"No, captain, it is not. It is merely a request."

"Then I accept."

Hard-headed female! Cecil thought.

Obstinate male! she thought.

Ben drove past Cecil's offices, on his final tour of the town before going home. He noticed the lights and smiled. Might be an interesting evening, he thought.

Now eighty strong, Tina's group laid out their perimeters and ringed themselves with Claymores. Guards were doubled and everybody ate quickly; cold rations. They had all heard the sounds of being surrounded by what they assumed were unfriendlies.

Tina darted from post to post, inspecting the hurriedly dug machine gun emplacements, chatting briefly with each person she came in contact with. On the east side of their position, Ham was doing the same.

They met at the top of the perimeter, facing north.

"When do you think Tina?"

"Anytime now. They're moving in closer. They'll hit the Claymores any second."

The night was suddenly shattered by several pounds of C-4 exploding, hurling out hundreds of ball bearings. Following the explosion, there came the screaming of the mangled and mauled and dying. The dim shapes that flitted around the perimeters were gunned down by expert rifle fire from the Rebels.

The east side of the encampment was ripped by

Claymores being fired, with more howling of the wounded and the wild cursing of those who were spared the round shards of death and went running back into the gloom of night's protection.

"Back, back!" A voice reached the ears of the Rebels behind the Claymores. "Another day, folks!" the voice called cheerfully. "We shall meet again, and that's a promise."

After a few moments, the sounds of vehicles being cranked up and driving away reached the Rebels.

Ham walked to Tina's side. "Now what in the hell do you suppose that was all about?"

"I don't know. But that voice sure sounded familiar to me. I know I've heard it before."

She radioed back to Ike's position, some fifty miles south of her own, and brought him up to date.

"And you knew the voice? You sure, Tina?"

"Positive, Ike. And not that long ago, either."

"Maybe it'll come to you. Which way did they go?"

"West. Toward the West Virginia line. And the way they were driving, I got the impression they weren't planning on coming back."

"Let's hope not. Wait for me outside of Roanoke, Tina."

"Ten-four, Ike." She turned to Ham. "Relax the guards some, Ham. Let's try to get a good night's sleep."

Twenty

It had been a dandy cross-burnin', Hiram thought. Plumb awesome. Made a man feel closer to God somehow. And this day was gonna be even more better, Hiram figured.

If plan C went as planned, those remaining loyal to Hiram would have slaves to do the housework and tend to the work in the fields. Then a man could do what a man was put on this earth to do: Fish, Fight, Fuck, and Hunt.

And pray ever now and then for all the blessings.

Hiram linked up with G.B. and Jakey and a few of the others. "Where is they camped?"

"Down there by the Simmons' place. They's about fifty of 'em."

"Slaves for all."

"And some good-lookin' wimmin wif 'em, too."

"Pussy for all!" G.B. grinned, squeezing and rubbing his crotch.

"Let's git 'em, boys!" Hiram ordered.

"Here they come, Emil," a young woman whispered. "Have you prayed to the Great God Blomm?"

"Yeah, yeah!" Emil brushed it off. Only god he

244

was interested in right at the moment was that goddamned AK-47 in his hands. "Pass the word for the others to get ready."

"Yes, oh, Great Emil."

Emil shook his head as she was leaving. Chick had a great ass on her but a head full of nothing.

Emil checked around him. He had four of his biggest and strongest people ready with hand grenades. If these rednecks wanted to get hostile — and Emil had never known a redneck who wasn't all-the-time hostile — he'd play the game one better.

"All rat!" Hiram shouted. "Come on outta there, you hippies!"

"Fuck you, redneck!" Emil shouted. Turning to his people, he said, "Remember, don't shoot to kill . . . not yet anyway."

"Ah thank we been insulted, Daddy!" Axel Leroy said.

"I ain't no redneck!" G.B. said, with considerable heat in his voice. "I's a civilized man. I go to *church*!"

"You'll pay for 'at, you heathern!" Hiram hollered. "Now do yoursales a favor and come on out of that there holler 'fore we drag you outta there."

"Lemme go git 'em, Daddy!" Axel Leroy started jumpin' up and down. "They ain't gonna fire them guns nohow!"

"Ah do believe the boy is rat," Jakey told him.

"Awrat, son," Hiram patted Axel on the back. "You go on down there and fetch some out." He looked at B.M. and G.B. " 'at there's a fine boy, y'all."

"Fine boy!" the both agreed.

Axel started his swaggering walk toward Emil and his intrepid little band. "Y'all better come on out now. Hit'll git rough ifn you don't."

Emil lifted his AK and put a full clip around Axel's feet, using quick trigger pulls. Axel jumped about three feet up into the air and started haulin' ass for the nearest cover, whooping and hollering all the way.

"Give 'em hell, boys!" Hiram shouted, and commenced firing his shotgun.

"Give the 'necks some grenades!" Emil yelled.

The chosen four began pulling pins and lobbing grenades around the bastion of knotted 'necks. The concussion from the first explosion knocked Hiram sprawling. He lost his shotgun and became slightly disoriented. "Don't whup me no more, Momma! I promise I won't peek in on sister no more!" Then he realized where he was and what he had just said and closed his mouth.

The other grenades rocked and rolled the ground, and G.B., his big fat ass in the air, took a piece of shrapnel in one cheek. He started roaring like a wounded water buffalo.

Donnie got so scared he pissed his dirty drawers and got so close to mother earth his buttons were imprinting on his chest and belly.

B.M. jumped to his feet; rather stupid thing to do with the air filled with lead and shrapnel. "Charge, boys! The reputation of the Klan is at stake here."

B.M. began running toward Emil's position. About halfway there, he looked around and found himself alone. He didn't know which way to go or what to do once he got there.

He froze upright, numb with fear.

Hiram's bunch couldn't fire for fear of hitting B.M. And no amount of yelling could get through to B.M. to get down, get on the ground — just get the hell out of the way, goddamnit!

"Hold your fire!" Hiram shouted, once more in full command of his faculties, miniscule as they were. "Y'all stop all that gun-shootin' and throwin' them bombs. Les' talk! How 'bout it?"

"Cease fire!" Emil yelled. "Don't toss no more grenades. What do you want, Rockingham?"

"What y'all doin' in our territory, hippie?"

"It's a free country, you cretin!"

"Whut'd he call me?" Hiram whispered to G.B.

"My ass hurts somethang fierce!" G.B. moaned. "Ah thank I'm bound for glory, boys. I can see the Pearly Gates now."

Hiram looked at him in disgust and ignored his ass-shot friend. "Why don't y'all jist come live with us, hippie? Ain't that a right nice neighborly thang to suggest?"

"I would sooner consort with hyenas! Now leave, before I call upon the awesome powers of the Great God Blomm!"

"Blomm?" Hiram looked around him. "What the hale is a Blomm?"

"Sounds nasty," Jakey said.

Hiram looked around him and assessed his situation. G.B. was moaning about his ass; Axel wasn't nowheres to be seen; Donnie Frank was babbling about the fires of Hell; and B.M. was froze solid with piss running down his pants' leg. Hiram allowed as to how he'd been in better spots.

247

Goddamn bunch of hippies shore had a lot of guns and stuff. . . . And then Hiram got the message, worming its way through the morass of his mind: Ben Raines done this. Just as shore as frogs fuck, Ben Raines done this.

"Ah thank we'uns will jist call a truce, hippie. You leave us alone, and we'll shore leave you alone. How's that sound to you?"

"That's just fine, Rockingham," Emil shouted. "We'll be here for a month, taking the cure."

That puzzled Hiram. Of course, most things puzzled Hiram. But this really puzzled him. "The cure for whut?" he yelled.

"The abomination of the ages! The scourge of mankind. And the tintinnabulation of the bells, too!"

"Sounds plumb disgustin' to me," Wilbur said. "Whatever it is."

"Now leave us be!" Emil yelled. "Go back to your hovels and do whatever you do."

"Ah still thank we been insulted," Wilbur said.

"Oh, my ass hurts!" G.B. moaned.

"Captain Gorzalka's people report gunfire down near where Emil and his fruitcakes are camped, sir," the aide reported as soon as Ben reached his office.

"Any word on dead or wounded?"

"No, sir."

"Thank you."

Ben rang up the como shack. "Any word from Ike or Tina?"

"Yes, sir. They pulled out just before dawn.

Everything is reported smooth."

Ben looked at his desk. It was clean. He had nothing to do. He told his staff he'd be back when they saw him, and climbed into his Jeep. He checked his Thompson and then looked in the back seat. Plenty of food and water. He pulled out.

"You," Ben's XO pointed at several Rebels. "Follow him. Keep your distance, but don't let him out of your sight. Report your position and I'll send an additional squad out to beef you up. Move!"

The Rebels scrambled for vehicles and pulled out, staying well behind Ben.

Ben checked his mirrors, knowing damn well somebody would be tagging along behind him. At first he toyed with the idea of losing them, but then resigned himself to his fate.

The country roads, bad even before the Great War, were now, a decade later, nearly impassable. He drove past the now falling-down shacks of the poor and the mansions that the rich had built. He took a small, selfish, grim satisfaction in the knowledge that they all were now equal in death.

Ben had never been much of a possessions-lover. He could have lived much more extravagantly than he had, back when things were more or less normal, but Ben had chosen to keep his life as simple as possible. He had lived well, but rather simply.

And he had taken some criticism for his life-style. Always a loner, Ben lived a very private life, almost never opening up to people.

"Well," he muttered to the wind and the bumps and ruts and holes in the road. "It's all moot, now, isn't it?"

He came to the great mansion of the Lantier family. Once home to Fran and Ashley, two spoiled and arrogant brats.

On impulse, he pulled into the drive and parked, getting out of the Jeep.

He stood for a moment, looking at the mansion. The windows had been smashed and the door kicked in. Pulling his Thompson from the leather boot, Ben jacked in a round and walked into the once-great mansion.

It was a mess.

Most of the furniture was gone; what was left was covered with bird shit and had been chewed on by rats and mice. He wondered, standing in the great hall, what the place might be turned into.

Nothing, he concluded. It was just too god-damned pretentious. Let it fall down . . . just like the Lantier empire.

He walked back outside and stood on the porch for a moment, then turned around and struggled with the door—or what was left of it—and managed, finally, to close it.

"End of an era," Ben said. And walked to his Jeep. He did not look back.

They seemed to be constantly running into each other; no matter where one turned, the other seemed to be there. Finally, it got to the point where Cecil had to motion Patrice into his office.

"Yes, sir?"

"Knock off the 'sir' business while we're alone. After last night it's a bit much, don't you think?"

"About last night. . . ."

"What about last night? Are you ashamed of what happened?"

"No. It's just that. . . ."

"Don't you want it to happen again?" Cecil sat down on the edge of his desk.

She seemed embarrassed. "I get the impression the entire base knows of it!"

"Why, hell, I'm sure everyone knows. You know about Ben and Holly, don't you?"

"Yes, but others have affairs and no one seems to know, or care."

"The 'others' aren't two of the three commanding generals of one of the largest standing armies anywhere in the world, Patrice."

"I'm a Moslem, Cecil." She formed her arms under her breasts. "We are two different cultures."

Cecil waggled his eyebrows. "Seems as though our cultures got along pretty well last night, don't you agree?"

"That isn't what I mean and you know it."

"Where is this leading, Patrice?"

"*You* called *me* in here, remember?"

"Do you want to be transferred out of here, Patrice?"

She turned away. With her back to him, she said, "I have never felt so attracted to a man in all my life, Cecil. And it scares me."

"Never had a boyfriend, Patrice?"

"Training camp affairs. There isn't much time for that when you're training to conquer the world." She said that bitterly.

"Is that what you think we—the Rebels—are trying to do, Patrice?"

She turned. "No. No, I don't think that at all, Cecil. I did at first," she added quickly. "And I was ready to report back to Khamsin . . . but I kept delaying my reporting, putting it off. I just wanted to learn more and more about you people. It was both fascinating and repulsive to me."

"Repulsive?"

"You have to understand, Cecil. Since I was a little girl . . . and my father was French, by the way. He died when I was very young. I have been taught that America was the great evil. The great Satan. It . . . took me a while to realize that was all a bunch of nonsense. It's just that you people are so much more free-spirited than we."

"And that's good or bad?"

She smiled. "Well, personally, I think it's a combination of both."

"And me?"

"What about you?"

"Am I good or bad?"

"I think you're a very good man, Cecil."

"And a middle-aged one, Patrice. While you are still a young woman in her twenties."

She became very flustered. "Last night was, ah, highly satisfactory for me, Cecil. I don't remember, ah . . . can we drop the subject, please?"

"Yes. Last night. The great myth is that we are noted for always performing well. We got rhythm, too."

She lifted her eyes. He was smiling at her.

Almost shyly, she returned the smile.

"The entire outer office is trying very hard not to

252

look this way. Why did you pick an office with so much glass all around it."

"Why? You got something in mind you don't want the others to see?"

"Taking my background into consideration, I could take that the wrong way."

"If we didn't trust you, Patrice, we'd have just shot you."

"Yes. Yes, I believe that, too."

"Can you cook?"

"I beg your pardon? Cook? Of course, I can cook. What a silly question. Why do you ask?"

"I thought you might like to come over and help me cook dinner this evening."

She looked at him for a long time. Then, slowly, she began to smile. "I have some marvelous Lebanese recipes."

"I thought you people didn't like the Lebanese?"

She shrugged. "We weren't fighting their food!"

Twenty-one

"There ain't no justice," Hiram mumbled, sitting under a tree with a few of his friends. "It jist ain't fair, boys. It just, by God, ain't far a-tall."

"Whut you mean, Hiram?" Donnie Frank asked. Donnie was down in the dumps, and not just from the humiliation at the hands of them hippies, neither. Donnie Frank missed his wife.

"All we wanted to do was to be lef' alone. Then that goddamned Ben Raines come around, stickin' his nose into our lives. It ain't fair."

"What cure is them hippies lookin' for?" Wilbur asked.

"Oh, hale-far, Wilbur! There ain't no cure down here for nothin'."

Hiram was damn sure right about that, although not in the way he meant.

"Then? . . ."

"Ben Raines sent 'em in here to aggravate us."

"Hiram?" Jakey asked. "Whut's so wrong wif gettin' some learnin'? I jist ain't gonna live lak 'is. Cain't have no fun no more. Ever'time you turn around, someones a-shootin' at you. We cut off from anywheres. I don't lak it here no more."

" 'At's whut Ben Raines wants, Jakey. Cain't you see 'at? He's a-tryin' to jam learnin' down our throats. Well, it jist ain't a-gonna work wif me. No sir. I ain't gonna stand for hit no more."

"Whut you gonna do, Hiram?" B.M. asked.

"I'm a-gonna kill Ben Raines!"

"Hiram," Jakey looked up at him. "Has it ever crossed your mind that maybe Raines is rat and we're wrong?"

"Hale, no!"

"Hit has my mind," B.M. said. "Look at the way we livin' when we don't have to live this here way. I been doin' a powerful lot of head-wrestlin' last two-three hours."

Hiram felt he knew what was next out of the man's mouth, and he felt sick at his stomach. His entire little empire was rapidly falling down around his dirty ankles. "And whut has you decided."

B.M. looked at him. "They's got to be somethang to this here learnin' business. If they wasn't, Hiram, there wouldn't be so many people doin' it. Ain't that rat?"

"No, hit ain't rat! It's all a plot. Hit's jist a damned commonist plot! And y'all so dumb you fallin' for hit."

Communist, B.M. silently corrected, remembering Ben Raines's words. And felt kinda good, him correctin' Hiram.

"Ben Raines ain't no common . . . communist," Jakey put into words what was in the minds of many sitting around Hiram.

"So this is the way hit is, hey?" Hiram looked around him. "Come down to this here. Y'all jist gonna turn your asses to me."

"Ain't no law that says you can't come along wif us, Hiram."

"You's all a bunch of goddamn traitors!" Hiram yelled. "Wal, jist go on; jist carry your asses away from here and me. I don't need you. Go on, goddamnit! I don't wanna see your yeller faces no more. Git outta here!"

"You on my property, Hiram," he was gently reminded by a friend.

Hiram glared at him. "You ain't no friend of mine no more, Bobby Joe. Not no more." He looked at G.B. "How 'bout you?"

"I'm wif you, Hiram. 'At goes wifout sayin'."

Several more of the older men rose to stand by Hiram's side. The younger men sat and squatted around B.M.

Even Wilbur elected to stay with the majority. And Wilbur summed it up. "What we all is, Hiram, is your fault. You and G.B. and L.T. and Carl and Jimmy John; all the older men. You hepped raise all of us up. You taught us to be what we is. But you taught us wrong. You knowed you was teachin' us wrong, but you done 'er anyways. You all. . . ."

"Shet your lyin' goddamn mouth, Wilbur!" Hiram yelled at him. "You cain't talk to me lak 'at, you yeller dog pup!"

"You bes' git along, Hiram." Jakey rose to face the man. "You jist bes' git, now!"

"Yeah, I'm goin'. I'll let y'all go join up with Ben Raines. Then y'all can smooch up to a bunch of niggers and Jews and China-people, and then y'all be jist as in-ferior as them."

"Seems like," Jenny Sue's man, Frank, said, "them in-ferior people can read and write and figure and build towns and schools and whilst doin' that, git along with each other in the doin' of it all. If you so smart an' all, Hiram, how come you didn't teach us to do them things?"

" 'Cause ain't none of them thangs necessary for a man to git on wif. I'm showin' y'all what hit takes for a man to git on wif."

"Like bein' fearful of Old Lady Pauly?" Jakey asked. "Ben Raines shore made her look like a fool, didn't he? Like being in town about a week and a half and already got the sewage and water runnin'? Like havin' phones workin' agin? If them's in-ferior people, Hiram, wal, I reckon I'll jist go on in and join them in-ferior people."

Hiram pointed a shaking finger at the men who elected to leave. "Don't none of y'all never come back to me wif your tail tucked 'tween your legs, a-beggin' for me to take you back. If I ever seen airy of you agin, I'll kill you!"

"Yeah, Hiram." Jakey refused to back down. "Just like you kilted your own flesh and blood. Ah think you bes' go on now, Hiram." He lifted his eyes to the road; the sounds of traffic. "Look yonder, Hiram. Don't that tell you nothin'?"

It was the wives of Hiram and the men who chose to stay with him, in rattletrap cars and trucks, heading for the Rebel outpost on the other side of the bayou. The women refused to look at their men as they smoked by.

"You carry your ass on back here, bitch!" Jimmy John hollered. "Goddamn you . . . you hear me?"

Hiram and L.T. and G.B. and Carl hollered and squalled and threatened until the caravan was out of sight.

"Well, hell, boys," Hiram said. "They jist wimmin. Wimmin ain't got good sense noways. We can always find us some more wimmin to stick hit in. Come on."

Hiram and his crew went one way, B.M. and the others following the road to the bayou and beyond. To get some learnin'.

"That's it, Ben," Cecil brought him up to date, "there may be ten, fifteen people, including Hiram left down there. What do you intend doing about it?"

Ben shook his head. "Nothing. Not unless Hiram breaks some rule or law of ours. And he probably will. We'll deal with it then. How are the new people taking to our way?"

Cecil smiled. "Although they won't admit it, they're scared. It's a normal reaction."

"How many you think will make it with us?"

"Too early to tell. I'd say seventy-five percent of them."

Ben nodded and tapped a communique on his desk. "I'm not certain I understand this, Cec."

"Nor I. Communications picked it up last night, then again this morning. They taped the last message. Have you listened to it?"

"No. I've been waiting for you."

Cecil punched the button on the cassette/corder. The men listened to the calm but clearly desperate voice coming out of the speaker. "Cut off. Running out of food and ammo." As the man gave his coordinates, Ben quickly checked a map of Michigan. "Need help desperately. If any Rebels are listening, please give us help. We're two hundred strong, but facing a force much larger. Approximately six to seven hundred of them. Please help."

"Right here," Ben said, pointing at the map. "If it's genuine, they've got their backs against Whitefish Bay. If it's real, Cec, we've got to help."

"I knew you'd say that. But Jesus Christ, Ben there isn't an airport anywhere near the place that I can see."

"Get Dan in here." As Cecil was leaving, Ben picked up the field phone and got the como shack. "See if you can reach these people up in Michigan. Patch them through to me."

"Yes, sir."

It took several minutes; by that time, Dan Gray was in the office, along with Colonel West. Ben and the mercenary smiled coolly at each other and that was the extent of it. They didn't dislike each other; just two men with a few philosophical differences. But West was a fine warrior, and Ben needed him.

"Go ahead, general." The radio operator's voice came through the receiver.

"Michigan? Who are you and what is your status?"

"Joe MacKintosh, general. We're a group of people who came together and settled up here about four years ago. Been growing steadily right along. Patterned our form of government much like yours. But now, we're really in a bind. We've known for a long time there were outlaws and warlords all around the area, but they always left us alone, for the most part. Now they've joined up and been hammering at us for days. Pushed us back all the way from Newberry to Whitefish Bay. Can you help us, general?"

"Ten-four, Michigan. Hold on. Stay close to the radio."

"Opinions, suggestions, and alternatives, gentlemen," Ben said, looking around him.

"Obviously, general," Dan said, "we're going to have to jump in. So that lets you out."

"What the hell do you mean?" Ben shouted.

"You've just had surgery on your leg and minor surgery on your feet." The Englishman was unruffled. "You cannot jump, and you cannot march. It's as simple as that. And there is absolutely no point in arguing as to who is going in. I am, naturally, and I would suggest Colonel West and his mercenaries. With General Jefferys commanding."

"I second that motion," Colonel West said.

"All right, all right!" Ben waved his hand. "You're all right. Goddamnit!" He was thoughtful for a moment. "The old birds have to have fuel; that's a pretty good distance. We know Memphis is clear." He jerked up his field phone. "I want one platoon of Rebels airlifted to the Memphis Airport and I want them moving within the hour. Get cracking."

"I'm scared of Chicago," Ben muttered, replacing the phone in the cradle. "And there is another problem: chutes. We don't have enough. One battalion is going to have to jump while the other marches in. But marches in from . . . where?"

West was studying a series of maps. "The only airport I can find that would be large enough to handle our birds is this Chippewa County airport.

That would put us about thirty miles from the battle, as the crow flies."

"All right, we'll have to see if it's clear." He called for an aide. "Stay with communications. Stay with the Michigan people all the way. Ask them about this Chippewa airport; if it's clear with perhaps some fuel there. Move!" He turned to Cecil. "Get with the pilots, Cec. Pathfinders out right now."

"Right, Ben." He turned to leave. Ben's voice stopped him. "Yes, Ben?"

"No prisoners, Cec. We can't turn them loose to regroup, and we don't have the equipment to bring them back here. No prisoners."

Cecil nodded and left the office.

"Dan," West said. "Not all my men are jump-trained. So I guess I'll get to march in. We've both got things to do, so I'll see you in Memphis and we'll finalize matters."

Dan nodded and the mercenary left.

"I ought to shoot that damn Lamar Chase for doing this to me!" Ben bitched, then grinned.

"You're needed here, general," Dan reminded him.

"I'm always needed in the places where I don't want to be. You don't seem to be in much of a hurry, Dan. Are your people that ready?"

"My people are always ready, general." Which was true. The ex-SAS man and his troops almost always spearheaded any hostile push. Dan demanded one hundred and ten percent from his people, and got it, or they cleared the outfit.

"When you clear the hostiles out, Dan, be sure to mention to this Mackintosh about our outpost system." There was no mention of *if* hostiles were cleared. There was no *if* to the Rebels. They just did it, and were never especially gentle about how they did it.

They were bringing law and order back to a shattered nation. One either obeyed the rules, or one was dead. It was as simple as that.

"Besides, general," Dan said, "I know perfectly well, short of divine intervention, there is nothing going to keep you out of New York City, right?"

"If it's still standing, that is."

"Oh, I think it is, general. As a matter of fact, I'd be willing to bet a month's pay on it."

"If we were getting paid!" Ben said with a laugh.

Ben stilled the ringing of the phone. Communications. "The airport in question, sir—Chippewa? It's in good shape, and this Mackintosh fellow thinks there is plenty of fuel there. But he suggests to strain it."

"Thanks." Ben looked at Dan. "The airport is all right, Dan. I know you're antsy to get going. I wish to hell I was going in with you."

"There is always The Big Apple, general." Dan grinned.

The field phone rang again. This time the radio operator's voice was subdued.

"General Raines. I have General Striganov on the horn, sir. From Canada. He would like to offer whatever assistance you might need in dealing with the problem in Michigan."

Twenty-two

Ben sat for a few seconds in shocked silence. Finally, he found his voice. "Georgi?"

"Ben," the Russian's voice was clear over the hundreds of miles from Canada. "First of all, let me apologize. I am terribly sorry for our past differences. And I am not asking for any forgiveness. Just listen to me for a moment, if you will."

"Certainly, Georgi."

"I and my people were wrong in what we did. Hideously, horribly wrong. Some of my staff realized it before I did. That is why we left California, for Canada, to start anew. All but three battalions of my army have been disbanded. They are now farmers and shepherds and the like; we are working hand in hand with the Canadians. And our form of government is much the same as yours. I have been monitoring your broadcasts with the besieged group in Michigan. I know these outlaws. We drove them from Canada. They are about two thousand strong, Ben."

"Two thousand!" Ben almost shouted the words.

"Yes. They are holding back most in reserve. They

know that eventually they can starve the good citizens out. They are also aware that your people are coming to help. Do I have to tell you what they've planned for you?"

"Ambush."

"Precisely. I have ordered two of my battalions and one battalion of Canadians out. By ship. They left about an hour ago. They will hit the shore by landing craft at Crisp Point and then proceed inland by fast march. Do you approve?"

"I certainly do approve, Georgi, and I thank you for your help."

"Colonel Stefan Rebet will be commanding the Russian battalions and Major Danjou the Canadian troops. Tell you the truth, Ben, I wish I was going in with them. I miss it. And I would like to sit down and talk with you."

"Hell, Georgi, I'm not going in either!"

"What? The old fire-breathing dragon Ben Raines is going to miss some action. You're not ill, I hope?"

"Oh, no. I had some old lead dug out of one leg and some work done on my feet. Why aren't you going in?"

"Gout," the Russian said, disgust in his voice.

As Ben and Georgi, once bitter enemies and now reluctant allies, began laughing. They were still laughing and chatting and Dan, smiling, quietly left the office.

Two hours before dawn.

The pilots were checking over their aircraft. Gear had been loaded on the cargo planes and the men and women of the Rebels going in stood quietly, in loose formation, chatting and smoking and sipping coffee.

Ben stood with his commanders.

"Striganov told me this afternoon that his country used experimental gases in those areas of the northeast. Most of the country got the Tabun, and it wasn't terribly effective. He said a lot of planes went down in that area of the nation; planes carrying God alone knew what kind of germ-warfare bombs. I just don't know. It may be that those citizens up there, those who survived, just said to hell with it and chose to remain safe and quiet. I just don't know."

"I heard that Russian planes carrying paratroopers went down in the far northeast," West said. "And the Russians, once they heard their motherland was gone, went on a rampage, killing anyone, man, woman, or child, they came upon. That could account for a part of the population."

"The drift of gases, the drift of radiation, the Russians, the outlaws that rise up after any major disaster." Dan shook his head. "Those left just may, like General Raines said, have kept their heads down and remained very quiet."

Ben shook hands all the way around. "Luck to you all, boys." He stepped back and saluted them all. He said to Cecil, "Keep your ass down, old man."

"I'm glad the intell we've been receiving about the Russian proved accurate," Cecil said. "There are certainly some strange twists and turns in war, gentleman."

"I'm glad to have him on our side," Dan said.

"Have you heard from Ike?"

"About fifteen minutes ago. Washington, D.C. is gone. Hot as a fireball. I'm wondering still about New York City. Do you men suppose the government, once it was re-formed, knew about New York City and just kept quiet about it?" Ben asked.

"It would have to be, Ben," Cecil said. "What was it that General Krigel said after he linked up with us after the battle for Tri-States? Let me think. Yes. President Logan had expressly forbidden any fly-bys over the eastern corridor. But if that's true, why?"

"I don't know. Easier to contain the people, maybe. But Logan was crazy, remember? Hell, he married Fran Lantier Piper, didn't he?"

The men laughed softly at that.

"But what about the people up in Vermont, Maine, New Hampshire, New Jersey?" West asked. "Surely someone would have gotten out to tell their story. It would have to be that way."

Ike and Tina halted their teams some sixty miles outside of what was left of Washington, D.C. and the Baltimore areas. Their equipment showed the areas to be hot with radiation.

Tina had pushed on ahead, staying well away from the hot zone. She radioed back to Ike.

"The Philadelphia area, Ike?"

"We'll have to check it out. Stay well west of the hot zone. Start cutting east at Hagerstown. Take the Gettysburg, York, Lancaster route. Have you found any survivors yet, Tina?"

"Ten-four, Ike. Plenty of them. But they're jumpy

folks. We know they're there; they've let us see them. But they won't approach us. Ike? I think we're entering a no-man's-land here. These people don't have any idea who we are."

Ike acknowledged her transmission and told her to stand by. He turned to Dr. Ling. "Doc, could a radiation belt have prevented, blocked, radio transmissions into and out of this area?"

The doctor hesitated. "Possibly," he finally answered. "But the more I think on the matter, the more I believe there has been a massive hoax perpetrated on these people. It could well be that they've been led to believe that anything out of this area is hot, and we've been led to believe that anything inside this area was off limits. That's only a theory, general."

Ike scratched his head, a puzzled look on his face. "But *why?* Why would anybody do something like that?"

Dr. Ling shrugged his shoulders. "I have no idea. As I said, it's only a theory. Perhaps that would account for President Logan's relocation efforts some years back?"

"Yeah. Maybe. Thanks, doc." Ike walked to the communications van. "You able to get through to Base Camp One yet?"

"Yes, sir. Just spoke with them again. It's firm. General Jefferys is leading Rebels into Michigan. Colonel Gray and Colonel West. General Striganov is sending three battalions in from Canada to beef us up."

"Ben not going in?"

"No, sir. And he's not too happy about that,

either."

Ike grinned. "I just bet he isn't. Thanks. Keep everything on scramble; pass the word. We don't want that Libyan fart-in-the-wind to learn how spread out we are."

The radio operator laughed. "Yes, sir," she acknowledged.

"Radio Tina to push on. Maintain no more than fifty miles distance between us."

"Yes, sir."

Ben had stood on the tarmac of the regional airport and watched as the planes took off, circled, then headed north. Holly stood with him. Off to one side, some distance away, stood Patrice, her eyes on the lights of the planes, watching until the planes were gone and the lights faded.

"Go get her," Ben asked Holly. "Let's have breakfast together."

"She's got quite a case on Cecil, hasn't she, Ben?"

"I think they share the feeling. Come on. I'm hungry."

The Rebel community, while numbering in the thousands, was, nevertheless, a close-knit community, and the mess halls were quiet that morning, with not much conversation. All knew that of the Rebels who had left, some would not be returning. But all knew that to face death was a part of being a member of Raines Rebels. They were dedicated to restoring order to a torn and lawless land, and that would never come easy.

Ben and the ladies sat at a table with Buddy and

Dr. Chase. The doctor looked glum.

"What's the matter, you old goat?" Ben asked him. "Your lip is dragging the ground. You didn't actually think I would send you up to Michigan, did you?"

"I could have flown in, and not jumped, Raines." His reply was testy.

"They'll be traveling fast, Lamar. Besides, like me, you're needed here until we get this area smoothed out. I'll make you a promise, though."

"Oh?"

"If New York is still standing, you and me, we'll be the first ones to go in."

"I'll damn sure hold you to that, Raines."

"It's a promise, Lamar."

"And me, Father?" Buddy asked.

"You'll be right in there with us, Buddy. It's going to take all of us. He cut his eyes to Patrice. "You want to come along, captain?"

She forced a smile. "I wouldn't miss it for the world. All my life I've heard about New York City."

"I can't even envision it." Buddy spoke after swallowing a mouthful of scrambled eggs. "I've seen pictures, but I don't think that a picture does it justice."

"What do you remember about it, general?" Patrice asked.

"Almost getting run over by those goddamn bicycle messengers on Park Ave."

Ben then realized that Buddy and Patrice had no idea what a bicycle messenger meant. He opened his mouth to tell them but was interrupted by a runner from communications.

"The platoon at Memphis, sir? They fought the Night People all night, but now report one runway of the airport is clear for take-off and landing. The Pathfinders have cleared the airport in Michigan and are moving now to set up the DZ."

"Thank you. Please keep me informed."

"How's your feet, Ben?" Lamar asked.

"Fine. The leg is a little sore, that's all. Has anybody heard how Emil Hite and his intrepid little band fared during the night?"

No one had.

Ben smiled. He wondered what Hiram was going to do next.

"Ah ain't livin' lak 'is," Hiram suddenly announced, startling those who had chosen to follow him. "We got to start thankin' 'bout them 'at's gonna foller us."

"Whut you mean?" G.B. asked, wincing as he shifted positions and felt a sharp pain in his wounded cheek.

"We had our way around these parts for years. 'At's whut I mean. Didn't obey no law 'ceptin' our own. Ben Raines has got to go. We'uns got to see to that."

"You mean . . . kill him?" Jimmy John asked.

"At's 'xactly whut ah mean. Jist lak we done them damned nigger-lovin' civil rats workers back when we was all young bucks. 'Member how we ambushed that old boy back in the sixties? Drug 'im out of his car and tarred and feathered 'im. 'At was rat good fun."

"How it was we done 'at?" G.B. asked. "I disremember 'xactly."

" 'Cause he were drivin' through this area and we done tole him not to do hit no more." Hiram smiled in remembrance. "This here is *our* country! And don't nobody have no rat to tell us hit ain't."

"You got a plan, Hiram?" Carl asked.

"Damned rat I does. We gonna tale Ben Raines—'er some of them Rebels of hisn 'at we want to talk 'bout joinin' up. Once we git him in here, then we can kill him."

"Ah lak hit!" G.B. said.

"Naturally," Hiram replied. "I thunk hit up, didn't I?"

Ben was working at his desk when his phone rang. Communications, advising him that Hiram had sent word he wished to speak with Ben, at the bayou bank. Wanted to talk about joining the Rebels.

Ben laughed. "Sure he does," he told the woman. "What he wants to do is pull me down into his territory and then kill me. Hiram is a die-hard redneck, lieutenant. So full of hate it's finally consumed him. All right. Advise Captain Gorzalka. I'll be down to see Hiram in about an hour."

Ben rang the hospital, to see if Holly wanted to ride down with him. Then he changed his mind; might get dangerous. He sent a runner after Buddy and waited until the young man entered his office.

"Where's your weapon, son?"

"In my Jeep."

"Get it. And meet me at my Jeep. We're going to

finish a twenty-year-old game."

Heading out, Buddy asked, "What game, Father?"

"One might call it many things, son. Good against evil. But to Hiram's way of thinking, I'm the evil one. One hardhead against another hardhead. Each one thinking he is in the right."

"And who is in the right, Father?"

"Intellectually, I am. Morally, half and half. Socially, the way we—the Rebels—envision our society, oh, give me sixty points and Hiram forty. Add that up, son."

"Giving how many points per issue?"

"One hundred."

"Two-ten to ninety."

"That's the way I figure it."

"But how much is a man worth, Father?"

"At last count, about four dollars."

"Are you *serious!*"

"Yep. The average man has that many minerals in his body."

"Ah!"

"But that isn't what you meant, is it, son?"

"No, sir."

"The worth of a person, son, depends, to my way of thinking, how much that person contributes to society, and how much they take away from it."

Buddy thought about that for a moment. "That sounds logical, Father. But doesn't Hiram have as much right to judge you as you do to judge him?"

Ben smiled. He hadn't sired a dummy. "That's the way it would be in a democracy, son—on paper, that is."

"What do you mean?"

"It never worked out that way. Justice was supposed to be blind; but in a lot of cases, she wasn't."

"So I have heard my mother mention, time after time," the young man said drily.

And Ben knew what he was talking about.

"Did your mother think to tell you that I contacted the attorney representing her and told her I would share in the expenses of the child if she would just prove that the baby really was mine?"

"No. Least I don't think she ever mentioned that to me." He waved a hand. "That's over and buried, Father. We found each other, finally, and we are together. That is all that really matters, is it not?"

"Yes. What do you think of Holly?"

"A very nice lady and a more than capable physician, I believe."

"That's a nice, safe reply."

"If you're waiting for me to start calling her Mother, you are going to have one hell of a long wait — sir!"

Ben laughed and reached over, jerking Buddy's bandana over his eyes.

Buddy grinned and folded his arms across his massive chest. "Fine. I'll just nap. Wake me when we reach this odious individual's position."

"I couldn't have said it better myself."

Twenty-three

"Hiram," Ben called across the brackish bayou, "you must think I'm a damned fool!"

"Don't neither, Raines. Jist wanna talk is all. Why don't you come on acrost? Is you scared of me, Raines?"

"No, Hiram. I'm not afraid of you. Where are your asshole buddies? You have them positioned around the bank to get a shot at me?"

That shook L.T., lying in the deep grass with a rifle. How the hell did the man know that? Hiram's plan had seemed so good at first. Now L.T. was just plain scared.

The Rebels under Captain Gorzalka's command shifted nervously behind their guns; not a one of them liked this worth a damn. The general was too open, too vulnerable.

And the enemy could not be seen; but all knew Hiram's followers were hidden in the thick underbrush of the bayou bank.

"He has his rifle cocked back," Buddy whispered to his father.

"You got sharp eyes, boy."

"Thank you."

"Never did trust none of us folks from around here, did you, Raines?" Hiram asked.

"Never did, Hiram. And don't now."

"You thank you so goddamned high and mighty, don't you, Raines?"

"No, Hiram. I simply believe there are social and moral codes one must follow along with the legal written laws."

"You goddamn son of a bitch. You took my power away from me. You took my younguns."

Ben noted that he mentioned power before his kids.

Hiram jerked up his rifle just as Buddy jumped, knocking Ben to the ground. Another rifle barked, then others joined in. Ben heard the bullets hit Buddy's body; felt his son's blood leak onto his flesh. He rolled over, protecting his son with his own body just as the Rebels opened up with every gun at their disposal.

Crawling, Ben pulled Buddy behind a tree and tore open his shirt.

It was bad. One slug had hit him in the chest, another had taken him in the shoulder, and yet another one had torn a chunk out of his head.

"Captain! Get Buddy out of here and into the hospital. Medic! Get over here and do a patch job. Let's go!"

Hiram and his crew had slipped away, heading for deep cover.

Ben paced the hospital corridor. It was growing

275

dark when Chase finally came out of the OR and walked up to Ben. "I don't know, Ben. It's too early to tell. If he makes it twenty-four hours, he'll pull through. And no, you can't see him. He's in recovery and he is unconscious. All we can do is wait and pray."

Ben nodded. He looked at Holly, who had just come out of the OR. "Change the dressing on my leg, Holly. Paint it good and make it as waterproof and dirt-proof as you can."

"All right. I gather you won't be home for dinner."

"You got that right."

Ben stood on the Rebel side of the bayou as Emil Hite and his followers were boated across. Emil had heard about Buddy, and he knew not to say anything to Ben. He and his followers quietly melted away into the darkness.

"Captain Gorzalka, start ferrying my equipment across and caching them in the spots I told you," Ben ordered.

"Yes, sir."

Ben turned to his XO, Joe Williams. "You're in charge, Joe. Cecil and Ike have already been notified."

"Yes, sir."

"I should have just killed him when we pulled in here," Ben spoke quietly. "I knew it then. I know it much more deeply now."

No one said anything; they knew Ben was not expecting any reply.

Holly had arrived in a Jeep, driven by Patrice, and the two women walked to Ben's side. "You could just send in troops and flush them out, Ben," Holly said.

"Yes. I could do that." He turned to Gorzalka. "Captain, ring the area once I'm in. None of Hiram's people come out. If they manage to kill me . . . there are orders in a sealed envelope on my desk. If they kill me, secure this area by any means possible. But don't burn it. That would harm the wildlife. . . ."

Holly looked at him in total amazement.

". . . Is my equipment across?"

"Yes, sir."

Ben glanced at Holly. "Take care of my son, Holly."

"All right, Ben."

He kissed her quickly and walked down the bank, stepping into a waiting boat.

The darkness soon swallowed him.

On the far side, Ben stepped out of the boat and slipped up the bank. He looked back at the Rebels in the boat. "Go back to the other side and resume your duties."

"Yes, sir," one said reluctantly, and the boat pushed off.

Ben straightened up and stepped away from the bayou treeline. At the edge of a clearing, he looked up, getting his bearings. The night was filled with stars, perfectly cloudless. Ben located Orion. Keeping his eyes straight, he lifted them and found Little Bear; the last star in the configuration would be the Pole Star, with Plough to his left and Cassiopeia to his right.

Now he knew the points. Ben had a compass with him; but this was just as easy.

He walked on, stopping every so often to cut a short pole. When he had his arms full, he walked on, whistling as he went, sometimes singing songs from the nineteen-sixties and -seventies. He found a place to make his camp and then went to work securing it.

On the north side of his camp, Ben rigged a dead fall snare, using a log and a piece of rope and a small stick. He laid the loop on the ground and covered it with leaves.

On the south side of his camp, Ben rigged a staked dead fall, using a smaller log and lashing three sharpened stakes to the log, fastening the trip wire to a sturdy bush.

On the east side, Ben found a natural depression in the earth. He quickly deepened it with a small entrenching tool and rigged a spear pit, covering the pit first with small limbs, then leaves and dirt.

On the west side of camp, Ben rigged a grenade trap by first removing the pin and securing the spoon with wire, just enough tension to hold the spoon in place. He rigged it waist high between two trees. Then he cleared an area and built a fire. Then Ben slipped back a couple of hundred yards and crawled up under some thick brush.

He waited, eating cold rations and sipping from one of his two canteens. There was a grim smile on his face.

He did not underestimate Hiram's ability in the woods, nor any of the others'; they were all good hunters and trappers. But that expertise could also work against a person, making them too sure.

Ben lay to the north of the small fire, just able to see it from his position. He did not think it would take long for the trash to appear, and he was right.

The slight sound of a twig snapping under weight reached Ben's ears. It was only a very small sound, carrying no more than fifty feet. But animals don't step on twigs unless they are running in fear. This was an animal, but not the four-legged kind. Only cutting his eyes, not moving his head, Ben picked out the dark shape of a man approaching the fire from the north.

A few more feet, and whoever it was approaching the fire would be in for a very painful surprise. The man's foot dragged into the loop; Ben heard the brace slide out from under the supports. Then a scream ripped the night as the log came down on the man's lower back, driving him to the ground, breaking bones and crushing flesh.

"Jackson!" A hoarse whisper came out of the darkness. "Whut happened, Jackson?"

"Cain't move my legs!" the man under the log croaked. "Cain't feel nothin' from the waist down." He started crying under his pinned position.

"Jimmy Luther!" Hiram called. "You see anything around that there far?"

"No, sir. I'll take a look."

"Do 'at. But take Raines alive. I want to hear him holler when we cut off his pecker."

Ben smiled grimly. He had pinpointed Hiram's position; could have easily sprayed the area and probably taken the man out. But that would be too easy.

It was to be Jimmy Luther's last look at anything. His knees hit the black trip-wire and the spoon popped free.

"Whut's the hale's 'at!" Jimmy Luther hollered.

The full force of the grenade, a Mini-More, actually a pocket Claymore, hit Jimmy Luther waist-high and spread parts of him all over the area.

"Jimmy Luther!" Hiram squalled. "Jimmy Luther! Boy, you answer me now, you hear?"

But the only person Jimmy Luther would ever answer to would be God, on Judgment Day.

"Ah'll fetch 'im!" another voice called.

"There ain't nuttin' to fetch, boy!" another man called. " 'At 'ere was a gree-nade, Charlie."

"Go see 'bout your brother, boy," Hiram shouted.

Charlie hit the punji pit at a full run, the sharpened stakes driving into his legs and feet. He pitched forward, half in and half out of the deadly staked hole. Ben had wished, building the pit, that he had some monkey shit to dip the points in; but he figured he'd done pretty well with what he had in hand.

Charlie's screaming was cut short as the pain became too much and the young man passed out.

"Goddamn you, Raines!" Hiram screamed. "Is you there?"

Ben lay quietly, silently, his breathing slow and even and noiseless.

"Come on out and fight lak a man, you bassard!" Hiram yelled.

"Ah'm paralyzed!" Jackson moaned. "I cain't move my legs, boys. Oh, Lard, Lard, hep me! I don't wanna die. Mr. Raines! Mr. Raines! Hep me, please. Ah didn't really mean you no serious harm."

Sure, Ben thought. Sure, you didn't. When the chips get down, your kind always rolls over. And back when the world was whole, more or less, you always had some smooth-talking lawyer to help you. Now I'm putting into play what the courts should have done years back.

Fuck you!

"Hep me, Mr. Raines!" Jackson began sobbing. "Don't leave me out there. The wolves'll git me sure."

Wolves! Ben thought. It's cocksuckers like you who killed the wolf out years ago. And now they're back, and once again, silly assholes like you are scared of them.

Ben remembered from his writing days that no one had ever been able to prove that a grown, healthy wolf had, unprovoked, ever attacked a human being.

"Axel Leroy?" Hiram called.

"Yes, Daddy?"

"Kill that yeller-bellied son of a bitch, boy."

"Yes, sir."

Ben heard a single shot, and Jackson's blubbering abruptly ended.

"I got 'im, Daddy!" Axel yelled proudly.

You raised a fine boy there, Hiram, Ben thought. Just a real jim-dandy.

"Good shootin', Axel Leroy," Hiram told him.

"Ah don't thank Raines is nowhere around heers," a man called out. "Ah thank he jist suckered us all in heer."

"Ah thank you rat, Sonny boy." Another voice was added. "Whut you thank, Smithy?"

"He long gone these parts."

"Oh, God, please hep me!" Charlie squalled, once more adrift in a sea of agony, the stakes punching through his legs and feet with each movement. "Oh, Lard, ah can't stand hit!"

"Vince," Hiram called. "You closest to 'im. You wanna try 'er?"

"Ah'll do moreun 'at," Vince bragged. "Ah'll do 'er!"

And you have to pass right by me to do it, Ben thought, smiling. He slipped his razor-honed long-bladed knife from leather and waited. He heard Vince coming closer, crawling toward the sounds of Charlie's bawling and hollering. Ben had slipped to the edge of the brush, holding the knife in his right hand.

Ben waited until Vince was at his position with his right arm fully extended, fingers digging in the dirt. He drove the blade into the hollow of the armpit, all the way to the hilt, and twisted the blade savagely. Vince screamed hideously. Ben jerked out the knife, coming up on his knees. He drove the blade into Vince's neck, all the way through, at least six inches of the blade driving into the hard ground, pinning the flopping man where he lay.

Then, working quickly, Ben did a little surgery on Vince.

"Vince!" Hiram was hollering. "Oh, Vince-boy! Whut's goin' on over thar?"

"Cover me!" a man yelled. "Ah'm a-gonna git Charlie."

282

Amid the banging of wild shooting, Ben dragged the body of Vince back into the brush and covered it. Then he made his way out of the brush and was a good mile away before the shooting stopped.

Ike was so mad he almost broke the radio mic. Calming himself, he handed the mic back to the operator and stalked away to find Tina.

She noted the dark look on Ike's face. "What's up, Ike?"

"Buddy's been hard hit, Tina. That trash that Ben told us about ambushed Buddy and Ben. Ben was unhurt, but now he's gone on a rampage, alone, hunting them that did it."

"Is Buddy going to make it? And tell me the truth, Ike."

"I wouldn't lie to you, Tina. Chase said that last night he wouldn't have bet either way. But now, Buddy is awake and stronger and it looks good."

"Thank God!" She put her arms around the man she had called Uncle Ike for most of her life and placed her head on his barrel chest. "Now tell me about Dad."

Ike brought her up to date.

She pulled away, wiped her eyes, and composed herself.

"It's no time to be brave, Tina," Ike told her. "If you want to cry, go right ahead."

She shook her head. "It wouldn't do any good, Ike. And it wouldn't help us get the job done. My father is tough as a boot, Ike. Both mentally and physically. And I don't have to tell an ex-SEAL that mental is the key to a good portion of getting the job done. Those redneck trash will regret the day they ever heard the name of Ben Raines."

Ike smiled at her. "Honey, I think they've been doing that for years!"

"All right. Do we go into downtown Lancaster?"

"Yeah. Let's see what's goin' on with the Yankees."

L.T. woke up at dawn, a strange weight on his chest. He opened his eyes and began screaming hysterically, almost insanely.

The head of Vince, bloody and pale, with the eyes wide open in the shock of death, sat squarely on L.T.'s chest, staring at the man.

Twenty-four

Carl jumped up to run over to where L.T. lay thrashing around on the ground, his dirty feet kicking at the head of Vince. Vince's head rolled down the small incline to land with a soft plop in a fresh puddle of cow shit.

Carl felt a series of hammer-blows on his back. It was the most peculiar sensation he had ever experienced in all his often-peculiar life. He felt himself falling, falling, as the white-hot pain began spreading all over the line of .45 caliber bullet holes.

The last thing that Carl would think of was: We shoulda done whut Ben Raines wanted us to do.

L.T. managed to get to his knees before the .45 caliber slugs of social justice stitched him from his right side to his neck. He died on his knees, hands at his side.

William Watson lay hunkered in a ground depression. He had the time left to piss his dirty underwear, and when the grenade landed just a few inches from his nose the 60mm fragmentation grenade blew parts of William Watson all over the yard, some of them smacking Jimmy John in the face.

"Yukk!" Jimmy John said, wiping his face. As he turned to find his weapon, his eyes met those of Ben Raines. Ben stood by a huge old oak tree. Jimmy John thought he had never in his life seen nothin' that looked so savage.

Ben shot him in the face, the copper-jacketed hollow-nosed .45 slugs making a dreadful mess in the early morning.

Jimmy John was literally lifted off his feet and slung to one side.

Ben took that confusing time to run to his right, circling the camp, staying in the deep brush, popping out the half-empty drum and fitting a full drum into the belly of the Thompson. He slung the SMG long enough to pull the pins of two grenades, one in each hand, holding the spoons down. Ben's leg was aching, but he did not really notice the slight pain.

Ben came face to face with a man; he could smell the fear-stink of the 'neck; smell the awful odor of rotting teeth and bad breath panting out of the man's wide open mouth.

Ben dropped one cannister down the 'neck's shirt front and drove his elbow into the man's face, knocking him down. Ben ran behind a tree just as the grenade exploded, sending bits and pieces of human body all over the forest. He stepped out from behind the tree, his head aching and his ears ringing from the explosive sounds of battle and tossed the second grenade in the general direction he'd seen a 'neck run. The grenade blew and Ben watched as an arm floated lazily up into the air and then dropped to earth.

286

A bullet sent pieces of bark into the side of Ben's face, ripping open the skin, bloodying his face. Ben turned and dropped to one knee, leveling the Thompson and holding the trigger back. Efrom Silas and Axel Leroy went jerking and dancing the macabre steps to the Stygian shore.

"You'd never make it on Dance Party, boys." Ben voiced a soldier's grim humor. "Not original enough."

Ben squatted beside a tree and tallied it up, his eyes touching briefly on each sprawled body. He found a blanket-covered body and thought that must be Charlie. The punji stakes had done their work; probably bled to death.

He did not see Hiram, nor G.B., nor the last son of Hiram; Bubba Willie, the retarded one, had been taken into town by his mother. Ben saw them then, the three of them, running across a meadow, heading for the bayou. He watched as they disappeared into the woods.

Ben backed off from the site of carnage and rested, eating a can of cold beans and crackers for breakfast, sipping at his canteen of water.

There was a grim smile of satisfaction on his face.

"Hell of a damn battle just went on in there," Captain Gorzalka remarked.

"And look over there to the west," a Rebel pointed out. "Buzzards circling."

"The general must have done that last night. He sure was some kind of pissed-off."

Holly had waited the long night, Chase insisting

she stay. One thing the Rebels had was a fine staff of doctors; Buddy would be well taken care of. She had slept in the back of a truck; the gunfire and explosions had wakened her.

"Oh, Lardy, Lardy, Lardy!" The shout was faint. "Halp, halp!"

The Rebels started laughing, as much from relief as anything else. They knew then that the general was very much alive and well.

"Come on, Grover Neal!" Hiram's shout could be heard. "Git your ass a-movin', boy!"

"Ah'm a-gonna kill Ben Raines!" Grover shouted. "Ah'll go down as a big man. Ah'll be a hero, Daddy! Ah'll be. . . ."

The chug-a-chug of Ben's Thompson rattled out the voice.

Hiram and G.B. appeared on the far bank.

"Y'all got to hep us!" G.B. squalled, his voice shaky with fear. " 'at 'ere man's plumb crazy. He's a devil. He's done kilt ever'body. He cut off Vince's haid and crept up in our camp lak a snake and poot it on L.T.'s chest. Then he jist come out of the mist and started killin'! Oh, Lard, ya'll got to hep us!"

The Rebels stood on the high side of the opposite bank and looked on in undisguised disgust as Hiram and G.B. begged and groveled.

"Ain't y'all got no mercy in ya?" Hiram yelled. "Whut kind of people is y'all anyways?"

G.B. screamed in fear as Ben appeared on the high bank above them. He fell to his hands and knees near the water. "I'm sorry, Mr. Raines. I'm sorry for all the bad thangs I done." Then he began confessing to the most heinous of crimes. Torture and rape and perversion over the years. Incest with his daughters. Civil rights violations. He was blubbering and snorting as he finally wound down his list of atrocities.

Hiram began puking on himself as Ben leveled the Thompson and held the trigger back. G.B. was flipped over into the dark waters of the bayou, blood leaking out of a dozen or more bullet holes. The blood drifted, attracted those who lived in the dark waters.

With puke staining his chin and his shirt, Hiram began cursing Ben. Both Ben and the Rebels noticed a slight stirring of the brackish waters. Hiram finally paused for breath.

Taking a deep breath, Hiram screamed, "I hope your son dies, Raines. I hope he suffers and hollers and cries. I hope you git the cancer. I hope your dick rots off."

Then he whirled and dove into the bayou.

"Hold your fire!" Ben shouted.

Hiram made it to the middle of the bayou. Water splashed high into the air as a 'gator took him by the legs and twisted, pulling Hiram down. Hiram surfaced once, his eyes wide with fear, his mouth open, water pouring out of it. The tail of a huge old mossy-back flipped out of the waters.

And then the waters were still.

Holly did a quick repair job on Ben's face, sliced open his field pants and redressed his wound, giving him a shot of antibiotics. Ben endured it all silently.

He had asked about Buddy, and had been told it

looked good. He was going to make it.

"General?" Captain Gorzalka asked. "Do you want us to start rebuilding the bridges?"

Ben shook his head. "No. This will be a place for the animals to run free, safe from man. We'll do this in every state. Someday, probably, man will fuck it all up again; but it won't happen in our lifetime. This area will be off-limits to anyone except game management people." He turned to an aide, who, he supposed, had been waiting all night for his return. "Make that an official order, Mary. Type it up and I'll sign it."

"Yes, sir."

"Ben Raines!" Holly said. "You are a walking contradiction, you know that?"

"Sure. Always have been."

"I swear to God, I think you care more about animals than you do about humans."

"Some humans, yeah. You're right. You want a lecture on animal rights, Holly?"

"Hell, no! Thank you just the same. Damn you, Ben Raines, you are the most infuriating man I have ever known. I swear that's true. . . ."

Ben fished in his pocket and found a biscuit, munching on it while Holly ranted and raved and cussed him . . . in a ladylike manner, of course.

"Don't you know that people *care* for you, Ben Raines? That people *worry* about you and some of these dumb stunts you pull? Well, do you realize that?"

"Yep." Ben chewed.

Before she could get steamed up and started again, the radio-person hollered out, "Dr. Allardt?

290

Dr. Chase on the horn."

Muttering, Holly walked to the vehicle and spoke with Chase.

"She really likes me," Ben said to Captain Gorzalka, motioning toward Holly.

"If you say so, sir," the captain replied dubiously. "How many did you off in there, general?"

Ben thought for a moment, mentally counting it up. "About fifteen, I think."

"General? That old lady in there, that hoodoo woman, Pauly, or whatever her name is?"

"What about her?"

"She's still in there. She refused to come out with Emil and his fruitcakes."

"She's harmless. We'll check on her from time to time. I think she likes being alone. Captain, you know of anybody who likes animals and who would like to be in charge of this area?"

Gorzalka grinned.

"All right." Ben returned the grin. "You've got the job. Course you might be pulled away from it from time to time."

"Suits me, sir."

Holly walked back over. "Buddy was just taken off the critical list. Upgraded to serious. He's going to make it, Ben."

"Think he'll be ready to go in twenty-four hours, Holly?"

Holly lost her temper—again. "What in the hell are you babbling about now, Raines? Twenty-four hours! How about two months, you hardhead?"

"Calm yourself, dear. I was just joking a bit."

"I didn't laugh!"

"I noticed that. I'm very quick about that sort of thing. Humorless, that's you."

"Ben Raines, you just killed about a zillion people in there!" She waved her hand. "And you're making jokes!"

"Fourteen, actually, I think. The 'gator got Hiram. Captain Gorzalka, you have any bicarb with you?"

"Yes, sir."

"Toss it in the bayou. The 'gator is going to need it."

Laughing, the Rebel walked away.

"Jesus Christ, Ben!" Holly yelled. "And what about this twenty four-hour-business. What the hell are you planning? Come on, you've got something up your sleeve."

"I think we could use another combat doctor, Holly. You want to come along with me? It's going to be a unique experience. Have you ever worked in a field hospital?"

"I swear to God, Ben, you're babbling out of your skull. Did I miss a wound? Did you receive a blow to the head?"

"I'm fine, Holly. My, but it's a glorious morning, isn't it?"

"It's lovely. Beautiful. Where are we going, Ben?"

"You sure you want to come along, now, Holly?"

"Yes, Ben. I'm sure. Now where are we going?"

Ben smiled at her. "Michigan!"

Twenty-five

"I don't blame you, Ben," Lamar Chase said, sitting in Ben's office, watching the man field-strip his Thompson and carefully clean and oil each part. "I just wish I was going with you."

"We're all going to New York City, Lamar. If it's standing. I'll probably leave no more than two companies here."

"Buddy is fully conscious now. He's in some pain, but he's going to be just fine. It was a very close thing."

"I'm going to see him late this afternoon. Was he informed of my foray into Hiram's territory?"

"Yes. He said that didn't surprise him a bit; only wished he could have gone along with you."

Colonel Joe Williams, Ben's XO, stepped into the office. Ben looked up. "You're in charge here, Joe, effective 0400 tomorrow morning."

"Yes, sir. Wish I was going with you."

"I know you do. Just keep the Big Apple in mind." Ben leaned back in his chair. "Joe, it's all running smoothly and I know you'll keep it that way. When Buddy gets ambulatory, start going over leadership courses with him. He's a good boy, but he's still got a lot to learn about commanding personnel. At your recommendation, I'll commission him when I get back."

"Yes, sir."

To Chase, "You're sure you don't mind Holly coming along?"

"Of course not, Ben. I'm falling over good doctors. She'll be needed up in Michigan. I've taken the liberty of packing some extra materials that I think she'll need."

"Good. All right, people. That about wraps it up. I'm going to clean up, get something to eat, and then start lining up the people I'm taking with me."

The office emptied.

The Rebels ran into a solid and well-manned barricade on the Interstate. About ten miles outside of Lancaster. Tina radioed back to Ike and she was ordered to hold, not to attempt to advance.

Just after crossing the Susquehanna River, the Rebels had begun to notice well-kept homes and neat fields and gardens. It was eerie in a reverse sort of way, after what they had been seeing on their journey.

"Amish?" Ham asked.

"I don't think so," Tina told him. "The people we've seen so far are all well-armed and look like they mean business."

They made a quick camp by the side of the road and ate a cold lunch, then rested, always conscious of eyes on them.

"Keep your weapons close by, but don't make any hostile moves. I don't think these people mean us any harm. I think they're just curious." Tina opened her lunch packet. "At least," she added, "I hope I'm right."

Then they were all conscious of being surrounded, on all sides. The weapons in the hands of the men and women were not pointed directly at them, but held at the ready.

"We don't mean anyone any harm," Tina called out. "We're part of Raines Rebels, heading east to check out New York City."

"That is a lie!" A man returned the call. "General Raines was killed more than ten years ago."

"General Ben Raines is my father," Tina said, raising her voice. "And I just kissed him good-bye about a week ago in what was called Louisiana. I assure you all, Ben Raines is very much alive and well."

Whispers reached the ears of the Rebel Scouts. They continued their eating of lunch, outwardly showing no signs of fear.

"You say Ben Raines is alive," the same man called. "Prove it!"

"You've heard of General Ike McGowan?"

"Everyone knows of the exploits of General Ike. And of the vice president, Cecil Jefferys. What about General McGowan?"

"He should be here in about forty minutes. I'm sure you have good communications; you know there is a large force coming up behind us."

"This is true," the man acknowledged.

"We'll share our food with you," Tina offered.

"We'll share with you. We have fresh-baked bread and meat and vegetables."

"That would be very nice. But we don't want to strain your supplies. Ike is coming up with more than three hundred personnel."

"We have more than enough." The spokesman stepped out of the line of trees and walked across the ditch, up to Tina's position. He gazed at her. "You do not look like General Raines. There is no family resemblance."

"Ben adopted me and Jack. My brother was killed during the fighting over the old Tri-States. My father's flesh-and-blood son, Buddy, is with him at the new Base Camp One."

Men and women began bringing fresh-cooked food to the Rebel Scouts, and it was a most welcome sight. After a week of, if they were lucky, one hot meal a day, the Rebels welcomed the hot food.

While the Scouts ate, the spokesperson for the community asked, "Why would you risk going into a hot area, and how did you come *through* the hot areas?"

"What hot areas are you speaking of?" Ham asked, around a mouthful of ham sandwich.

"You say you came from what was once Lousiana; how did you pass through the radiation belt?"

"With the exception of what was D.C. and Baltimore," Tina told him, "there are no other hot areas."

The men and women looked at each other; it was evident that none of them believed a word Tina had just said. Something odd about these people, Tina thought.

Tina got her map case and showed them all the

route they'd taken in getting this far. "You can see our route: Jackson, Mississippi to Memphis, Tennessee. Then to Nashville, Knoxville, Bristol, Roanoke, and on up here, skirting the D.C. and Baltimore area."

The spokesperson shook his head. "But we were told that everything from the Pennsylvania line south and everything from the old Interstate Eight-one west was dead. And would be hot for centuries to come. And that everything north of the old Interstate Seventy-eight, and everything east of Philadelphia, including that city, was off limits."

Ike and his contingent pulled in and were introduced all around. While they ate, something that Ike did very well, Tina brought him up to date.

"Who told you all this crap?" Ike asked the spokesperson. "And when?"

"Just after the bombing; the Great War. Just after President Logan's relocation plans came through."

"Yes," a woman broke in. "It was President Logan himself who came to see us. I remember it well. He had a . . . well, *person* with him. A robed and hooded person; eyes all white and face horribly disfigured. The President said that this, meaning the burned person, was all that was left outside of tiny pockets like ours, and we must never, never leave the designated areas." She shrugged. "And we have not. The government told us it was unsafe."

Ike snorted and accepted another fine ham sandwich from a rather plump lady. Rich, homemade mustard, pickles that made his mouth water, and thick slices of still-warm homemade bread. Ike chewed and sighed with contentment. "So this is it, then—you people have never left the designated confines?"

"No, sir. We believed it wasn't safe. The government told us so."

Ike didn't want to bit the hands that were feeding him, and feeding him well, so he didn't tell them that with somebody like Hilton Logan, you couldn't believe a word out of his mouth. "But surely you have radios! You've heard us talking back and forth; you've said so."

"Certainly," the spokesman said. "But what could we do? How to get to you? No Rebel contingent ever came this way, so we could but assume the way was blocked."

Ike leaned against a fender. "Yeah, it's all beginning to fit now. You're too young to remember, Tina; but Logan evacuated the cities, placed them off limits, and relocated the people. We'll probably never know for sure, but my guess would be he struck a deal with the Night People. I'll give the liberal son of a bitch credit; maybe he thought he was doing the right thing."

Dr. Ling said, "I can imagine, after the bombings, that his medical advisors told him to do this; to separate the bomb-blast people from those so-far unaffected."

"All right," Ike nodded his head, "I'll accept that. And to make it work, a story had to be concocted."

"Sure." Tina jumped in. "And what better story than to tell the people about so-called Hot areas of the nation. He even went so far as to forbid pilots from flying over the designated areas. Ike, do you know what this means—really means?"

298

"Yeah, in more ways than one, kid."

The residents of the area were standing quietly, listening to the Rebels talk. To a person, all wore shocked looks on their faces.

"General McGowan." The woman gave him a huge piece of apple pie. Ike looked at it, smacked his lips, and took it. "What do you mean in more ways than one?"

"It means, ma'am," Ike chewed and then continued, "that with the exception of D.C. and Baltimore, the nation is clean. Everything else was just a big damn lie on Logan's part."

"Tell me something, any of you, all of you." Tina faced the crowd. "What's the closest any of you have ever been to Wilmington or Philadelphia?"

"No one goes into the cities, Miss Raines," the spokesman informed the Rebels.

"Why?" Ike asked, knowing what Tina was leading up to. He had spotted something very odd; might be a coincidence, but he rather doubted it. So had Tina.

Ike turned to face a Vietnamese man and spoke to him in his own tongue. Ike ended with something that sounded like, "Do mamma money eye," which, loosely translated, means "these mother-fuckers are lyin'!"

The small man nodded and turned away, walking through the ranks of Rebels, speaking to them softly. The Rebels began to fan out.

"Why won't you go into the cities, mister?" Ike asked, turning to face the spokesman, who wore sunglasses. They all wore sunglasses. And even though the day was hot, all wore long-sleeved shirts.

"The cities are unsafe. They are filled with radiation."

"You're a liar!" Ike told him, then reached up and ripped the sunglasses from the man's face.

There were tubes running into Buddy's arms, but his color was good and the nurse said he was getting stronger with each passing hour. Buddy smiled at his father.

"You had me worried, boy. Thank you for saving my life."

"You're welcome, sir. I hope I didn't hurt you when I knocked you down. A man your age . . . well, bones break easily." There was a twinkle in his eyes.

"I think, boy, when you get up out of that bed, I'm going to whip your ass!"

Buddy laughed softly. "So you are going to Michigan, sir?"

Holly stuck her head into the room. "Yes, we are, Buddy. And Patrice is going, too."

Ben opened his mouth, then closed it. This would be as good a time as any to check Patrice out to the fullest.

"Any comments, General Raines?" she asked sweetly.

"Not a one."

"Will surprises never cease!" She walked on down the hall.

"Are you going to hold on to this one, Father?" Buddy asked, cutting his eyes toward the open doorway.

"I haven't the vaguest idea what you mean, boy. You've been listening to too much camp talk. I am really a one-woman man, at heart."

"Father?"

"Yes, son."

"You are as full of shit as a Christmas goose!"

The man's eyes were chalk-white and dead-looking. He screamed as the light struck his eyes. His screaming abruptly ended as Ike, left-handed, shoved his CAR-15 under the man's chin and pulled the trigger.

The Rebels, fully alerted and on guard, cut loose with automatic weapons at nearly point-blank range. For many of the Rebels, especially those closest to Ike and Tina, it was too close for guns; they grabbed knives and camp axes and went to work. Blood began to spurt from gaping, horrible wounds. The Night People, many of them losing their ultra-dark sunglasses in the fighting, were blinded by the bright sunlight. They ran screaming off up and down the road and into the fields. The Rebels cut as many of them down as they could.

"No pursuit!" Ike yelled. "No pursuit! Let them go. Gather 'round, gather 'round."

The Rebels gathered around him, a few meters away from the blood-soaked and body-littered ground, Ike said, "I got a hunch, people. And if I'm right, it isn't gonna be any fun. But it's something we have to do. So listen up."

After Ike's orders, they broke up into teams and began going house to house, farm to farm. Ike had been right.

One Rebel, a veteran of a hundred battles, stepped out of a barn and bent over, puking up his lunch. He wiped his mouth and pointed toward the barn. "Ike was right, Tina. Take a quick look in there. The smell gave it away."

Trying to breath as shallowly as possible, and through her mouth, Tina took a quick look inside the barn. Human bones were piled up, some piles reaching as high as the floor of the loft. Tina backed out and fought to keep her lunch down.

When she knew she wasn't going to toss her lunch, she lifted her walkie talkie and said, "Shark, you were right. I'm just east of your position. Can you get up here?"

"Ten-four."

"Holy Mother of God!" Ike said, backing out of the barn. He took a deep breath and closed the double doors. "Some of those bones are no more than a day or two old. We've got a major war on our hands, people, and I don't just mean us. It's going to take everybody to whip this."

Dr. Ling, wearing a face mask, entered the death-barn. He did not stay inside for long. When he stepped outside, he looked at Ike. "The worst is now reality. They're spreading out of the cities, probably by the hundreds; perhaps by the thousands. Looking for food. Burn this place, Ike."

The barn was doused with kerosene and gasoline and set afire. The heat was so intense it backed the Rebels clear out of the yard.

"The way I figure it, gang," Ike said, his Rebels gathered around him, "the more normal-looking Night People are being sent out to infiltrate the villages — in search of food. Then the . . . others join them. So that means the really disfigured and deformed ones are here, in hiding, in the dark, probably in the cellars."

"Aw, shit!" one Rebel exclaimed.

The others laughed, relieving the tension.

"And one more thing," Ike said, raising his voice. "The town just up the road once held some sixty thousand people. That means there're probably some being kept alive, and fattened up . . . the survivors had a pretty good farming community going here. So we've got to find them. And we got another problem: this very well may be a group of people whose religious convictions forbid them from fighting. If that's the case, we'll cut them loose and then they're on their own. I'm not going to fuck around with a bunch of people who won't fight to save their own skins. Any of you who don't agree with that can carry your ass, or asses, and do it now."

The Rebels stood tight.

"OK, people. Take a breath while I get on the horn with General Raines. He's got to know about this scam of Hilton Logan's." He walked away muttering, "Hilton, you sissy-pants craphead, what have you done to us?"

303

Twenty-six

"Well, Ike," Ben spoke over the long miles. "I'm not going to blame Logan for this; he wasn't smart enough to dream this up by himself. And those who advised him probably thought they were doing the right thing, for the majority. We'll probably never know for sure."

Then Ben told him of his decision to go to Michigan.

"Ben, goddamnit! Can't you sit still anywhere for ten days?"

Ben laughed at his friend. "Ike, there is nothing for me to do here. I've just been told that after learning what happened to Hiram and his bunch, Lamumba and his crew quietly pulled out. I don't know where they went, and I don't really care, as long as they stay out of my way. Everything is kopasetic here. I'm not needed. I'll be pulling out at oh-four-hundred in the morning."

"All right, Ben. I've got to go root around in some cellars. You watch your ass, partner."

"Same to you, Ike. I'm leaving Joe in charge down here."

"Ten-four, Ben."

Ike broke it off.

Ben set about gathering equipment. He did not envy Ike and his Rebels the task that lay before them.

The sounds of gunfire rattled through the afternoon as the Rebels carefully and cautiously searched the darkness of the homes, usually finding the Night People huddled in stinking groups in the dark cellars.

It was not a pleasant job, and none of the Rebels enjoyed it a bit; the only thing that made it bearable was that there were no children found among the groups of Night People, and that fact puzzled them all.

Taking a break from the grisly job, Ike and Tina sat and talked.

"No kids, Ike."

"Yeah. These people are savage and cannibalistic, but they're smart, too. I think when the kids are of a certain age, they're farmed out; taken to a safe spot. These people know that at full strength we're only six thousand strong; and every time we establish an outpost, there goes another platoon. They know they outnumber us, Tina. And as we get closer to what I believe is their home base, New York City, we're finding them well armed, not just with sticks and stones and bows and arrows."

"Ike, what are we going to do when we find the kids?"

"God help me, Tina. I don't know. I think if they're young enough, we can take them and teach them . . . I hope," he added.

Neither one of them cared to pursue the other side of that issue any further. And each of them knew that the final decision would have to be made by Ben.

Tina's walkie talkie crackled. Ham. "Tina, we've located the prisoners. They were being held in a warehouse close to Lancaster, and the city is full of those . . . creatures."

"What kind of shape are the civilians in?" Ike asked.

"Rough. They were being force-fed, like geese."

"Leave the city for now. Bring the people to our position, Ham."

"Yes, sir."

It was as Ike had feared. The men and women were of that religious sect that would not fight. Ike paced up and down in front of the hundred or so men and women; the kids were being looked after by Rebel medics.

He kept looking at them, shaking his head and muttering to himself. Ike was not alone in his dilemma; no Rebel could understand any group of people who would not fight to stay alive.

"I don't know what to do with you people," he finally told them. "I'm over a barrel. You obviously are good people; hard-working. I can see that by your farms. But I don't have the time, the inclination, or the personnel to protect what is rightfully your responsibility."

"The Lord will provide, our faith will sustain us," a man said.

Ike disliked him immediately. Reminded him of one of those TV preachers of past years. Smug and sanctimonious . . . and thoroughly obnoxious. "The Lord will provide, huh?" He pointed toward the still-smoldering remains of the barn. "Then what happened to those people?"

"Obviously, their faith was not strong enough to sustain them."

"Suffer the little children," Ham muttered, just loud enough for Ike to hear.

"Yeah," Ike returned the muttering. "And that's what's got me all knotted up inside."

Ike walked over to Tina. From the look on her tanned face, he knew she felt the same as Ike about the just-rescued civilians. "You know what Ben is going to say if I ask him for an opinion, Tina?"

"Sure. I can just hear him. 'You're a big boy, General McGowan. You handle it.' "

"Yeah. Right. How many kids under, say, twelve are there?"

"About fifteen."

"I'm not going to leave the little children to be eaten by savages."

"I was hoping you'd say that."

Ham had joined them. "What about the city, general? Do we clean it out?"

Ike shook his head. "No. I'm not going to waste any more personnel on a group of people who won't fight for their own lives. Order all personnel to regroup; cease our searching for the remaining Night People."

"Yes, sir."

As Ike once more faced the lines of just-rescued civilians, the spokesman said, "The Lord provided you people, didn't He?"

"Only momentarily, partner. We're pulling out within the hour."

Panic crossed the man's face. "But you can't just *leave* us unprotected, sir."

"You got two hands don't you, mister? Pick up a gun and fight!"

"We cannot."

"You won't, you mean?"

The man shrugged. "Where are our children?"

"We're taking the younger ones with us."

"You can't do that!"

"There is one way to prevent that."

"How? We'll do anything."

Ike turned to a Rebel. "Give him your weapon."

The Rebel walked to the man and offered his M-16. The man shook his head. "I will not touch that thing."

"Let's go!" Ike shouted. "Mount up!"

"And you call yourself a Christian!" the man sneered at Ike.

"I call myself a realist, mister. And you all seem to be forgetting one message from the Bible: The Lord helps those who help themselves."

As Ben looked up at the star-filled sky, an old song came to mind; something about a starry, starry night. He couldn't remember much else about it; except that he'd always liked it. Couldn't remember who sang it. Fellow had a very pleasant-sounding voice.

His team was loading up, moving toward the planes, heavy with battle gear.

"Everyone present and accounted for, sir," James Riverson said.

"OK, James. Thanks. What's the latest word from Cecil?"

"They have engaged the enemy only sporadically. They've taken some of the pressure off those trapped, but it's turned into a cat-and-mouse game."

"Another dirty little war."

"Yes, sir."

The engines of the planes began coughing into life, making conversation difficult. Ben spotted Holly and Patrice and pointed toward a plane, motioning them to get on board.

"Good luck, sir!" Colonel Joe Williams shouted.

"Thanks, Joe. You take care."

"Yes, sir."

Ben walked across the tarmac and boarded, finding his canvas seat. The engineer handed him a headset and Ben plugged it in. Ben and James had been the last to board. "Ready when you are, captain," Ben said.

The interior lights flickered twice and the door was locked closed.

Ben looked across at Holly. "You ready for a little combat, doctor?"

"Not really. But whither thou goest and all that stuff."

Ben laughed at her. "That's what I like, Holly. A woman who knows her place."

She gave him the finger.

Twenty-seven

"How's it looking in your sector, Dan?" Cecil radioed.

"Buggers won't stand and fight, Cecil."

"Colonel West?"

"We've linked up with Colonel Rebet and Major Danjou, general. At your orders, we'll begin securing everything from Brown's Lake south to Murphy's Creek, and then push east."

"Are you in position, Dan?"

"Ten-four, Cecil."

"I'll be in position in a few hours, gentlemen. But we're going to be spread very thin. We desperately need someone at the easternmost sector. Hang on, a runner just handed me a message. Son of a bitch!" they all heard the usually calm Cecil yell.

"What's up, Cecil?" Dan radioed.

"Ben. He's on his way with two companies; left at oh-four-hundred this morning."

"You owe me a pound of tobacco, Dan," Colonel West said. "I told you!"

"Don't rub it in. Cecil? Shall we wait for Ben. His bunch can plug up that eastern hole."

"Ten-four. Let's hold what we've got. Ben should be here in about eight hours. As soon as they land, he'll start stretching south to north. We'll shove off at dawn."

Some of the spirit of adventure, of heading into the unknown had, for a time, left the Rebels under Ike's command. It would return, but for now, they were mostly silent as the miles slipped past. They all knew it was a hard thing to take people's children from them. But they all knew, at least in this case, it was best for the kids. What other alternative did the Rebels have? If the adults of the community wished to be eaten alive, that was their choice. It was unfair to ask a child to be devoured for the parents' philosophy.

And while the Rebels, to a person, disagreed with what the civilians they had rescued were doing, they also respected religious rights; that was just one of the things they were fighting for. Some of what the Rebels did was unpopular, and, had there been other laws, would have been illegal. But they were fighting to restore a nation, and somebody's rights were going to be stepped on for the good of the majority. As General Ike had said, "Tough times call for tough people."

That's just the way it was.

They had skirted Lancaster, and according to Tina and her Scouts, who were now ranging only five to six miles ahead of the convoy, the area before them was deserted . . . except for Night People, who they were sure were holed up in the small towns.

311

They made the run from Lancaster to Philadelphia without incident. Probably because they did not stop to investigate any of the towns they rumbled through.

"How about Philadelphia, Ike?" Tina radioed back from her point position.

"Any blockades, Tina?"

"Negative, Ike."

"Next exit, Tina, work north over to Interstate Seventy-six. Take it to the loop. That's . . . Two seventy-six. Stay on it until we cross the river. 'Bout . . . four or five miles past the river you'll hit the Jersey Turnpike. We're going to shut it down and make some plans just inside New Jersey."

"Ten-four, Ike."

The planes refueled at Memphis and Ben dropped off some much-needed supplies for the beleaguered little garrison defending the airport.

"Sure am glad to see you people," the lieutenant in charge told Ben. "It was hell for a time. Had to nap during the day and stay alert at night."

"Better now?"

"Much better, sir. With these Claymores you brought us, we'll all feel better. We're gradually pushing them back. We've cleared about a quarter of a mile in any direction, working in two-person teams during the day."

"You've all done a good job. I'm very proud of you all. Just hang tough until we get this mess cleared in Michigan, then you can be relieved."

"Yes, sir. I don't think they're going to bother us

much after today. We rounded up all the portable generators we could find; got about half of them working. No point in juicing wire or fences; they've learned to short them out. We found a whole bunch of floodlights. That pretty much keeps them away. Caution your team, general, not to walk anywhere except on the paved areas. The rest is heavily mined."

"Will do, Kitty. Thanks."

The planes were refueled and airborne in less than thirty minutes, the tanks topped off to the last drop; the next stop was lower Michigan.

The convoy pulled over in a rest area, Ike briefed his people. "All right, gang, listen up. I was going on north, but I changed my mind. I want to investigate some military bases: Fort Dix, McGuire Air Force Base, and the Naval Air Station. We might luck up and hit treasure. Tina, follow the route I marked on the map. Let's roll. If all goes right, we'll spend the night at Dix. Move out."

The bases were a mess, having been looted and picked over many times, but Ike knew there were treasures to be found . . . if one knew where to look, and Ike knew where to look. He began assigning teams.

"Sid, take your people and start piecing some trucks together. If I remember correctly, the motor pool is over yonder somewhere." He grinned. "You'll find it."

"Thanks a lot, general. What if we find Night People?"

"You got a choice, Sid. Kiss them or kill them."

"Thank you. The options are simply delightful."

And that broke whatever tension and depression might have remained after the other day's grisly work and the taking of the kids. Laughing, the Rebels gathered around Ike and Tina.

"We're going to find a lot of things that we can use, gang. Things that looters would bypass, thinking they couldn't use them. On all of these bases, we're going to have to blow the concrete and steel doors leading to the underground complex. It will be well worth the effort, believe me."

It came as a surprise to them all, and a very pleasant surprise, but they found no traces of the Night People. What they did find were long, dark corridors filled with numerous accouterments of and for war: radios, rifles and machine guns, hundreds of vases of ammo, rations, C and MREs, still good. They found spare parts for nearly everything imaginable. Nearly every base had such underground warehouses; it's just that the public didn't know about them.

They found underground fuel tanks filled with gasoline. They found portable generators, camp stoves, Tommy cookers, and Ranger stoves; boots by the hundreds of pairs, and uniforms by what looked like the thousands.

Ike stepped into one huge room and smiled. "Well, now, lookie here, lookie here!"

"What is it, Ike?" Tina asked.

"Old flame throwers. I want all of these loaded now. We can mix our own fuel. They'll come in handy."

She grinned. "I know what you're thinking, Ike."

"You bet. The Night Creepers ain't gonna like none of what these old babies can put out."

"You're a mean man, Ike McGowan."

"I ain't bad for a Mississippi white boy!"

Several black Rebels standing nearby groaned.

Ike walked away, grousing. "First man ain't got a chance around you rhythm aces!"

To an outsider, the bantering might have seemed tinged with ugly racism. It was not. That would not have been tolerated by anyone of any color in the Rebel ranks. It was offered good-naturedly, and taken the same way. That was not to say that Ben Raines had eradicated all racism within his army. But all were trying very hard, and it appeared to be working.

Only a fool makes the statement that he or she can look at someone of another color and not see it. Ben's philosophy was: See it all you want, just accept it for what it is—all Rebels bleed the same color.

Ike stood outside the tunnel entrance, his eyes looking north. Tina climbed out to join him and to get a breath of fresh air, for it was stale and musty in the tunnels.

"It's right up there, Tina. We'll exit off at Perth Amboy and hit Staten Island."

"Will I see the Statue of Liberty, Uncle Ike?"

"Yeah, from the north end of the island, if it's a clear day."

She was gazing at an old map of New York City and shaking her head.

Ike grinned at her, knowing, or at least suspecting,

315

what was going on in her head. "What's the matter, kid?"

"I can't even imagine what this place is like, Ike."

"It's a monster, kid. But one time it was a great place to visit. Lots of things to see and do."

"You ever live there, Ike?"

"*Hell,* no!"

She laughed aloud at the expression on his face. "Why, Ike?"

"Too damn many people. I was always glad to visit, but just as glad to get gone."

Ham joined them. "Sid's got some vehicles running, general. And we're loading up and tarping down the equipment you wanted loaded. We're welding the doors closed now."

"All right. Post guards and set up camp. We'll take it easy the rest of the day and relax some. Get me about a half-dozen big ol' boys, Ham. I want to go over the nomenclature of those flame throwers."

"Right away." He turned and walked off.

"I want everybody to learn how to operate these old M2A1s, Tina. But they're heavy old bastards. About seventy pounds."

"How do they work, Ike?"

"All it is is thickened fuel that's propelled by gas under pressure. They have a range of about forty yards. It's about the most effective thing we can use against the Night Creepies. Come on, let's get something to eat. I'm hungry!"

"You're always hungry. Would you like another ham sandwich? I saved some of the food that was prepared for us by . . . those people yesterday."

"No. Just the thought of who fixed it makes me

gag."

"Yeah? There is something else, too, Ike."

"What?"

"How do we know it was really ham?"

Ike glanced at her and belched. "I just lost my appetite!"

They refueled at a small airport in lower Michigan, and dropped off supplies for the small team of Rebels who had flown in and opened the strip. While there, Ben used the radio to reach Cecil.

"Be there in about two hours, Cec. How's it looking so far?"

"Not bad. So far, though, we've been fighting shadows."

"It's your show, Cec. Where do you want me and mine to set up?"

"Plug the gap between Dafter and Sault Ste. Marie, Ben. South to north. We'll start putting the squeeze on the outlaws at dawn. I'm giving you that sector because of the smallness of your team."

"Ten-four. Where are the others?"

Cecil brought him up to date.

"I'll start getting into position as soon as we land, Cec. What do you hear from Ike?"

"He's at Fort Dix, Ben."

"Son of a bitch! For a decade we've lived under a myth."

"Exciting, isn't it, Ben?"

"To say the least. So let's get this little foray wrapped up ASAP, buddy. I want to take a bite out of the Big Apple."

Cecil laughed over the miles. "You'll never change, Ben. If there's action, you just have to be there, don't you?"

"Damn right!"

"See you soon, Ben. Hawk out."

"Let's go, let's go!" Ben hollered, waving toward the planes. "It's kick-ass time!"

"Most impossible man I have ever encountered," Holly muttered to Patrice as they boarded the planes.

Patrice grinned at her, belting herself in. "But never a dull moment around him."

"That's what has me worried; I'm beginning to enjoy it!"

Twenty-eight

"Does anyone even know who the hell it is we're fighting?" Ben asked the small garrison of Rebels at the Chippewa Airport.

"Some warlord by the name of Monte. And he's a bad one, general. Just as bad as, maybe even worse than, Sam Hartline."

Ben looked at the sergeant. *"Nobody* is that rotten, sergeant."

"Beggin' your pardon, sir, but this one is. He's cut a path of terror wherever he goes. According to the intelligence we received from the Russian colonel, Rebet, and from Major Danjou, this Monte is working hand-in-glove with the Night People."

"How can that be?"

"Here's what we have on him, general. He was twenty years old when the Canadians put him in prison—life sentence—for multiple murders, rape, torture, the whole dirty ball of wax. A year later, the bombs came. He and a bunch of others busted out during the panic; they linked up with a bunch of cons from the States. They've been growing larger ever since."

They waited until a plane had landed and taxied away.

"This Monte, so it seems, has struck some sort of deal with the Night People. He supplies them with humans, for food, in exchange for the best-looking women they capture, and he's also agreed to protect them against any large-scale attack. He's just a real nice fellow, general."

"Certainly seems that way. Give me the rest of it, sergeant."

"He's also reported to have worked out some sort of nonaggression pact with Khansim. That was done only a few days before the people up here called for our help. And," the sergeant sighed, "rumor has it that he's got one hell of a detachment somewhere around the New York City area."

"Has Ike been notified?"

"No, sir. We can't get through to him. The frequencies are being jammed."

"Goddamnit! Now you're going to tell me this Monte's army is a hell of a lot bigger than we were first informed." Not a question.

"Yes, sir. By about several thousand."

Holly and Patrice were standing close by, listening. Patrice said, "I never heard of anyone called Monte, general. Where has this person been all the time?"

"A damn good question, captain." He looked at the sergeant.

The man shrugged his shoulders. "We can only guess, sir. Working somewhere between Toronto and Montreal, intelligence thinks. Just beginning his push west. It's said that Detroit is crawling with these creepy bastards."

"I should have destroyed the shells of cities," Ben muttered. "I had a plan to do just that and didn't put it into effect. This is what I get for it."

"You can't be expected to think of everything, general," Patrice told him. "We'll just have to take it one problem at a time."

Ben smiled, picking up on the "we." He glanced at her. "Yes, captain, we'll have to do that. James!"

"Yes, sir," the big sergeant major called.

"Start moving the people out, head them north."

"Yes, sir."

Ben looked toward the east. "Hang tough, Ike. Hang tough."

"It's no use, general," communications informed him. "I've heightened the antenna to where I should be able to talk to Mars. I can't break through. I think we're being jammed."

"Jammed! Who's doin' it?"

"I don't know, sir. Somebody with equipment that's just as sophisticated as ours."

"Well, now . . . that's just lovely." Ike motioned his XO over. "Tom, I think we're in for a fight. Have Ham stop welding those doors closed. We might need some of that equipment in there. Have the people start laying out perimeters; but don't make them so broad we can't defend them. I want mortars right here!" He pointed to the ground, then pointed out other emplacements. "I don't think there is anyplace for us to run. I think we boxed ourselves in. I did. Tell Sid to stop whatever he's doing and get his people working on bringing up those Bradley tanks we found. Just get them running somehow. Get your 40mm cannons up and placed. Fifties ringing the area. Claymores out. Move, Tom!"

He turned to Tina. "Get some of your Scouts out, Tina. But don't range too far off the post. Tell them quiet is the word and to keep their heads down."

"I'll take a team out now, Ike."

"No, you won't." He stopped her cold. "I need you here. We've got about three hundred and fifty people, Tina. And I got a hunch we're going to be heavily outnumbered. Take the south end. Move!"

She was off at a run, shouting orders.

Ike glanced at the sky. "Two, maybe three hours of good light left," he muttered. "Then all hell is gonna break loose." He grabbed a running Rebel and spun her around. "Lou, get me some boys to tote those flame throwers up here. I wanna start juicin' them up. Go, girl!"

Ike grabbed another Rebel. "Get several six-bys and tow those goddamned tanks into position, Lutty. All I need is the electrical system working so we can swing the turrets. Go, boy!"

Ike's walkie talkie crackled. "How many of these goddamned old bastard brutes do you want, general?" Sid asked.

"How many do you have down there, Sid?"

"Ten."

"All of them. Are the port-firing 5.56s still intact?"

"They're inside. I can mount 'em."

"Get on it. We'll stagger the tank positions to give the gunners something to shoot at."

"Ten-four. Rolling."

The twenty-ton behemoths were dragged into place while Sid's crews were still working on the giants, struggling to replace batteries and get the 500-horsepower Cummins VTA-903s running. The firepower of the tank was enormous; inside the tank were: 900 rounds of 25mm cannon shells, 3150 rounds of 7.62 ammo, 6720 rounds of 5.56 ammo, 7 TOW/Dragon missiles, and 3 LAW.

"You, Ham!" Ike yelled. "Get some trucks and round up all the fifty-five gallon drums you can find. We'll fill them with dirt and sand and gasoline; use them for light tonight. We can make Foo-gas bombs out of the others!"

"Yes, sir." And Ham was off and running.

"Sid! Check those turrets. They're supposed to traverse three hundred sixty degrees continuous."

Sid looked at him in disgust. "Yeah, I know, gcneral."

Ike grinned at him. "Sorry, Sid."

Sid grinned and gave Ike the thumbs-up signal, then disappeared into the tank.

Ike looked around him; things were beginning to take shape very quickly. If he set this up right—and he fully intended to do just that—his three hundred fifty-odd force would stand off a force five times greater.

And he had a hunch just about that many would be coming at them at full dark.

He began walking the egg-shaped perimeters. Bunkers were being quickly built, dug deep and fortified with anything the Rebels could find that would stop a round. Mortar pits were dug and were being bagged. Then he heard the sounds of tanks being snorted and farted into life. But they were not Bradleys. The tanks rounded a bend and Ike began smiling. Old Dusters. M-42s. He hadn't seen one in a long time. The Dusters rumbled to a halt.

"Where the hell did you find these?" Ike shouted over the rumble.

"Over yonder," Ham said, waving a hand. "We were looking for fifty-five gallon drums. There's eight more Dusters where these came from. I figure about half of them will run. I got an idea, general."

"Lay it on me."

Ham climbed down. He and Ike walked away from the rumbling. "We pull these Dusters well outside the perimeter area. God knows, there's enough ammo in the tunnels to refight the war. We tuck 'em in close to buildings, and if we're lucky, we can catch the enemy in a crossfire."

"All right, but strip some gun shields and mount some .60s up there. Good idea, Ham. Get moving on it."

Ike stopped a Rebel. "Pass the word, son: any ammo taken out of the tunnels be sure and check for corrosion. We can't afford any jammed-up weapons tonight."

"Yes, sir."

"Sir!" A runner from communications panted up. "The Scouts have advanced as far as the Interstate."

"What the fuck are they doin' rangin' that far out? Goddamnit, you tell them to get the fuck back here on this fuckin' reservation and to stay here!" Ike roared. "And you can quote me on that!"

"Yes, sir!"

The runner turned and Ike grabbed him by the

seat of his field pants, turning him around.

"Did you have any message for me other than that?"

"No, sir!"

"Fine. You tell the Scouts that the attack is probably not going to come from that direction, anyway. You tell the lookouts in the airport towers to start using Starlites at dusk and to keep an eye on the Garden State Parkway." He pointed. "That's over yonder, son."

"Yes, sir!"

"Move."

Ike grinned as the young Rebel sprinted toward the communications van. He had a hunch the attack—if one was coming, and he felt it was—would be coming at them through the old Naval Air Station. And there was no point in trying to lay Claymores anywhere other than in proximity to their perimeters. The post was just too damned big.

And Ike did not expect much in the way of artillery, with the exception of perhaps mortars; too much equipment was rusting around the post. The enemy—as yet, unknown—either did not know how to operate it, or felt it useless. Either way, that made them less formidable, and probably meant a ground attack . . . human waves.

He continued his walking of the garrison's perimeters, correcting this, okaying that, lending a hand here and there.

"I want every post to have plenty of flares," he ordered. "You people sure you know how to operate those flame-tossers? All right. Good. Looks like it's goin' to be a great night for a cookout."

He walked on, inspecting the machine-gun posts and the mortar pits. "Lots of Willie Peter, boys and girls." White Phosphorous. "One of the greatest mortar rounds ever invented. Give the Night Crawlers something to think about."

Ike knew he should eat, but he hadn't gotten his appetite back after that crack Tina had made about the sandwiches..

He rinsed his mouth out with water from his canteen. And that reminded him of fresh water. He looked around and spotted Tina, and walked over to her.

She noticed the canteen in his hand and said, "We're bringing up water now from the base supply. It tested all right. But we're still running it through purifiers just to be on the safe side. Heard my Scouts got a little carried away."

"I told them to carry their asses back here." He looked around him. "Light is going to be a problem tonight."

"I got an idea, Ike."

"Let's have it."

"If Sid's bunch could get that road-scraping equipment running, we could cut trenches in the earth around our perimeters. While that's being done, have some people start gathering up scrap wood and fill the trenches, then douse it with gasoline. It would serve two purposes."

"Right. Give us some light plus burn the shit out of the creepies. I'll get on it." He checked the sky. "Have the people start eating in shifts, Tina."

"Right." She smiled. "I'm kinda hungry myself." She dug in the pockets of her field pants and handed

Ike something wrapped in a paper napkin. "I'll share with you."

"Oh, gee, thanks, Tina. I guess I could eat. What is it?"

"A ham sandwich from down the road." Then she whirled and took off, running as fast as she could.

She still couldn't escape Ike's cussing.

Twenty-nine

"Traffic on the parkway," the lookouts reported from the airport towers. "And a hell of a lot of it, too."

"Get out of there and get the hell back here!" Ike ordered.

"Yes, sir! With pleasure."

"Ham?"

"Here."

"You got your Dusters in position?"

"Ten-four."

"Do not. Repeat: Do not fire until I give the order. You copy that?"

"Yes, sir."

"I don't want you people giving away your positions until you absolutely have to. Understand?"

"Yes, sir."

"All Dusters outside the perimeters test-crank your engines."

One failed.

"Sid!"

"I'm going, I'm going!"

"And don't run into a goddamned Claymore, either!" Ike ordered.

"I will absolutely, positively do my dead level best to comply with your orders, general, sir."

The problem solved, Sid and his crew raced back inside the compound and took up their positions.

Ike glanced at his watch: eight-thirty.

"It's going to be a motherfucker, people," he said, speaking into his walkie talkie. "No one gets an itchy finger; no one fires until I give the order. All posts acknowledge that."

All posts ten-foured the order. The garrison lay still and quiet. Now the sounds of the many vehicles could be heard. Then the engines were cut off. The night lay silent as death around the Rebels.

"There will be a mighty big bang any second now," Ike muttered. "Just a little closer, you creepy cannibals."

Claymores began sending out their deadly cargo of ball-bearings, shredding the life out of any in its KZ. Hideous screaming echoed in the night.

"Hold your fire," Ike whispered into his walkie talkie. "Hold your fire. Let them come on."

The point people of the still-unseen enemy ran into Claymores all around the little garrison's perimeters. The night rocked first with blasts and then with the howling and shrieking of the mauled and dying.

"They've reached the first of the ditches we scraped out, general," Ike was informed by a Rebel standing close to him, a headset covering her ears.

"Do not ignite the gasoline. Negative on firing the gasoline, Jersey. Pass it down."

She whispered the orders down the line and they were acknowledged.

The advancing enemy were so many, so thickly crowded together, the Rebels could now smell the stink of their unwashed bodies as they advanced closer.

"Yukk!" Ike whispered.

Jersey turned to Ike. "Major Broadhurst says they're so close he can see the snot dripping from their noses, general."

"Well, let's wipe their noses with some lead, Jersey. Outside tanks do not fire. Outside Dusters, Do Not Fire. All others . . . *fire!*"

The ground literally shook as the Rebels opened up with rifles, machine guns, rocket launchers, mortars, and 40mm cannon. The night was illuminated as Rebels released the thickened gas in the tanks of the flamethrowers, the fuel setting clothing on fire and sending robed men and women running into the night, moving, shrieking balls of fire, until they fell, their brains cooking, eyeballs turned to liquid, running down charred faces. Burning dots littered the battleground, allowing the Rebels to see the hundreds of men and women who faced them outside the smoky perimeters.

"Not yet, Ham," Ike said into his walkie talkie. "We'll save you people until last. Acknowledge."

"Ten-four," Ham whispered. "Some crews are reporting Night People crawling all over their Dusters. They're unaware anyone is inside."

"Ten-four. Stand tough, Duster crews."

Beside him, Little Jersey, all four feet, ten inches of her, stood steady as a rock, relaying orders and receiving acknowledgments, passing them on to Ike.

Ike grinned down at her. "Hangin' in, Jersey?" he

shouted over the din of battle.

"It's better than a kick in the ass, sir!" she returned the shout, grinning.

Ike laughed, the sound lost amid the barrage.

Jersey listened for a moment, then turned to Ike, shouting in his ear, "Ham reports a larger force moving up, sir. Not Night People. Ham reckons battalion size."

"What type of weapons, Jersey?"

She asked. Ike bent down so she could reach his ear. "Light weapons and machine guns, sir. None of the Duster crews report any sign of mortars or artillery."

"Tell Ham to crank up and fire when he's ready, Jersey. See if they can drive them toward us."

"Yes, sir."

The rattle of twin-mounted .60s joined the head-splitting din. Twin 40mm guns added their crashing to the night battle.

"Heads down in the compound until the Dusters turn the enemy toward us, Jersey."

She nodded and relayed the orders.

The retreating Night People ran into the advancing forces, creating havoc in the night.

"Flares up!" Ike ordered.

The night turned surreal with starbursts.

"Compound snipers pick your targets."

Jersey relayed the orders.

"Mortar crews adjust. Free-fire past the Dusters."

Those who were coming up behind the Dusters felt the sting and lash of Willie Peter rounds as they exploded in a shower of flesh-searing shards.

"Bradleys pick up the gap between the Dusters,"

Ike ordered. "Keep the sky bright, flare crews."

Jersey relayed the orders and the night was white-bright as the flares exploded, 25mm cannon fire and 7.62 machine gun fire roaring and hammering and disintegrating the now-confused and disoriented enemy, who found they had no place to run.

With the 25mm cannon ten feet off the ground, the Bradley's gunners were able to pinpoint fire over the heads of those in the compound and literally blow the enemy to bloody rags of once-human beings.

Outside the compound, in the darker areas of the immediate post, but well outside of the free-fire zone, the crews of the Dusters wheeled and clanked and crushed to death any enemy who happened to be unlucky enough to come into view in the flare-filled night. The massive steel treads mangled and mauled human flesh, leaving bloody indentations in the ground, splattered with bits of human flesh and bone.

"They're running, general!" Ham radioed to Jersey. "Do we pursue?"

"Only for a short distance," Ike ordered. "They'll be back as soon as they regroup and map out a plan. Finish off what you can and then get back inside the trenches."

"Ten-four."

"Cease firing!" Ike yelled. "Cease firing!"

The firing gradually waned into silence.

"Machine gunners, rake those piles of wounded. Scraper operators, stand by to push the bodies into the trenches and douse with gasoline; they'll give us a few more minutes of light when we need it."

"Disarm the Claymores at compound point, Jersey. Remine outside the trenches. Leave the Dusters room to get back."

"Yes, sir."

"Check for wounded, Jersey."

Ten hit, none seriously.

Ike patted a Rebel on the shoulder. "Start here. Every other Rebel stand down for fifteen minutes. If you want to smoke, move back from the main perimeter. Pass it along. Let's go, Jersey."

The little Rebel with the backpack radio walked with Ike as he made his way through the shell-casing-littered compound.

Ike stopped by Major Tom Broadhurst's position. "Did you wipe their noses, Tom?"

"Damn sure did, Ike!"

Ike patted him on the shoulder and walked on, coming to Tina's position. He looked at the body-littered field in front of her position. Stinking bodies were piled up like scattered firewood. "You a mean motor-scooter, kid."

"I don't like these people, Uncle Ike."

"No kidding! I never would have guessed."

Ike and Jersey circled the camp, stopping every few meters to chat with his people. Ham and his Dusters were clanking back into the outer compound, wheeling around, guns facing the darkness.

The treads were dark and slick with blood.

The scrapers were shoving the bodies into the trenches around the outer edges, touching the dark unknown. Following the earth-moving equipment were Rebels with containers of gasoline, dousing the bodies that were piled up on the scrap wood in the trenches.

Ike turned to Jersey and the little Rebel held up a small hand, signaling for silence as she listened intently through her earphones. She looked up at Ike.

"What's up, Jersey?"

"The jamming has stopped, Ike. I think we can get through now."

"How many casualties did you sustain, Ike?" Ben asked.

"Ten. None serious. We lucked out, Ben; caught them by surprise and really creamed them. Hit them hard. I'd guess we offed between six hundred and seven hundred fifty. I think they're through for this night."

"I think I wasted my time coming up here, Ike. Scouts report this Monte person's troops are pulling out as quickly as they can slip through. I'm thinking, Ike, that this was a diversion action to suck us up here so we wouldn't be able to come to your rescue. And I'll be willing to bet you a bag of tobacco that this Joe MacKintosh does not exist. It was just reported to me that the area where they were supposed to be is deserted. How about them apples, buddy!"

"Yeah, it looks like you've been had. What's next, Ben?"

"Can you hold, Ike?"

"For how long, Ben?"

"Until I can get some people on a plane and get over there. How long will it take you to clear a runway?"

"Give us a couple of days at least, Ben. The runways looked pretty bad to me. But we really haven't had the time to check them out."

"Ten-four to that, Ike. I've got to get Chase up here, anyway. I promised the old goat we'd enter New York City together."

"Ben? I think we'd better save Manhattan for last. We'd be defeating our purpose to go in there first. We'd better secure the areas surrounding it first."

"All right, Ike. Tighten up your hold at Dix tomorrow and then get on the runways."

"That's ten-four, Ben. You want a suggestion?"

"Have at it."

"We're gonna need a lot of equipment, Ben. And I mean a *lot* of equipment."

"I see what you're getting at, Ike. All right. I'll start the trucks rolling ASAP. My people report lots of vehicles in pretty good shape around here. So we'll start getting them in good order and drive over to the Big Apple. I think this operation up here is nothing more than a fart in the wind."

"Maybe your reputation scared them off, Ben."

"Sure, Ike, sure."

"And everything is settled with Hiram and his rednecks?"

"Hiram is dead."

"I figured it was coming to that. You should have done it twenty years ago."

"It wouldn't have been legal then. Moral, probably, but not legal. Hang on, here's a runner."

When Ben came back on, his voice was filled with disgust. "It's over up here, Ike. Dan and the Canadian troops report the area is clear. Monte's people bugged out."

"Which direction, Ben?"

"They slipped across at Sault Ste. Marie and were reported heading east, staying in Canada."

"You know where they're heading."

"Sure. New York. Hang tough, Ike. We're on the way."

"Shark out."

Ben turned to Holly. "Get some sleep. We've got a long haul, starting in the morning."

"Where to and how?"

"We're driving. I'm going to see if we can pull anything out of the ashes of New York City."

Thirty

There was no containing Ben when he had the itch to travel, as Holly found out several hours before dawn the next morning.

He rudely shook her awake.

She looked at him. "What's the matter?"

"Nothing. We'll be pulling out in half an hour. Move it."

"What time is it?"

"Three."

"In the *morning!*"

"Yes. Quit your bitching. You wanted to come along, remember?"

"It's cold, Ben!"

"So get up and move around and you won't be so cold. Shake a leg, lady—time's a-wasting!"

Outside, Ben started hollering for his team. A group of mechanics—who, fortunately for them, were not going with Ben's team east—had worked all night long getting Jeeps and trucks ready to roll. They were still fine-tuning engines when Ben started hollering, rousing the camp.

"Get them up and moving, James! We pull out in half an hour. Let's go, let's go, let's go!"

"The person is a madman!" Holly bitched, lacing up her boots.

Cecil came running out of his tent, his M-16 at the ready. He relaxed when he saw Ben. "Good God, Ben!" he called. "When is the last time you voluntarily slept past dawn?"

"I can't remember, Cec. I'm taking my team and half of Dan's group, including Dan. You and Colonel West wrap things up here and come on behind us."

Dan came staggering up, rubbing his eyes. "My word. What a perfectly ghastly hour for a human to arise from sleep."

Ben grinned at him. "We pull out in half an hour. So get your tea in your belly and the lead out of your ass, Dan."

"I shall be functioning as smoothly as a well-oiled machine in ten minutes, general!"

"I knew I could count on you, Dan." He stepped back and eyeballed the Englishman. "My, but you do cut a dashing figure in your long handles."

Dan drew himself up and with as much dignity as he could muster, did an about-face and marched off toward his tent.

"Your backflap's open, Dan!" Cecil called.

Dan reached around, jerked up the flap, and quick-stepped to his tent.

Riding in a Jeep, crossing the Straits of Mackinac, with Lake Huron to the east and Lake Michigan to the west, Holly really started bitching about the cold.

"I'm cold! I'm hungry! I want some coffee! And why in the *hell* can't you drive a pickup truck like a normal human being, Ben Raines?"

"Are you uncomfortable, Ms. Allardt? Is that what you're trying to tell me?"

She kicked something that was rattling around on the floorboards. "What is that?"

"That's a thermos of coffee, Holly. I thought you might like some. And pour me a cup, too, will you?"

A hundred and fifty miles after pulling out from the old airport, Ben ordered the convoy pulled over at an old National Guard base, outside of Grayling.

"Breakfast time, boys and girls!" he called. "Those wonderful MREs. James, first bunch to finish eating, send them into that old Guard camp; see if they can find anything worth salvaging."

"Yes, sir."

He sat down beside Holly and grinned at her. "All comfy now?"

"Raines, you are possessed, you know that? Can you ever just sit still and relax?"

"Too much to do, Holly. And not nearly enough time to get it all done."

"And when it's all done, Ben? . . ."

"It never will be finished. Not in my lifetime. In case you haven't noticed, dear, while I am not yet in the twilight of my years, I ain't no spring chicken."

"You're still a few years away from a wheelchair, Raines," she said drily, stirring some glop in a cup and eating it. "And I hesitate to ask exactly what this is I'm eating."

Ben picked up the empty wrapper. "Well, it was packaged in 1985."

"This stuff is seventeen years old, Ben!"

339

"Relax. They'll keep practically forever. I've eaten rations that were packed back during the Korean War. They were OK, except for those green eggs."

She put down her cup and stared at him. "Green eggs!"

"They weren't bad as long as you kept your eyes closed."

Tina walked up to Ike, her hands in her pockets. "If you come out with another ham sandwich," Ike warned, "I swear I'm gonna belt you!"

She laughed at him and pulled her hands out, empty. "Our teams have gone in all directions, Ike. No sign of any Night People. They're ten miles outside the post now, in all directions. How far do you want them to range out?"

"That's far enough. I think they've pulled back into the suburbs and the city. By the way, your dad pulled out of upper Michagan at oh-three-thirty today."

"How far is it from there to here, Ike?"

" 'Bout a thousand miles, give or take a hundred Knowin' Ben, he'll be pushin' it hard."

"Dr. Chase and his people?"

"They'll be up in about a week, Lamar said. Your brother is doing fine, by the way."

She nodded and jerked her thumb. "Those bodies are beginning to stink, Ike."

"Burn 'em. Let's shift positions to the airfield."

"Desolate," Holly murmured. "Ben, where are the

340

people?"

They were heading south on Interstate 75, just north of Bay City. "I don't know, Holly. It's bothering me, too. There should have been survivors in this arca. I'm guessing this Monte person — and probably the Night People — picked this area clean."

She shuddered.

"For food."

"I get the picture, Ben!"

"Probably hold them prisoner and fatten them up like hogs."

"All right, awready!"

"Point to Eagle," Ben's radio crackled.

"Eagle. Go ahead."

"Smoke from fires in Bay City, Eagle. You want us to check it out?"

"Ten-fifty. Wait for us, Point."

The people ran when they spotted Ben and his Rebels, and no amount of hollering and calling out that they were friendly would slow them down.

"Scared," Ben said. "Spooky of any strangers. I suppose it's understandable."

"You *suppose?*" Holly asked.

"Holly, in every other home you can see, stretching either way from here to both coasts, there is at least one gun of some sort. The military bases are littered with weapons. They're rusting, many of them. These people could have become organized and armed. Why they didn't, or wouldn't, remains one of the great mysteries to me."

"Well . . . we have to help them, Ben."

Ben picked up his mic and ordered the Scouts out. He put the Jeep into gear and rolled on, heading back to Interstate 75.

"Where are you going, Ben?"

"I help those who help themselves, Holly. If they'll just help themselves a little bit, I'll help them a lot. But these people are just standing around, waiting for somebody to do it all for them; waiting to die at the hands of warlords or outlaws, or what-have-you. If you tried to give one of them an order that you felt might save their lives, they'd stiff their necks and proclaim, 'I ain't takin' no orders from nobody.' To hell with them, Holly. There are too many fine, decent people out there in the ashes who want help for me to screw around with a bunch of losers."

She didn't say another word to him until they were on the outskirts of Saginaw.

"Are we stopping here, Ben?"

"You have to go to the bathroom?"

She did her best to wither him with a glance. It had no effect on Ben. "You know what I mean, Ben."

"No, Holly. We are not stopping."

She muttered something that sounded extremely vulgar.

The smell emanating from Flint told them all that to enter the city would be useless. The smell told them the place was crawling with Night People.

An hour passed in silence, the rush of the wind flapping the canvas top and sides of the Jeep the only noise. As they drew closer to Detroit, the land became more desolate; one could practically feel the human void; the emptiness of human life.

"We're going to have two choices." Ben broke the silence. "We're either going to have to go into the cities and kill them during the day, while they sleep, or we're going to have to napalm the cities and drive them out and shoot them." Without waiting for Holly to reply, Ben picked up the mic. "Stay on the Interstate heading dead south. No one leaves the convoy. Let's just get the hell out of this state."

About an hour before dark, Ben ordered the convoy to pull over and make camp. They were about twenty miles from the Ohio line. Dan walked up to Ben and Holly.

"General, they have to have left the cities and set up in the country. I simply refuse to believe that all the survivors are dead."

"It is my fervent hope that you are correct Dan. If you're not, we're facing total annihilation. There is no way a force as small as ours could ever hope to cope with what appears to be hundreds of thousands of these people. It's mind-boggling."

"Ben," Holly said, looking first at Dan and then at Ben. "As a doctor I've got to say that I find it impossible to believe that chemicals or radiation — what little there was of it — could have killed thousand of these people. I just do not accept it."

"Nor do I, Holly."

"Then? . . ."

"There is no doubt they have good communications. As good as ours. That means the ability to communicate around the world, right, Dan?"

"It would seem that way."

"So why didn't our communications people pick up any of their traffic?"

"Hard directional?"

"Maybe. But in what direction?"

Dan was thoughtful for a moment. "East, to the European countries."

"Exactly. We know for a fact that there is a small radiation belt circling high above us that tears up radio communications, right?"

"That is correct."

"And it doesn't always stay in the same place, right?"

"Atmospheric conditions affect it. I think the belt remains pretty much stationary. Yes. I see what you're getting at. But, general, that would suggest a very high level of intelligence on the part of these . . . cannibals."

"Yes. But why shouldn't some of them have been engineers, scientists, whatever, before the war?"

"Yes." The Englishman spoke softly. "Indeed. Why not?"

"And what part of the world took the hardest hits of radiation?"

"Europe, of course." Dan stroked his pencil-thin moustache. "General, are you suggesting that there might have been some sort of flotilla from Europe?"

"It's one answer."

Dan leaned against a fender of a truck, sipping at his late afternoon tea. "It's certainly something to think about. And we must not overlook the possibility of recruits, too."

"Yes."

Holly was horrified. "You mean . . . you're suggesting that *normal* people would voluntarily join something this . . . this hideous?"

"We weren't that far removed from barbarism, Holly," Ben told her. "Besides, total despair and no

344

hope for the future will drive many into doing things that in a civilized, ordered world would be unthinkable to them."

"That's monstrous!"

"Yes. But I'm afraid it's also reality. Dan, double the guards. Keep fires burning all night. Tell the sentries to call out only once for recognition, then open fire."

"Yes, sir."

"It's going to be a long night," Holly said, looking around her at the gathering pockets of darkness dotting the land.

"You're safe. Are you beginning to understand why I preach organization and unity and strength?"

"Of course. I always have, Ben. But there are many people who don't like that type of society. And that is their right. Or do you disagree with that, too?"

"Certainly not. But do you know where many of those types are?"

"I'm sure you'll tell me; not that I really want to know."

"Being eaten alive because of their stubbornness." He held out a can. "Care for some beef stew, Holly?"

Thirty-one

The Night People made their presence known during the gloom, but they were cautious not to get too close to the Rebel encampment; not after a group of them stepped in front of a Claymore and were spread all over the area, in dripping chunks and pieces of raw meat. After that, the Night People pulled back and stayed far from the camp. Later, sentries would report that several hours before the first fingers of dawn began spreading silver over the land, the Night People began withdrawing, slipping away, back to their dens of darkness to sleep away the dreaded light.

The Rebels ate a quick breakfast and mounted up. All wanted to be away from that place.

They skirted Toledo and Ben pulled the convoy over at a junction, waving Dan up to him.

"We're going to avoid the cities, Dan. We've got to find out where the people have gone; besides into the stomachs of the Night People."

"You do turn an eloquent phrase, general."

"Thank you. It's going to be a meandering route.

346

But we're going to check out the small towns. We'll take Highway Twenty over to Norwalk, there we'll pick up Eighteen; take it to the Interstate. Pick up the Turnpike; follow that to Youngstown. From there, if all goes right, we'll pick up Eighty and take it all the way across. Advise your Scouts and have them move out. Stay ten miles ahead of the main columns and keep in radio contact."

"Yes, sir."

They checked the towns out as they came to them. Nothing. Nothing. Nothing. Nothing. It became a game to the Rebels: who would spot the first living being.

But none were found.

Outside of Norwalk, Ben pulled the convoy over and walked back to Dan.

"Let's add it up, Dan; see what we can come up with. What have you noticed?"

"Brass. Lots of empty brass. The citizens aren't taking it quietly. They're fighting back and doing a pretty good job of it."

"That's what I think. I think they've moved south; away from the lake, away from the cities. Down in the central part of the state. Communications reports some radio traffic, in code, coming from that area."

"Have they broken the code?"

"Oh, yes. They're wondering who we are; whether we're part of Monte's bunch. We'll noon here and try to make contact with them. Tell the people to stand down and relax. Guards out."

"Yes, sir."

But the people refused to respond to the Rebels'

calls. Finally, exasperated, Ben took the mic.

"This is General Ben Raines. I'm with a contingent of Rebels near Norwalk. I am not asking you to give away your position; just advising you who we are and if you are in need of anything. Will you please respond to this?"

Ben waited; tried again. This time he got a reply.

"Ben Raines is dead."

"Ben Raines is not dead. I assure you I am alive and well. Will you give me some travel instructions?"

"What do you want?"

"Is the Interstate between Cleveland and Akron safe for travel?"

"Negative. Skirt south of Akron. And take the loop around Massillon and Canton. Are you really Ben Raines?"

"Yes. Do you people need anything?"

There was a long pause. "Yes. Some help."

"In what form?"

"We've got to have someone help us with security; we're farmers and businessmen, not soldiers."

"Give me your twenty and I'll send a team down to assist you."

"Negative. We'll meet you in Ashland. That's southeast of your position."

Ben looked at Dan. "We're going to have to change routes anyway. Mount them up, Dan."

They were a haggard-looking group of people, but they were well armed and the weapons were well cared for.

The leader of the group stared hard at Ben. "By God! You're really Ben Raines!"

"Alive and well." Ben shook his hand. "Now bring

me up to date on what's been happening around here."

Using the scrapers, Ike's Rebels soon had a runway cleared at the old military base. Then the Rebels set about crushing stone to fill in the potholes that had developed over the long years of disuse.

Ike had been sending teams out, five to a team, to start cleaning out the immediate area around the old reservation . . . . cleaning it out of whatever creepies might be holed up during the day waiting to prowl at night.

Surprisingly, the teams had found very few of the Night People. Upon questioning them, Ike learned they lived in the cities, mainly, coming out several times a week to hunt for food. The ones who had been captured had not been careful of the time, the daylight trapping them, forcing them to seek whatever dark shelter they could find.

"What's the number in the city?" Ike had asked.

But the Night People would only smile, the evil shining through their eyes.

Ike had ordered them shot.

"Inspect their bodies," he ordered.

No traces of radiation could be found anywhere on the two men. Their eyes were normal. Dr. Ling and his people did autopsies on the bodies. No abnormalities could be found.

"Son of a bitch!" Ike cussed, heading for the communications building.

* * *

"Yes, I had reached that conclusion, Ike," Ben said. "There were just too damn many of them for all of them to have been affected by the blasts. Now what?"

"We wait for you, Ben. Then we hit the suburbs and start cleaning them out."

"Going to be autumn in New York soon, old buddy," Ben said with a smile.

"No play on words intended, though." Ike's voice crackled through the speaker.

Holly, standing nearby, did not have the foggiest idea what the men were talking about.

"An old song, doctor." Dan brought her up to date.

"What's your location, Ben."

"Just preparing to pull out of Ashland, Ohio. I've left a squad of Rebels with a local resistance group. They're heading down to Mansfield and will begin establishment of an outpost."

"Ten-four, Ben. Talked with Chase; Buddy is getting stronger by the hour. But he's going to take a while recovering."

"Ten-four, Ike. See you in a couple of days. Eagle out."

Ben and his people rolled eastward, making camp that night just to the west of the Pennsylvania line and a few miles south of the Pennsylvania Turnpike. At dawn, they began a gradual swing to the north and linked up with Interstate 80. They would take that all the way into Ike's position.

Ben used a series of country roads, most of them in deplorable shape, which slowed the convoy down to a mere crawl. Finally, after a series of frustrating detours, Ben linked up with the Interstate just west of the Allegheny River and the convoy began to move out. Smartly, as Dan would say. They had gone only a few miles when the forward Scouts reported a roadblock.

Ben, with Holly by his side, pulled up to the roadblock within minutes after receiving the message.

"Scouts back," he called.

"What is it, Ben?" Holly asked.

"I don't know. I don't like it. I just don't like it."

"You have anything of substance to base that on, Ben?"

"A gut hunch."

"General!" a Scout called. "That sucker is made out of *steel,* carefully fitted and welded together, too. It'd take a hell of a bang to move that."

"Are you going to blow it, Ben?"

"No. It isn't worth the risk involved. The thing might be wired to blow if tampered with." He picked up his mic and gave the orders for the convoy to turn around, head back to the first exit.

"North or south, general?" Dan asked.

Ben hesitated. A strange smile flitted over his lips. He checked his maps. "North," he radioed. "And head's up, people. I think I know why the blockade."

"Why?" Holly asked.

"It's a trap. And we're going to just bust the hell out of it."

Ben picked up his mic. "All units to scramble frequency." He waited until they had time to change frequencies. "I have a hunch we're about to hit some outlaws or warlords, people. I think that's why the barricade. Scouts, you should be coming up on the town now. What do you see?"

"Be there in about two minutes, general. But you're right, I think," the lead Scout reported back. "Seeing lots of vehicles on both sides of the road. OK, general, we've got the town in sight; some pretty hairy-looking people lining the streets. Orders?"

"Stop right there. Let us catch up."

Ben passed the convoy and took the lead, despite Dan's frantic callings to stay back and let others handle it.

Dan and James and several Jeeps with rear-mounted .50s and twin-mounted .60s raced to catch up with Ben. Holly was holding on for dear life; she was still holding on as Ben slid to a stop in front of what used to be some sort of general store. He looked at a character lounging on the porch of the building. A brute of a man, wearing a black leather jacket with the sleeves cut off, dirty jeans, and heavy boots. His massive arms were covered with tattoos.

Ben and the brute sat and stared at each other. The brute was not too happy to see all the Rebels coming up fast behind Ben. His piggy eyes noted the professional manner in which the Rebels swung their vehicles, covering all sides of the street.

Ben stepped out of the Jeep, his Thompson in his hand, off safety, on full auto. He stood by the Jeep.

"Whut you wont, soldier-boy?" Brute asked. There was an M-16 lying on the porch floor, right side.

"A bit of civility would be nice, don't you think?"

"Haw?"

352

"Good morning to you. Now you say good morning to me."

"You crazy, boy!"

Ben lifted his Thompson, the muzzle pointed squarely at the brute's chest. "Say good morning, sir."

"Ah . . ." Brute rumbled. "Good mornin', sir."

Ben lowered the muzzle. "That's better. Did you put that barricade on the Interstate bridge?"

"Shore did."

"Why?"

The question seemed to confuse the human animal. " 'Cause I wanted to, that's why."

"Not good enough." Ben was approached by a Rebel. He whispered in Ben's ear. "Thank you. Take a team and free the prisoners."

"Yes, sir."

"Hey, now!" Brute hollered. "Whut you people gonna do?"

"Free all the men and women you're holding for whatever reason. And while we're doing that, you may send some people out to clear the Interstate."

"I ain't doin' jack-shit!" Brute bluntly informed Ben. His hand dropped carelessly down, closer to the M-16. " 'Em people is ourn. Slaves is legal now."

"By whose orders?"

"There ain't no one givin' no orders no more, Mister-Whoever-in-the-Hell you is."

Ben smiled thinly. "I do so hate to resort to violence, lard-ass. Ruins my entire day."

"Sure it does," Holly muttered. She had gotten out of the Jeep and had the vehicle between her and Ben and the brute. She was ready to drop to the street the instant the shooting started.

"Who you callin' lard-ass?"

"You, whale-butt. Now send some people out to clear the Interstate."

Brute's face darkened with hate and rage as streams of people began moving up the street. They were ragged and dirty and all showed signs of having been physically abused.

"Question them, Dan," Ben said. He cut his eyes back to Brute. The man wasn't sure exactly what he should do next. He knew only that he wasn't gonna sit still and let this soldier-boy free his slaves.

"Mister, you ain't got no right to come in here and throw your weight around. I . . ."

"Shut up!" Ben told him. "We can do this easy or hard. It's up to you."

Dan stepped up to Ben's side. "The women have all been raped repeatedly and sodomized. So have the men prisoners," he added, disgust in his voice.

"Stand ready, Dan," Ben returned the whisper. "See the outlaws on the second story of the buildings?"

"Oh, yes. I've alerted my people."

"Whut you two a-whisperin' about?" Brute hollered, his hand moving closer to the M-16 on the porch floor.

"We were discussing the Emancipation Proclamation, asshole," Ben told him, his eyes studying the man. About forty, Ben guessed. Old enough to have completed all types of schools. And no reason to be what he had become. "What have you had the prisoners doing?"

Brute grinned. "We fuck the women—and sometimes the men — and use them in the fields, to grow our food, wash our vehicles and clothes, and take care of the houses . . . if 'at's any of your goddamn business."

"And if they refuse to become your slaves? . . ." Ben asked.

Again, Brute grinned. "We strip 'em naked and drop 'em in the hog pens. 'At 'ere's good fun."

"You are one sorry excuse for a human being. As a matter of fact, I'm offended by having to share the same air with you."

"Whut's 'at mean!"

"It means I'm going to kill you." Ben's voice was low-pitched.

"Whut's your name, sucker?" Brute asked, his right hand only inches from the M-16.

"Ben Raines."

Screaming, Brute jerked up the M-16. Ben's Thompson chugged and spat a death song, the big .45 caliber slugs knocking Brute out of his chair, a bloody line of holes working left to right, from his hip to his jaw, the slugs tearing away the lower part of the man's face; teeth bounced and rolled on the porch floor.

Brute lay on his back and pissed his jeans as he died, his final breath the greatest act he had ever done for society.

Over the hammering of heavy machine guns from the Rebels, Ben muttered, "You and Hiram have a good time, Brute. You two deserve each other."

The machine guns mounted on the Rebel vehicles made quick work of the outlaws who thought they had gone undetected on the second floors of the town's business district. Teams of Rebels went building to building, using grenades to clean out what was left of the outlaw gang. Some forty-odd surrendered, most of them in shock at the swiftness of what had gone down.

Ben lined them up and ordered them under heavy guard.

Holly had crawled under the Jeep. It took Ben a few minutes to find her. He squatted down and peered under the vehicle, smiling at the doctor. "Did you decide to take a short nap, Holly?"

"Raines, I wish you would warn me before you decide to start a damned war!" Her face was greasy and her hair disheveled.

Laughing, Ben helped her out and brushed her off. "You haven't seen a war yet, Holly. This was just a little exercise, that's all."

She glared at him and looked at the rows of outlaws, their hands on the tops of their heads, fingers interlaced. 'What are you going to do with them, Ben."

"One good deed deserves another, Holly. You'll see. You and the medics set up a hospital; check out the former prisoners. I'm going to prowl around some." He walked off, humming an old song. Holly didn't believe she'd ever heard it.

"The Good, The Bad, The Ugly."

Thirty-two

Ben walked the town, a squad of Rebels split up, some in front of him, some behind him. He paid them no attention; he was used to it. Holly and the Rebel medics had set up shop in an old drug store. At her insistence, she was patching up the wounded outlaws. Ben had shrugged; her option, if she wanted to waste her time on trash.

Ben and his bodyguards had found no more outlaws, although all had heard the sounds of racing motors as some carried their asses out of there when the shooting started and it was soon evident the outlaws would lose. Typical trash-action. In a mob, surrounded by their buddies, they're all bluster and toughness; put them by themselves and their true colors are soon flying. Yellow.

Back on the main street, Ben told Dan, "We'll spend the night here. What about the prisoners you've talked with?"

"They're a pretty spunky bunch, general. I approached them about an outpost system and they jumped at it. It would be my suggestion that we move them up the road to the town of Clarion."

"Bigger town than this?"

"Much bigger. Some of those who were held prisoner told me that there is a group there who are pretty damned tough. Edgar. . . ."

"Who?"

Dan smiled. "The fat warlord you offed."

"Oh."

"Edgar's bunch has never been able to whip them. They've got a good organization of solid, steady men and women. With schools, general."

"My kind of people, Dan."

"How about the outlaws we captured, general?"

Ben looked at him and walked off.

Dan smiled. "Right-oh, general."

The Rebels buried the outlaws in a mass grave, and with what had once been county earth-moving equipment, scooped dirt over them. Ben had sent Holly and a detachment on to Clarion before the last of the outlaws joined Edgar and the others. He would tell her . . . if she ever asked him. But he doubted she ever would.

Ben had met the people of Clarion. Even before meeting them, he knew he had found a group of people whose ideas matched his own. Coming into the town, he noted the streets were all clean, with no shacks of burned-out buildings. The lawns were well-tended and everyone had a large garden, not all the people growing the same thing. Shops were open, and the barter system was back in play.

Ben asked for volunteers from his ranks, and a full squad stepped out. They would stay with the townspeople for a time, helping them rearm and set up defenses. And learn the Rebel way of meting out justice.

Ben and his Rebels pulled out the next morning, heading east on Interstate 80. Ben had asked the leader of the several hundred men and women and kids where the next large gathering of people was. The man had smiled sadly.

"No where near here, general. I heard there was one over around Williamsport, but I can't be sure of that. And it's a long, dangerous trip over there."

"We'll check it out and report back to you. Good luck."

The Rebels found several hundred people in Williamsport, but they were nothing like the bunch back in Clarion. What they found was a bunch of losers, with no organization, no signs of progress, and leaderless. They were a sullen, dirty bunch, with no thought for the future, living hand to mouth, day to day.

Ben ordered the kids under thirteen rounded up; he had heard that south of there, around Milton, a group had settled in and were doing wonders. They would take the kids and see if they could find a home for them there.

"We glad to be rid of the little squallin' fuckers," a woman told Ben.

Ben resisted an urge to shoot her.

Milton was almost a carbon copy of Clarion, and the men and women said they would be happy to take the kids and raise them decently. And they were, to a person, after a town meeting, very receptive to the suggestion of becoming a part of the outpost system. Once more, a small team of Rebels, all volunteers, all single, were left behind when Ben and his people pulled out the next morning.

They were slightly less than two hundred miles from Ike's position when Ben called a halt and ordered camp set up for the night.

Ben radioed Ike that evening. "Give me a safe route to your position, Ike."

"Come in east of Trenton, Ben. You're going to have to wind around some. Planes have begun landing here. And Chase is waiting for you. So is Cecil; they flew in last evening. I'll brief you when you get here."

"See you about noon tomorrow, Ike."

Before dusk, Ben walked the camp, stopping to chat with many of his Rebels. They were a tired bunch, and badly needed rest. He made up his mind they would push on to Ike's position the next day, and then rest and re-equip before beginning the bloody sweeps of the area.

Even though that much time had not lapsed, it would be good to get together with the gang again.

Ben's team rolled onto the old military post amid cheers and shouted greetings the next day. Even though Ben could not see it, he was very much aware of the massive presence of New York City, to the northeast, some forty miles away as the crow flies.

Ben cut the engine to his Jeep and called for James Riverson.

"Stand them down, James. Rest them for a couple

360

of days. No details during that time. Just sleep and eat and gossip."

"Yes, sir," James grinned.

Ben kissed his daughter and shook hands with Ike and Cecil and Chase; Holly had gone with her medics over to the base hospital.

"Cecil, before we sit down to jaw, radio Base Camp One. I want a battalion left down there. All others start pulling out for here. I spotted some tanks; good — we won't have to truck ours up here. Ike, I want a complete list of all parts needed to get the tanks all ready; we'll have those trucked up. How about the fuel situation up here?"

"All kinds of underground tanks untapped, Ben. All over the area. It looks pretty good."

"It's going to be fall before we're fully ready to make our push into the city." Ben looked around him. "We're going to need winter gear." He looked at Ike. "How about the base reloading equipment?"

"In pretty good shape. I got it cranked up and producing."

Ben nodded. "The base hospital?"

"Not bad," Chase said. "Ike's people did a god job of cleaning it up."

"We'll use this hospital for the most serious cases; get them away from the combat zone. We'll need a field hospital for the less seriously wounded."

"I have one picked out, Ben," Ike told him. "It's small but still in good shape."

"Good." Ben looked around him, sighing. "It's going to be a bitch, people. A screaming, bloody bitch. And we're going to lose some people. But we've got to find those people called the Judges and destroy them. We've got to find the radio equipment and knock it out. So much to do."

"Ben?" Chase asked. "What in the hell are we going to *do* with New York City once we do clean it out?"

Ben laughed long and hard. "Damned if I know, Lamar!"

"One thing about it, Ben," Ike said drily. "Once we do clean it out, it'll be the first time true justice has prevailed here for fifty years!"

Thirty-three

"Let's go home now, Carol Ann," her husband said, taking her by the arm.

"You better turn me loose, boy," she warned him.

"Carol Ann, I found us a nice little place down clost to home. You fetch the kids and come on now. The house needs cleanin' up."

"Clean it up your own damn self!"

"Girl, don't talk to me lak 'at. Took me three days to find you. What happened to yore hair!"

"Me and the others had it cut some and done up. You don't like it, that's tough!"

The others were having the same problems with their wives. They just couldn't get used to the change in them. The girls seemed different; kind of tough-actin'. And they wasn't takin' no orders worth a damn.

"Misty," B.M. pleaded. "Whut the hale's come over you? I ain't never seen you act lak this here 'fore."

"You got us a new home all picked out, B.M.?"

"Shore. Nice one. Just a-waitin' for you to come clean it up."

"Your arms broke, boy?"

"Haw?"

"You ain't . . . don't have a damn thing to do, B.M. Now you want me to come back to you, you en-roll in school. You join up. We'll take the trainin' together and the housework we'll divvy up fifty/fifty."

"Hit ain't fittin' for a man to do a woman's work, Misty."

"Then carry your ass, boy!"

"Misty, you cain't mean 'at! I done said I was gonna do rat. Right. Whut more do you want from me?"

"Respect, B.M. The two of us pullin' together, not apart. The kids goin' to school and learnin' right from wrong and how to get along with other people. That and a whole lot more, B.M. Now, me and Jenny Sue and Carol Ann and Laura June and Billie Jo talked it over. That's the way it's gonna be, B.M. This place here, B.M., why it's a whole new way of life that I didn't even know was there. There ain't no hate here, B.M. I never seen, saw, anything like it. Everybody has a job, and they do it. Nobody steals, lies, breaks the law. Nobody is all off to themselves, thinking they're better than other folks. I like it, B.M. I'm stayin'. If you wanna stay . . . well, I'd like that. But if you don't think you can cut it, then you best haul ass, boy. 'Cause the first time you spout off some crack about somebody of another race or color or whatever, some of these ol' boys around here is gonna kill you, B.M. And I'd grieve if that'd happen. But I got to think that you're a grown man, and what happens, well, you brung, brought it on

364

yourself. Now I'm through talkin'. You gonna stay, or go?"

He looked at her for a long time, then slowly smiled. "You learned how to write your name yet, Misty?"

"Want to see me?"

"Yeah!"

With a stub of a pencil and a scrap of paper, she printed: MISTY. Then she printed: LOVES B.M.

"What do it say, Misty?"

She told him.

"Well, I think I'll give it a whirl, Misty. Think you can write something, some*thing* else?"

"What?"

He told her.

She printed: B.M. LOVES MISTY.

Thirty-four

Ben, Ike, Tina, and Cecil, accompanied by a company of Rebels, heavily armed, drove up Highway 9 to Perth Amboy and crossed over to Staten Island. They drove to the far north end of the island. They saw no one.

"Used to be able to take a ferry from this point," Ben said, showing them the half-submerged ferry.

It was just breaking dawn, the mist still clinging to the bay.

"I can't see it!" Tina said impatiently.

All turned at the sound of vehicles. Dan and a platoon of Scouts had been lagging behind, keeping a close watch.

Dan shook his head. "Nothing. And not a sign of anyone's ever having lived on the island."

Chase had ridden out with Dan. "Let's check out Sea View Hospital today," he suggested. "It would be closer and this is as good a jumping-off place as any. You agree, Ben?"

"Good as any, Lamar."

The mist was gradually lifting.

The silence was vast around them; only a few sea

366

birds soared and called.

"I wonder why that is?" Lamar said, his eyes watching the birds.

"Survivors probably hunted them and ate them," Ike said.

Lamar muttered something terribly vulgar under his breath. "Why didn't the city people leave and head out into country?"

"Perhaps they couldn't," Ben told them all. "Besides, they don't know any other life. The mist is lifting."

Everybody was straining their eyes, to be the first to catch a glimpse of the Lady with the torch of welcome.

Then the sun burst free, burning off the mist, and there she stood in the harbor.

Everyone was touched. Most of the Rebels had tears streaming down their face. Lamar Chase garumped a couple of times and cleared his throat. Dan honked his nose into a handkerchief. Cecil was openly, unashamedly, weeping. Tina was crying so hard she could hardly see the lady in the harbor.

Ike said, " 'Give me your tired, your poor, Your huddled masses yearning to breathe free. . . .' You know the rest of it, Ben?"

" 'The wretched refuse of your teeming shore, Send these, the homeless, tempest-tossed, to me: I lift my lamp beside the golden door.' "

Little Jersey was standing on the cab of a truck, so she could see over the heads of the Rebels crowding the dock. "That's beautiful, general; did you write that?"

"No, Jersey," Ben smiled. "Emma Lazarus wrote

that. It's from the 'New Colossus.' That's the inscription for the Statue of Liberty."

"You ever been up close to it, general?" a Rebel called out.

"Oh, yes. Just before the Great War. It's quite a sight to see."

"I don't think Emma had the Night People in mind when those words were written," Ike said.

"No." Ben shifted his Thompson. "I don't either. So let's go make sure that the next ship of people seeking freedom really finds that freedom."

The Rebels mounted up. Behind them, the sounds of many Rebels' vehicles, including the rattle of tanks could be heard.

Ben stood up in his Jeep and waved his hand. "Scouts out! Let's go!"